THE CREATION
CONUNDRUM

THE CREATION
CONUNDRUM

by

R Santosh

White Falcon
Publishing

www.whitefalconpublishing.com

The Creation Conundrum
R Santosh

www.whitefalconpublishing.com

The contents of this book have been timestamped on the Ethereum blockchain as a permanent proof of existence. Scan the QR code or visit the URL given on the back cover to verify the blockchain certification for this book.

Requests for permission should be addressed to
dr.rsantosh@gmail.com

ISBN - 978-93-89530-94-0

ABOUT THE AUTHOR

Dr. R Santosh was born in Pune. He did his schooling at the St. Vincent's High School, Pune. He did his MBBS at the BJ Medical College in Pune, followed by MD in Internal Medicine at the prestigious JIPMER, Pondicherry. He did his DM (fellowship) in the subject of Endocrinology at the premium institute, PGI Chandigarh.

He started his career at Apollo Hospitals, Hyderabad. After three years, he turned into an entrepreneur. He is one of the founder directors of the Magna Centres for Obesity, Diabetes and Endocrinology and is the Chief endocrinologist at the Filmnagar Hyderabad unit.

As a medical professional, he has thirty-five publications including four textbook chapters. He has spoken in more than five hundred scientific forums, which include international, national and regional diabetes and endocrine conferences. He has been an invited faculty member in six international conferences till date.

He has won the Abdul Kalam Award for excelling in the field of Endocrinology.

He has written three books, two of which have been commercial successes. The third book, the Subconscious was a self-published book that debuted at the number one position in the Amazon Best Sellers list.

He is a cult follower of Pink Floyd and has a keen interest in cricket and football. He won the crowd favorite award in the Karaoke showdown in Hyderabad in 2011.

Contents

PROLOGUE

The YouTube video had gone viral. The Captain couldn't resist playing it again.

"The only way to reach heaven from this *Kalyuga*... for sure, for all Hindus is simple – in your lifetime, you must visit Rameshwaram, Tirupati, Haridwar, Yamunotri, Gangotri, Dwarka, Konark and finally, Kashi. If you have done so and got an *Aarti* done on your and your family's name, you will have achieved complete *moksha*." The Great Guru Amar's voice was resounding and loud, thanks to the latest Bose Surround Sound Audio systems. The Great Guru looked as fresh as ever. He never looked tired. He was fifty-two years old, had a frail built, a shaven head, with vermillion applied on his head at all times. He wore a traditional saffron kurta and white dhoti each time. He always had the unmistakable reassuring smile on his face.

The audience roared in appreciation.

Recently, Amareshwar Nath, better known as the Great Guru Amar had started his nationwide tour. He started from his 100-acre Ashram at Dehu, a small town near the city of Pune in the month of March. After touring Mumbai, Bangalore, Mysore, Coimbatore and Chennai, he had returned to Pune, for the last sermon of the first leg of his tour. The Great Guru had strived to bring back religious beliefs in the minds of people, which were wilting away more and more. The Great Guru spoke extensively about the rich culture of the Hindus, the religion that spanned six millennia, more than any other religion in the world.

The Great Guru, however, spoke highly about all other religions as well. In all his sermons, he was particular to mention that God existed and all that people needed to do was to worship regularly. The Hindus need to visit temples and the Christians must attend Church. The Muslims must attend the prayers at the mosques and the Parsis at the fire temple; the Buddhists and Jains at monasteries and the Jews at synagogues. Every individual needs to find a place where he or she can connect to his or her messenger of God. God is one and he controls everything.

The Great Guru had embraced social media extensively, something that made him connect with many people instantaneously. He had a very active Facebook page, three million followers on Twitter and a large number of people subscribing to his YouTube channel. His sermons were often filled with a lot of jokes, wit and humour, which was the need of the hour to grab the attention of millions of people online. But his messages always had one moral: God exists, and everything that has ever happened in the world, and that will ever happen, will be the will of God. He fiercely opposed abortions, genetic studies and stem cell research, research that searched for the 'God particle', because he found them to be against the nature of God's creation. He, however, spoke well about the other advances made by man in medicine and communication. It was all God's wish.

In the present world, when it had been extremely demanding to make the common man believe in anything that suggested God exists, he had posted extreme questions catching the minds of even the youngsters.

If God doesn't exist and physics laws are true, then all matter needs to be finite on the earth. How is the human population increasing; where is the extra matter that is required for building billions of humans and other animals coming from?

What happens when you die? Does your conscious brain that is seeing, feeling, smelling and hearing everything, the brain that assimilated so much knowledge, suddenly blackout? How can a human completely blackout? He must get up somewhere… and that somewhere is where God wishes us to be?

Why are we civilized? Why do we follow rules set up by the civilization? We could break all laws, couldn't we? There could be total anarchy, couldn't it? Isn't it because we want to live happily and also help our fellow friends in society? Why would ninety per cent of people like to help others? What is there in us that makes us cooperate with fellow humans? What is stopping most of us from being cruel and do whatever we want? After all, all of us live only once... It is the power of God that instils this feeling in us, and the corollary is, it is the fear of God's wrath that prevents us from being merciless.

Hence he believed and wanted everyone to believe that God exists, and we must pray to him daily. Therefore, each Hindu must visit each temple to attain the liking of God.

A young girl, probably around fifteen years old had gotten to the mike in the audience. "Guruji, may I ask you some questions?"

The Guruji's chief assistant, Rudradevi, intervened. "Let Guruji finish his sermon please!" Rudradevi was always present in all the Guru's sermons. She was probably around thirty-five years of age or so. It was very evident that she was a very good-looking lady, probably from North or West India. She also wore the same patterned vermillion as her Guru and wore a saffron *sari*.

The Guru spoke, "No, Rudradevi, please let her ask. *Beti*, what's your name? How old are you?"

"I am Dipti Iyengar, I am fifteen years old."

"Yes, *beti*! What do you want to ask?"

"If God exists, then surely He must be everywhere? After all, he created the Universe?"

"Yes!"

"Then why should one go to all these temples?" The audience began murmuring.

"Well! It's true that God is everywhere! But the Devil is everywhere too; distractions are everywhere too. The only place where we can connect to him directly is in temples!" The audience roared again.

"Why do hundreds of people die while pursuing some sort of pilgrimage each year? Doesn't God like them?"

"Well..."

Before the Guru replied, Dipti ranted on, "Do all animals go to hell because they cannot connect to God directly? If humans must not kill humans or harm them, then why do we eat and kill millions of animals each day for food?

"We all know that all matter originated from the Big Bang, if NASA is able to capture a photo of the Big Bang, and nothing before it, then where is God?

"If God is so great, why did He allow the war between Protestants and Catholics to occur? Why is there unrest, today as well, between the members of different religions? Aren't they all God's children? I feel, Guruji, there is no God! If He was there, He would have taken care of all humans and animals, and ensured all lived happily during their lives. Thank you."

The fifteen-year-old had silenced the Guru and the crowd for a while. It was pretty evident that the fifteen-year-old had been taught all this and she was rattling something that she had learned almost by heart. Or maybe someone or both her parents had instilled this feeling in her right since she could comprehend anything. This was too much stuff for someone so young!

The Guruji had laughed and said that Dipti was a child and she, in the near future, may realise that God existed. But his expression said it all; he was worried. This was going to go live on all social media, and it would kick up a storm.

That's exactly what had happened. In the days of rampant use of social media, there were always people with the opposite ideology who could express their views clearly. The views of the teenager were widely denounced by some, but greatly appreciated by others; some of them even trolled the Great Guru massively. This video now had close to a billion views, much more than any of his previous videos.

The Captain smiled again. At least, now he was sure that a few thousand shared his views. He needed to bring this Guru down quickly.

Chapter 1

"This is your captain speaking from the flight deck. We are currently cruising at thirty-eight thousand feet above sea level and we have now begun to communicate with the Dubai Air traffic control. Dubai reports a temperature of nineteen degrees Celsius and has great visibility of six kilometres. We are about to begin our descent soon and expect to touch down in forty-five minutes; that is at 8:30 am local time. We hope you had a pleasant flight from New York and hope that our cabin attendants took care of you well. Crew, please prepare for landing."

The captain's announcement woke up Rajesh from a deep slumber. He rubbed his eyes and it took him just that extra moment to realise where he was. He witnessed a small commotion, as the stewards were busy collecting used blankets and headphones, while many passengers stood in line to use the washrooms. Most would have got up from a small nap or would have eaten the breakfast served just a while ago.

Well, there were some real benefits of getting the seat near the emergency exit. He could stretch his legs almost the entire duration of the flight. However, Rajesh could enumerate many disadvantages as well. One of them was the crowds near the washroom. He hated this. Also, the constant chattering of the air hostesses during meal times and the times before landing seldom allowed him to sleep deeply. Now is the time the babies in the bassinet seats next to him would start wailing loudly as mild air pressure changes start while landing. More disadvantages than advantages!

He stretched and looked at the person next to him, who was reading the latest Dan Brown novel. This neighbouring person, a Caucasian, was six feet tall, just shorter than Rajesh. Rajesh was six-one in height and many observers found it odd that he was taller than most Caucasians. He wore frameless glasses, had jet black hair, broad shoulders and a well-toned body.

The Caucasian looked up and smiled at Rajesh, "Had a nice sleep?" His accent was distinctly American.

"Yes! What about you?"

"Yes, did manage a little sleep… it's noisy here! Hi, I am Ken."

"Rajesh." He shook hands. "Where are you travelling to?"

"Singapore. What about you?"

"Returning home to Chennai. You know Chennai?" Rajesh felt rather odd asking this. He was surprised at the number of Americans who didn't know Chennai. Chennai is the fourth largest city in India. It is the 33rd largest city in the world by population, and the fourth Indian city overall in the top 35, after Delhi, Mumbai and Kolkata. Only three cities in the US made it in the top 35, New York, Los Angeles and Chicago. So it was strange that many Americans asked him where Chennai was!

"Yes, of course! There are great temples around Chennai. I have been there once. Also a long beach, the Mariana beach…"

"Marina Beach…"

"Sorry. Marina beach. Also, the food there is awesome. People are crazy about the local cricket team, the Super Kings, if I am not mistaken?"

Rajesh was stunned. This was the largest information about Chennai possessed by any American that he knew. *He knew about the Chennai Super Kings, damn it!* "Impressive knowledge!" One of the flight attendants interrupted them to take away their blankets. It was a cruel practice, Rajesh thought. *I could continue wanting to use it, couldn't I?*

"What do you do?" Ken asked him.

"I am a reporter for a national TV News Channel, Channel IBC News."

"Wow, impressive! You must be travelling a lot?"

Many people thought this way. Rajesh just smiled. "Not much, I am the local reporter for the channel. So my travels are mostly around Chennai and certain other cities in the state."

"Oh! Hectic schedule?"

"Yes, you can say so... It depends on the activity. There are some days that are cool. No news is good news for me. I just go to the office at 9:00 am and am back by 4:00 pm. Nonetheless, some days can be horrendous. The latest political changes in our state following the demise of our chief minister have kept me awake and working for almost eighteen hours per day last year!"

"Eighteen hours! That's a crime!"

"Not for us! It's our duty to bring out the latest updates to the nation. I enjoy doing it most times!"

"Oh! Still, it's tight!"

"So Ken, what do you do?"

"I am a yachtsman."

The answer took Rajesh aback. He wondered why. Well, he was born and brought up in a country where the top earners were managers, constructors, politicians, doctors, lawyers, cricketers, engineers and the likes. Any person you met in India was studying to be one of them. He couldn't digest the idea that anyone could be a yachtsman by profession. It just didn't sync with any of his brain cells! "Interesting job!"

"Yeah, I love it!"

"Are you from the US or Singapore?"

"Australia."

Oh! A yachtsman! From Australia... travelling from New York to Singapore via Dubai! Still hard to comprehend! "Wow nice, where in Australia?"

"Gold Coast."

Shit! "Gold Coast was a beautiful place to just visit even for a week. I had been there six years back. The beach and the national park were amazing! I envy you! Sorry to ask, is your job a well-paying one as one compared to your peers?"

"Well, no, when you compare to my peers. I enjoy my life this way." Ken chuckled.

"What are your working hours?"

"Same like you, it differs. During Regatta days, it may be five to six days a week for almost ten hours. There are ten regattas I participate in!"

"Other days?"

"I practise for four hours a day, five days a week. I guess that's about it."

"What! What do you do with all the free time?"

"I hit the beach!"

"What if you want to earn a bit more?"

"Yes, sometimes I want to. So I help the local metro construction guys for a couple of hours. We get paid well per hour there."

It was too much for Rajesh. *A yachtsman, who works not even thirty per cent of the time he works, enjoys on the beach almost every day! Speaking of the dignity of labour, or rather about its complete lack in India, this guy so proudly works in helping build the metro! Here he is travelling the world! What the fuck have we Indians gotten ourselves into? We are always tuned to working longer and longer working hours, giving lesser and lesser time to our health and family. And no matter how much we earn, all we are bothered about is earning that extra few rupees, at any level; be it a labourer or a rich constructor. All we want is to work and earn more. The Australian here is living his life...we are just surviving; just surviving!* "Going to Singapore for a Regatta?"

"Yes! If you have time you can catch up on its live coverage on TV or later on, on YouTube!"

"For sure, I will." Rajesh gave him thumbs up.

He returned to thinking, as Ken settled back with his book. *Balls, I will have any interest in seeing live coverage of some Yacht race, leave alone searching for it on YouTube!*

Ken was thinking something about else. *Balls, have I ever gone to the beach for profession or recreation in the last three years...*

Chapter 2

Sanjay Sharan checked his door twice after he had already locked it. He had this habit of checking the locks time and again.

This probably started after his hostel room was robbed in 1987. He was a student at the College of Engineering, Pune. He had slept one night with his window open, which in those days didn't have grills. The next morning when he woke up, his wallet and watch were gone. His father had toiled hard his entire life and presented him this expensive Rolex after paying the expensive excise duty when his son won a merit seat in Engineering. The loss of the watch hurt him deeply, and to date, he had an inherent feeling that he may be robbed again if he didn't lock his doors and windows right.

That was thirty-one years ago. He went on to study and become a commercial pilot in Delhi. He had served as a pilot in Indian Airlines, Air India, and for the last six years of his career, in the Emirates airlines. He chose to opt for retirement at the age of fifty-two and joined back the organization as a Deputy Operations Manager, something that he liked doing.

He looked at himself in the mirrors near the elevator. He had aged gracefully. His silvery-white hair, according to many, made him look better. He was five-nine in height and had a pretty sleek body structure. Many of his contemporary colleagues had put on a lot of weight by now.

He was pretty fond of his apartment at Greens Dubai. Although living close to the city, his eighth-floor apartment, overlooking the golf course and the pond, offered him some seclusion.

He got into his SUV, the Jeep. He could also hear one of his neighbours driving out as the car tyres of the car made huge screeching noises. *Something had to be done about the flooring of this parking lot. A normal braking process also sounded like a huge accident!*

Normally, people would have been directed by Google to drive on the Sheik Zayad road. However, he had lived in Dubai long enough to understand that this road would be chock-a-block with traffic at this time on a Tuesday morning. He decided to use the parallel Al Khail road instead, which was longer by distance but would take lesser time.

He drove his SUV at a speed of 100 km per hour, something that he could not imagine doing in India, especially within the city. It had taken him a long time to adjust to Dubai's speed of driving, which only had complicated the fact that he had to drive on the right side of the road, not on the left as he had for years before he came here.

He put on the radio, on which someone was blurting the football results first.

"Manchester City suffers its first loss of the season! It lost at Anfield to a resurgent Liverpool 4-3, in a match that saw seven incredible goals…"

Of course, he knew that! He had seen the match on TV on Sunday night. The news was already a day and a half old. Although the institute in which he worked, Emirates, was the largest sponsor of the English Club, Arsenal, he had liked Manchester City Football Club in recent times. His seniors didn't approve of this, especially because MCFC's chief sponsor was their main professional rival, Etihad! *Oh God, let me just enjoy football and the players!*

The radio had switched to the weather. "Dubai; expect a clear happy weather today. The maximum will be thirty-two degrees Celsius, while the evening would be nippy at sixteen degrees." Yes, that was the typical January weather.

Again, Sanjay smirked. Let this be heard by an Englishman and an Indian. Both of them would have wondered what is wrong with the weatherman.

How could thirty-two degrees Celsius be classified as clear happy weather? Well, considering that this city in summer could reach a horrendous fifty degrees Celsius, this weather was definitely something to ride home about!

How could sixteen degrees be classified as nippy? It's a happy warm minimum temperature. People would still use fans all over India. However, Dubai is right in the middle of a desert. Sixteen degrees would generate really cold unobstructed winds, which necessitate the closing of all windows at night and sleeping with a comforter and no fans!

The trip to the airport would take forty-five minutes, so he decided to call his daughter on his hands-free. His daughter Myra had just married a few months back. His wife had died in a terrible road accident a year back on the way to Abu Dhabi on a really foggy morning. After that, his daughter and he had lived together until three months back, after which Myra had moved out with her husband to Boston. Ever since, Sanjay had been living alone. Myra had asked him to move with her to the US, but he loved his job and he had rather preferred to stay here in Dubai.

Sanjay calculated that it may just be short of 11:00 pm in Boston and hence, he placed the call very well knowing Myra's habit of sleeping late.

"Hi, dad!" Her sweet voice answered back. He guessed that most fathers would find their daughter's voice sweet.

"Hi, Myra! How's life?"

"I can't say nice…it's snowing like crazy here and we have spent our entire Sunday at home. Yes, we did enjoy the movie *Singham* on Netflix, but generally, we were bored! How I went to work today, only I know! It was literally like ploughing the snow as the car moved up to the main road!"

Sanjay quickly calculated that it was Monday night in the US. "Ha! I am basking in abundant sunshine with good temperatures!"

"I envy you! I thought this snow would be great, but now I hate it!"

"Ha, ha! Remember how crazy you were about snow in childhood. The only access you had to some snow was your winter vacation to Manali in the seventh grade!"

"Yeah, and how thrilled I was! See here, only snow is visible outside my room and I hate to step out! Tell me, what's happening at your end?"

"Nothing, just another usual day will begin now. Today I am looking after the boarding area of Terminal One. We have a new airline inaugurating its first flight today, so a little excitement; that's all. A boring two-hour meet in the afternoon, then back home. Just routine!"

Myra knew that being at the boarding area posed the greatest challenge for any Operations in-charge. Passengers sometimes can be extremely pushy and demanding here, especially during the time when many flights take-off simultaneously. A cancelled flight could show what hell meant to all the staff at the airport. Nevertheless, her father had gotten used to all this. "Sure, sure, handling passengers! So routine!" Her voice was sarcastic.

Sanjay laughed again. Yes, he was beginning to handle irate passengers easily. So it would be a routine day.

Or so he thought...

Chapter 3

"You went to the US for a holiday, I presume?" Ken asked.

"Well, yes, and no. Part of this trip is business; I am doing a news cover on my next flight!"

"News cover on a flight?" Ken was surprised.

"The next flight I travel, the one from Dubai to Chennai, is the first flight of a new airline: Eastern Airlines. It runs its first flight from Dubai to Chennai."

"Wow! Really? It's a Dubai-based company? These guys are going great guns!"

"No. It's based out of India. Mumbai. Actually, its promoters are a group of people who belong not only to India but also Non-Resident Indians. One of the largest investors is from New Jersey."

"Oh, so you went to the US to cover the promoters for a news story?"

"Nope. The first part of the trip was a holiday. I went to the US to meet a friend," Rajesh answered.

"You came to the US all the way from Chennai to meet a friend! Must be someone really special, I guess!" Ken winked.

"Yeah, he is…"

"He?"

Rajesh laughed, "When I meant friend, I meant pal, not a soul mate!"

"Oh! Where in the US?"

"Manhattan."

"Okay good, he works there I guess?"

"Well, he works in Baltimore, at the John Hopkins Hospital."

"Okay, he is a doc."

"No, admin."

"Good, so how come New York?"

"That's some story!" Rajesh said. As he said that, the video started playing visuals of Dubai, which everyone had to see and hear. "You wanna hear?"

"Well, okay, it must be interesting!"

"Okay. My friend's name is Manish. He and I were friends when we were very young. Very young means since the earliest I can remember until the third grade. We were the closest of pals and almost inseparable. We were in the same school and also stayed in the same society. We played together, studied together, and we also travelled together. Often we went to each other's house for dinner as well."

"The Chennai pals!" Ken exclaimed.

"Well...no. I was born and brought up in a city called Pune. We stayed there."

"Okay, Pune, I know... it's near Mumbai!"

Rajesh was quite impressed with Ken's knowledge; it really pleased him. "Suddenly, out of the blue, one day his parents came over to our place and announced that they were shifting to the States soon; probably even before the end of the academic year itself."

"Oh, the Pune pals separate?"

"Yes! It was a heart-wrenching moment for us. Of course, he was excited at the prospect of living in the States, and I was envious. But yes, he and I were now going to go different ways.

"Just two days before he left, we made the promise."

"What promise?"

"It was the twelfth of January, 1988. We made a promise that wherever we were, whatever we did, we would meet exactly thirty years later, that is - 10:00 am on the twelfth of January in two thousand and eighteen."

"Oh wow!" Ken's expression was of genuine awe.

"But where would we meet? Would he come to Pune? No! I need to visit the US some time right? So we made a random choice based on the limited knowledge we had about the US at that time; we decided to meet near the left foot of the Statue of Liberty."

"Hey, that's really nice of you guys to connect and really meet up at the Statue!"

"Connect? My foot, connect! He left to the US at a time when there were no personal landline phones, leave alone mobiles, internet, Facebook, WhatsApp, email, video calling and the like. We both lost touch almost instantaneously after I bid goodbye to him at the Pune railway station. The family would go to Mumbai and then proceed. I did get a letter from him a month after he reached the US. But my reply never reached him, I guess, as he would have moved from where he had posted the first letter. Talk of communication in those days, it was a joke back then!"

"You mean, you lost touch completely with this dude? Yet thirty years later, both of you remember your promise, and actually met? You met at the left foot of the Statue of Liberty?"

"Well, that's what exactly happened!"

"Oh, man! Don't kid me! How would you even recognize a person after thirty years of no contact?"

"By shaking hands and introducing ourselves?"

"Holy shit! He really was there? What a fairy-tale! What friendship!" Ken rested back his head again on the headrest as another loud announcement about Dubai airport played on the common TV. Nonetheless, it was clear that he was amused by the story he had heard just now.

Rajesh too sat back and relaxed. His memories just rewound to last week. He had hurriedly booked his tickets to the US. His secretary, Rama, had wondered aloud why he was doing so.

The truth was that the previous night he was going through some old family albums. Luckily for him, the timing had been perfect. He had seen his and Manish's photos as kids. He rapidly calculated the date that he had promised to meet Manish and was surprised that the date lay exactly a week later.

Of course, he had considered chucking the prospect of going to the US just with the hope of meeting a childhood friend. The childhood friend had, in all probabilities, forgotten him completely. He was ninety-nine per cent sure of this. Many other people had come into his life at varying moments and many became closer friends.

However, he considered that one per cent chance of Manish being there. *If Manish did remember and he came, won't it be strange that he wasn't there? Isn't it he who still felt that he could meet his childhood friend?*

Okay, if he didn't meet him also, it would be a thrilling prospect of even trying to meet him. He would also check out New York for the first time. Although he had a ten-year B1 visa, the only time he had used it was a year back when he had gone to San Diego for a conference.

Little did he know that this was going to be a fairy-tale trip!

Chapter 4

Rajesh had landed in New York at seven in the morning. The trip had been long and exhausting.

As soon as he had stepped foot out of the airport, he experienced something he had never experienced before – the biting cold. Well, it was nice to see people decked up in warm clothes walking around New York streets in winter on TV and on the internet; actually experiencing it for the first time was horrendous. Immediately, his ears and nose hurt. His hands dipped deep into his pockets. He had prepared for this trip, but all his warm clothes were still packed in the bag!

An Asian person stopped him and asked him if he wanted a taxi. Well, this was common in Chennai. The same sort of approach by taxi drivers here in New York surprised him! He was really cold and he said yes. He waited at his designated place, still shivering. He was relieved to see the car, and surprised too, as the car that pulled up said 'Taxi' but was a BMW seven series. He got into the taxi and proceeded to the 95th street in Manhattan, where he would stay with his college friend, Ravi. He learned that the driver was from Pakistan. They chatted all the way and he readily paid the seventy dollars with a receipt; only to realise later that he could have had this trip with only forty dollars had he chosen the regular cab!

His friend Ravi was a doctor and had conveniently rescheduled his appointments to have a weekly off on this day. Rajesh spent the day chatting with him, had a small nap, and in the evening, this time better dressed, headed to the Times Square with Ravi and his wife. They had met another college friend of theirs there. Overall, the first day in

New York had been a great day and he had some great and some not so good memories of that day.

The real day was going to be the next day though, 12th of January, 2018. *Would Manish have even remembered about it, leave alone care about it?*

Well, he decided he wanted to test that. Anyway, if Manish wasn't there, he would enjoy the day out in New York. As per Ravi's advice, he had left at 8:00 am on the Subway and found his way to the ferryboats to the Statue by 9:00 am. The number of tourists who had lined up in spite of this being a fiercely chilly morning surprised him. He had waited for twenty minutes in the line before getting on. (Later, he had learned that in summer, people often waited for up to two hours!) On the boat, it was even colder. As it reached the statue, he was surprised to see another ferry coming from the direction of New Jersey, also full of tourists. He briefly looked around to see if he could see someone who resembled Manish. Well, that was going to be futile, he knew it.

Although it was still fifteen minutes to ten, he proceeded to the left foot directly, instead of moving around the statue in an anticlockwise direction as many of the tourists seemed to do.

As he reached the place, he found a few sitting benches there. No one was sitting on them as it was too windy and too cold. Well, he sat on one of them, with hopes against hope.

He waited there. The time ticked to 10:00 am and passed it too. He started getting restless. *He knew Manish was not going to come.* Although he had made his mind up for the same for long, and also planned alternative agendas, he still was greatly disappointed.

What the shit? Why am I overreacting so much? It's just some childhood friend! He must have long grown up and moved on. He may not even be in the States anymore. Why was he feeling so disappointed?

The ten minutes that he waited there past 10:00 am was like eternity. He gave a huge sigh and got up from his bench. He looked around. Tourists were walking past the statue. All of them walked past it; well, almost all of them. He saw one man looking over the railing facing the sea and smoking. He seemed to be an Indian… could be a Pakistani or a Bangladeshi too.

He walked up to him and just tried his luck, "Manish Kumar?"

The man looked back at him, and to the enormous surprise and happiness of Rajesh, he replied, "Rajesh?"

Rajesh was stunned. Here was Manish, standing five feet seven inches tall, stocky man with a fully grown French beard. Someone whom he had last seen thirty years back as a nine-year-old, third-grade kid; with whom he had no communication whatsoever for these many years. The only thing that brought them together was a promise. It turned out to be an equally important commitment to him. Amazing, to say the very least.

Manish was taking equal time to let the situation sink into him. He too was gauging Rajesh's physical appearance.

It was a whole of fifty seconds before the two long lost pals hugged each other affectionately. They then shook hands and patted each other, not knowing exactly how to react.

They decided to walk around the statue and then proceed to the mainland for lunch. As they did that, they caught up with each other. Rajesh had studied in the same school until the twelfth grade and then proceeded to do engineering in a college in Pune. However, to the disbelief of everyone around him, he decided to pursue his career as a journalist. He had decided to join the upcoming news Channel IBC News. Ever since then, he worked for the same news channel. He started as a reporter, and although he was offered promotion multiple times, he took the financial incentive doing the same job as he loved what he was doing.

Marriage? To cut the long story short, no, he wasn't ever married! He had liked a girl named Rakhee in Pune; he had hung around with her quite a bit during engineering days.

In fact, he had deeply loved her, and she liked him too. But there were some sacrifices they both were not willing to make. She loved late-night clubbing and partying. She loved wearing short skirts. She loved having more than a couple of drinks each night and also smoked once in a while.

He tried adjusting to her lifestyle, he genuinely did. She was wonderful during the day, but come evening, she would be a party animal. He tried to be one too. She took him to a few late-night parties. After exactly six of them, he decided he couldn't stand it. He was not made for this at all.

To be very honest, she too had tried to sober down for him. But moving around restaurants for a quiet dinner and walking down the Main Street of Pune just didn't seem to excite her one bit.

They split once, but they got back together, as they did love each other much. They decided to give each other space. They would separate in the evenings and get back in the morning not asking what the other person did the previous evening.

However, the hectic study schedule meant that evenings were the only time they could actually meet, and this was just not happening. Rajesh had taken up drinking and scholastic performance was dipping. Rakhee too appeared unhappy. One fine day, their close friends took the call for them. They arranged for a meeting in the college canteen (of all the places!) and they talked them out of the relationship. Although they loved each other, they were made to accept that they were just not made for each other.

They split, but they continued to be friends, although that too was a little clouded now. Even before he moved to Chennai for the journalism course, he had come to know that Rakhee was now dating a boy from the Armed Forces Medical College. They seemed to be getting along well.

Instead of feeling angry, he had just resigned to his destiny. Funnily enough, he had dated three girls in Chennai, but none of his relations reached a serious stage. He saw that he enjoyed his work much, and besides, none of them could wipe off Rakhee from his memory. To the utter angst and disappointment of his family, he remained unmarried to date.

He had also never met Rakhee ever since he moved away. She most probably would have married the army chap and have had three kids by now. Well, he had decided not to care. *Did he or didn't he?*

There was a sudden thud. Rajesh snapped back to reality. The Emirates Flight had just touched down and was speeding on the Dubai runway. He looked up at Ken who smiled back at him, apparently still surprised by his story.

Chapter 5

Rajesh knew Dubai airport well. This was the fourth time he was flying Emirates. He had flown to London twice to cover a cricket tournament as a Rookie, and once to San Diego before. He knew by now that it would be at least another ten minutes to the parking bay.

He remembered the twelfth of January again.

Manish had taken him to Chinatown to grab a meal at one of his favourite restaurants. He had keenly listened to his friend until lunchtime. He knew that it was his turn to speak up now.

Manish and his family had first moved to New York, where his father got his first US job in a finance-consulting company. It was not at all a great moment for them. They had moved from a relatively poor country, whose money reserves were quite less in the 1980s. The money that they brought with them dwindled quickly as they realised the high cost of living here in the US. They had to rent a house, buy furniture, monthly groceries, lots of new clothes due to the cold weather and the biggest drain was the two kids' school fees; his sister's and his.

They had come to a hand-to-mouth situation and were severely in debt for almost two years. They lived in a small one-bedroom flat, which, according to Manish, was probably smaller than the living room of his house in Pune. The American dream had collapsed. They hated their decision to move to the US and considered moving back to India several times.

However, their financial situation was too bad to be able to return to India. Even if they had, they would be much poorer than how they had left India, and it would also have been a great social shame.

After two years, as both parents settled in their jobs, they were better off, and their debts were now greatly reduced. They moved inland to West Virginia and now had a bigger, albeit still rented house. They had a car after two years in the US. Life had improved.

He himself had done a bachelor's degree in computer engineering and then went on to do an MBA in a not-so-great Management School. Nonetheless, it was enough to land him a job in the academic event management section at John Hopkins Hospital in Baltimore, which was not too far from here.

He too was not married. In the US, there is never a social pressure to get married. He said he had a girlfriend, whose grandfather was from Tamil Nadu and grandmother was Polish. Her name was Cynthia. She also lived in Baltimore and they hung out quite often, but none of them had discussed marriage yet.

Manish invited him to Baltimore, but he said he couldn't meet Cynthia as she herself was leaving to Hong Kong the next day.

Rajesh would have of course loved to spend time with Manish in Baltimore, but he had promised to meet his maternal uncle in Boston the next day, before getting back to New York after a couple of days and then leaving back to India. Little had he actually expected to meet Manish.

Manish accompanied Rajesh to the Empire State Building and Wall Street. They discussed random stuff. Finally, it was time to say goodbye as Manish dropped him to a nearby subway station. It was indeed a sad moment, but the friends made up plans to be in touch now, having exchanged mobile numbers and email IDs. Manish promised he would definitely make it to Chennai the next time he came to India, which he said could be as soon as later the same year.

Rajesh had gone on to Boston and enjoyed his time with his uncle and his cousin, who had made a surprise visit with his family for the weekend from Chicago. On Monday morning, he flew to the JFK airport in New York and almost immediately boarded the Emirates flight to Dubai.

He looked out the window as the flight crawled to a halt and the crew was instructed to disarm all slides of the doors. The sun shone bright and he assumed that it must be quite warm here contrary to the freezing cold in the US. Anyway, he was not going to step out in Dubai. He would be at the airport and then back into the Eastern Airlines Chennai flight after six odd hours.

"Nice meeting you, mate! Catch you soon!" Ken said.

"Same here, Ken. I'll see you on TV or YouTube real soon. Look out for my comments on YouTube!" He almost kicked himself for saying that.

Ken laughed loudly. "My eyes will be open!" Having said that, he started moving with the crowd to the exit of the plane. Rajesh just took that extra few moments to check if he had taken all his belongings. He lost sight of Ken. *Nice chap.*

CHAPTER 6

Sanjay Sharan reached his office, where a cup of warm coffee always welcomed him. Lucy, his secretary from Manipur, had been spot on all these years. The first thing he needed to start each working day was coffee.

As he sipped on it, he checked the latest status report. He was in Terminal One today, the Terminal for all flights besides Emirates airlines. The Air India flight to Delhi and the Chinese Western flight to Beijing were delayed by three hours each due to fog in the international airport. Delhi flights were delayed often in winters, and the passengers who went there were almost always resigned to the fact. The Beijing flight was delayed for the same reason. Again, the passengers here always cooperate.

Last Sunday, he was in Terminal Three, the terminal for Emirates Airlines. It was hell. The flights to Bangalore and Chicago were unexplainably delayed and there was a commotion in the airport. Bangalore, of all the places, had reported fog. The flight to Chicago had developed a snag during the refuelling stage. The passengers on both the flights least expected the delay and let their frustrations out loud. He was posted at the boarding gates and had placed the staff with the cool mentality there. They too were flustered. Some passengers could get exceptionally angry and abusive. To their benefit, they handled it well. Passengers failed to understand that the delays were beyond anything that the ground staff could do, yet *they* were the people who had to face the brunt of the passengers.

Lucy, the extremely smart and confident secretary, entered with a bunch of papers. It was a list of the staff working under Sanjay and where they were posted today. It could have been viewed on the system, but Sanjay preferred the old fashioned printout.

"I see that Roshan is working under you today. Good luck!" Lucy said.

Sanjay smirked. Roshan was, well, a sincere person. He was from Sri Lanka and had worked with Emirates Airlines for three years. He was too sincere and could not take the slightest of deviation in passengers' behaviour, which time and again led to scuffles between him and the passengers, often to be rescued by his seniors. He was subsequently sacked.

However, no case could be proven against him, as he always went by the rulebook. It was his interpersonal relationship that failed to gel. He applied for the job at Eastern Airlines and was immediately picked up at his first interview as he had immense knowledge in Ground Staff duties.

Well, today was interesting. It was Roshan's first day at the new Airlines. He had to ensure things were smooth. Although Sanjay had heard that no dignitaries would be travelling on the flight, there would be some media coverage and some hullabaloo surrounding the commencement of operations of this airline. He hoped Roshan didn't pick up a fight with anyone.

After having his coffee, Sanjay picked up the papers and headed off to where the action was – the boarding gates.

As he reached, he saw it was already extremely crowded there. This was the time when many flights landed. Most passengers who would have connecting flights made their way into the main terminal.

Of course, this is the time the food and beverage outlets thrived, and so did the Dubai Duty Free shops. Dubai Duty Free shops always had a lot of crowds, much more than any other airports he knew. Well, Dubai was a global shopping destination, but even after globalization and the same shops being available at all airports, the maximum crowd always showed up here in the territory that was now under Sanjay's control. Hopefully, no passenger created a scene in a shop or a restaurant. People were usually upset with long waiting queues and sometimes racial discrimination. However, most fights here were due to language barrier.

The real drama was always near the boarding gates; for obvious reasons.

He went to the area where he always hung around, and most people knew where to find him. He was near Gate C13. Most people considered this unlucky, but if you ever wanted to reach Sanjay, this is where he was mostly found.

His cell phone buzzed. The first distress call, he guessed. Although his walkie-talkie was always with him, it was always filled with other chatter. When someone wanted to reach him urgently, they always called.

He guessed it right, and it was from a staff member, Manikam, at the Thai Airways flight. He went near the gate C26, and a passenger to Bangkok was creating a scene.

He rushed and found the young man appear exasperated. A young Asian couple stood next to him, looking quite animated.

"Yes, Manikam?"

"Why, hello sir!"

"Hello, sir and madam, I am the terminal manager. What seems to be the problem?" Sanjay turned to the couple.

"Ask this guy what his problem is!" the Asian replied angrily. He was quite noticeably from the subcontinent.

Sanjay glanced at their passports and saw that they were from Pakistan. He quickly changed the language to Urdu and spoke to them. The change of language itself somewhat comforted the couple. "Sorry sir, I'd rather hear it from you!"

The Pakistani gentleman explained that his wife and he had chosen to carry one hand baggage each. He showed Sanjay the bags. They were small.

Fair enough, thought Sanjay.

However, they were tempted to buy some perfumes for their daughter-in-law, a bag for their son and lots of chocolates for their grandchildren in Bangkok.

They could do that, of course, but Sanjay knew where all this was heading to. He looked at their Dubai Duty Free shopping bags. They were so huge that they were equal to the hand baggage of at least six other people. Manikam would have rightly stopped them from carrying so much baggage on to the flight.

The couple insisted that it was not their fault that Dubai Duty Free offered so much variety and they wanted to carry all on board. But Manikam, who was doing the check-in formalities, informed them that they would need to check the baggage in and will receive them back once landed. However, they refused and this chap would just not listen and argued rudely with them.

Sanjay sighed. This was a common scenario. Of course, this was a relatively simple situation, but in all possibilities, this couple didn't know English. Manikam did not know Hindi or Urdu. His language sounded rude to them.

"*Gustaki muhaf* (Sorry for the mistake)" Sanjay replied slowly. He explained about the limited room in the economy class for each passenger to store their hand baggage. As a policy they could allow around 7 to 9 kilograms of luggage per person, otherwise, there would be mayhem inside the carrier. Even if he made an exception for them, other passengers would complain and create a ruckus, he explained. He also assured them very politely that their shopping bags would be very safe and would be handed over to them at the Bangkok airport. He shared his number with the couple and asked them to call him if they faced any trouble at all.

The polite language and the handing over of the phone number eased the couple immediately, and they agreed. "But ask your fellow to be more polite!"

"Of course, I will!" Sanjay smiled. But he knew all that Manikam needed was perhaps some Hindi classes. Hindi or the similar-sounding Urdu was probably the second most widely spoken language among the passengers travelling to and from this airport. It was even more widely spoken than Arabic.

The couple left their bags in exchange for a receipt. The person whom they dealt with was Sanjay and no one else. They gave one final glare to Manikam and made their way to the boarding area.

Manikam was visibly ready for firing by the airport operations head and a complaint to his airlines. "Sir, I am…"

However, Sanjay chuckled, much to his junior's relief. "Learn Hindi, my boy! Maybe I'll recommend to the management that they should give you all some Hindi classes!"

Well, the day had begun; the same old routine had started. Ninety-nine per cent of the processes would run smoothly without Sanjay's interference. Nonetheless, he was there to bail out the remaining one per cent screw-ups. He returned to his favourite spot, wondering if this was the day that he won't be disturbed again. *Ha! How I wish such a day existed!*

CHAPTER 7

Rajesh made his way out of the aerobridge onto the Dubai airport. This was the eighth time he was setting foot here, having done so twice each on his previous trips to the UK and the US, and once on his onward journey to New York. But even then, this airport didn't seem to cease to amaze him. There were thousands of people visible, yet everything seemed streamlined.

He followed the sign that said 'connecting flights'. After walking a short distance, he saw 4 LED Televisions lined up that were displaying the gates of the connecting flights. He checked his flight that was scheduled to leave in the afternoon 2:40 pm, EA 001. The flight was supposed to leave from C22.

The Terminal One gates were some distance away. He had to proceed to a train that took him there. The train trip was simple and nice. These modern airports were so huge. London Heathrow had an internal train, so had the JFK airport at New York and of course, Dubai.

After getting off the train, he proceeded to the security gates. Although the line was long, it seemed to move at a relatively quick pace, in stark contrast to the security holds of Chennai and New York. A rather simple concept; you are supposed to strip yourself of all metallic contents until the metal detector just doesn't buzz as you walk past. Men were usually through very fast; some women were frisked because of some jewellery they may have been wearing.

The most boring delay was on the other side of the security hold, as he had to wear his belt, watch and make sure his wallet, mobile phone, and keys were safely back in his pockets. He had to wear the shoes, which he had removed. *Well, to win something, you lose something!*

He followed the sign to the Terminal One, for which he had to go up the escalators, and he joined the really crowded boarding area. He proceeded to the Dubai Duty Free area where he picked up some chocolates for his nephew and an Absolut Raspberry flavoured Vodka for himself.

He then headed over to a reclining chair, where he made himself comfortable. This was going to be a three-hour wait before boarding the next flight. He would begin taking pictures for his flight story exactly fifteen minutes before departure, he decided. Right now, maybe he would read a book, or he would just take a nap for a couple of hours before he would grab some lunch.

He rubbed his eyes. They seemed to itch a little. He hated the dry air of a flight, which gave him a headache, a dry mouth and often dry eyes. He never enjoyed a drink on board, as the dehydration always meant he had a headache. He rubbed his eyes, blew on a handkerchief and applied it onto them. He needed a nap; his eyes and body were probably signalling the same.

He looked at his neighbour on to the right, a Chinese gentleman deep asleep and snoring slightly. The reclining seats were always spaced adequately so that people could doze off comfortably.

As he prepared for a snooze, someone moved into the seat onto his left, which was vacant thus far. It was a lady. He was forced to give her a longer than usual look. She was good-looking, most probably European or American. She was dressed in jeans and a half-sleeved dark blue top. She was probably five-seven or so, with a perfectly toned figure. She too looked tired, as if she too had made a long journey.

To his embarrassment, she gave a look back at him. He just smiled at her. He needed to say something, as it was quite obvious that she had caught him checking her out.

"Good morning, have a nice day," he greeted sheepishly.

"Good morning," she said in perfect English and stopped. She too seemed lost for words.

"You too look very tired, take some rest. I'm headed to dreamland," he said and laughed.

She smiled.

To avoid any further discomfort, Rajesh pulled over his eye cover and closed his eyes. He turned over his backpack and made it lie on his stomach while putting his hands through the back straps; as if he were hugging a baby. The last thing he wanted was someone flicking his bag and his passport. He knew this was unlikely in this heavily guarded airport, but he wanted to be careful nevertheless.

He again pulled down his eye cover, again checked out the damsel next to him... she was cute! He then pulled out his cell phone and set the alarm to 12:50 pm. This would give him around an hour and forty minutes of sleep, the phone said. After that, he would grab some food, and head towards the gate for boarding. He again rubbed his eyes, pulled his eye cover and closed his eyes moving into an instantaneous slumber.

CHAPTER 8

Gabriela Fabregas looked at the guy next to her, as she made herself comfortable on the seat at the Dubai airport. Yes, he was just one of the millions who checked her out. *Guys!* It was since her fifth grade that she was used to guys ogling at her.

She smiled as she remembered the guy in the Leesburg School who first proposed to her. She was in her sixth grade and her parents had been quite amused, although they warned her not to give in to any guy too soon.

Gabriela's parents had migrated from Argentina just after their wedding in the late 1970s. Gabriela was the elder of the two sisters. She was born in Denver, after which their parents had shifted to Leesburg in West Virginia. Her sister was born here. Both parents worked in companies in Washington. Her father was a civil engineer in a company that frequently received federal contracts and her mother was a chef in a restaurant.

She snapped back to the present time. The guy next to her had pulled down his eye covers and was fast asleep, hugging his backpack like a baby. He looked Indian, for sure. Most of her friends couldn't make out the difference between South Asians. But she knew for sure. This guy had facial features of a South Indian to be precise.

She knew because of two reasons.

Her present job was in an Indian Company, Infosys, in Basking Ridge, New Jersey. Her job as a business consultant meant she needed to travel to and fro to India quite often, and also to offices based in Hong Kong, Malaysia and Singapore. Her frequent visits to India, particularly to the South Indian cities of Bangalore, Chennai and Hyderabad made her familiar with the features of South Indians.

The other reason was the friend's circle of her billionaire boyfriend, Steve Mehrotra. Steve Mehrotra was from India but was an American by all means. He lived in a lavish house spread over two acres of land in the northern part of New Jersey. His friends were mainly other Indians, a horde of them from different parts of India. She used to socialize with all of them almost every weekend at Steve's lavish Friday night parties, which used to well extend until the early morning of Saturday.

Anyway, she didn't want to remember Steve now. The main reason she jumped into this extempore project by her company was Steve. She had to face the brunt of one of his temper tantrums last Sunday. She was relieved when her project leader had asked on Monday for any volunteers to leave immediately to complete a project in Hong Kong and then Chennai. She left late last Monday night.

To be fair, Steve had called thrice that evening and apologized to her. However, she had already committed to her team that she would leave for this two-week trip. She had taken the Emirates Flight to Dubai and then flown further to Hong Kong. After a gruelling week in Hong Kong, she had left this Monday (that is the day before), to Dubai where she would now further connect to Chennai for the second leg of her tour.

This was the time to make it up to Steve.

Steve had recently invested heavily in this new airline called Eastern Airlines. It was going to make its maiden flight from Dubai to Chennai today. In fact, he was the highest investor in this project.

She was going to take this flight today. She knew for sure that Steve was not coming to chug this flight off, but he would be coming for the larger inauguration ceremony at Mumbai airport a week later. So it would indeed be a surprise for him to know that she had travelled on this flight. She would send some photos on WhatsApp to him, as video calling was not permitted in this country.

However, this new flight meant she had no access to the regular Emirates lounge that she was so used to. She had the option to use the paid lounges, however, she decided against using them. Instead, she decided to use the seats near the boarding gates, something that she had done before only once in her life.

She looked at the guy next to her again. Just a moment ago, she had thought that the time she would spend here would be horrendous with this guy trying to hit on her. To her relief, she saw him fast asleep, deep in his dreamland as he himself had claimed. He was a rather tall Indian, a bit more than six feet in height, she guessed, and he did look rather...hmm... smart.

She smiled and decided to follow suit. She set the alarm to a quarter to one as she hugged her handbag the same way the guy next to her. Actually, this was a good idea, she felt. She too decided to catch twenty winks and fell asleep.

Chapter 9

Rajesh got up at quarter to one, to a loud sound, and looked around. It took him just a few moments to realise that it was an alarm; the phone of the lady next to him. He was irritated but soon he cooled down mainly because the girl was really good looking. Secondly, it was just enough time to grab some lunch before entering the flight.

"I'm sorry!" said the lady.

Oh, what a sweet voice! "That's okay, madam. I needed to get up now anyway."

She smiled.

Oh! What a sweet smile! Rajesh knew that this had to end here, unfortunately. He steadied himself, got up, and picked up his belongings. His eyes were still itching, *damn it!* He waved the lady bye, and to his happiness, she too waved back. He headed to the nearest restaurant where he had to wait in a small queue. He picked up pasta and headed to a table. He checked his boarding pass, and the boarding time on it. Boarding would begin in twenty minutes.

He looked up and saw a familiar person rush across him, probably in a hurry to get onto his flight. It was Ken, the Australian yachtsman, running to catch his flight to Singapore. Rajesh again smiled when he remembered his job profile.

Again, his eye itched. *Oh God! Hopefully, it's not conjunctivitis!* He had had conjunctivitis twice before, and both times he was quarantined in his room for four days! He needed to report to work tomorrow.

He looked around.

The person who sat two tables away from him was strange; two things struck familiar.

One: He knew her. She was the chick who sat next to him for two hours in the reclining chair. *Wow! She seemed to be following him everywhere!*

Second: She was doing something coincidentally similar to him – rubbing her eyes strongly.

Well, from his limited knowledge, he knew conjunctivitis was a disease that could spread like anything. His folks believed that it spread only by looking at another person having the same problem. Yes, if that logic was true, she had seen him eye to eye a few times. The vice versa was also true. The disease could have spread in either direction.

However, what his doctor friend had told him was a little different. Conjunctivitis usually spread not by looking, but via hands... rubbing eyes, and then shaking hands or using the same towel, cutlery, clothes or even furniture. Rajesh was sure he did not touch this girl, nor had they shared common towels or even furniture. *Then how did they both end up having itchy eyes?*

Maybe they had sprayed something toxic in the airport... but then everyone should have been having red eyes. No one else seemed to be bothered.

The girl looked up and gave him a glance. She smiled again but immediately looked back at her own phone and rubbed her eyes yet again.

Well, whatever. Rajesh just sighed. *So, a beautiful chick and I have itchy eyes! There ends the matter. No need to prod further. She goes her way and I go my way. There ends the story.*

He ate his pasta while checking out the latest news on the Times of India app. It was strange as to why his company, channel IBC news, still didn't have an app as yet. Well, anyway, the same old news flashed on the app – The ruling party at the central government and the opposition party at the central government had different representatives who were publically screwing the opposite party; nonsense to the say the least. He shut it off, scrolled Facebook and shut it off too.

He got up, gave one final glance at the girl, who was still concentrating on her phone. She still was rubbing her eyes. It felt strange parting from her as if she was a long-lasting crush whom he would probably never see again. He sighed heavily and proceeded to his gate, C22.

He used the washroom nearest the gate. He looked at himself in the mirror. He was taken aback immediately at his reflection. Both his eyes, but especially his left eye, were red. It was most surely conjunctivitis. *Shit!* Now he had to miss work for another few days, and his boss was going to be one angry man!

He went to the gate where his boarding pass was scanned. He requested the man at the counter if his seat could be changed to the one at the emergency exit.

"No. Full flight," said the guy at the counter.

Rajesh felt it was rather rude. The least he could have said was 'No, *Sir!*' Rajesh scorned at the fact that this guy was not all courteous, inspite of this being the maiden flight of the Airlines, *damn it!* He looked at the nametag. *Roshan.* Was it racism? He knew for sure that these Sinhalese guys from Sri Lanka hated Tamilians, even though they pretended that they don't. *Fucker!* He probably needed to mention his rude behaviour in the story he wrote. Anyway, he was in no mood for the slightest altercation.

He saw the person who was getting his passport checked by the other staff on duty, to see whether she was equally rude as this person here. The staff there seemed courteous. This guy, Roshan, was an exception!

He was about to proceed further when he suddenly looked back at the passenger on the other side. He walked with a limp, but that was not it, his face looked somewhat familiar, however, Rajesh was not able to place him. Well, as a reporter, he had probably interacted with countless people before... but this guy was different. He was not a person from Tamil Nadu, his features seemed North Indian, or at least from Maharashtra or Gujarat. He tried to strain his memory but decided to give up and proceed to the work he had been assigned: to cover the maiden flight of Eastern Airlines.

Rajesh moved on to the waiting hall at the gates where a small celebration was going on. There was a cake being cut by an elderly lady, probably a passenger, while some of the airline staff clapped. Rajesh pulled his camera out and took some snaps. After that, without further ado, the boarding began. Each passenger was handed over a small gift as they crossed towards the aerobridge from the waiting area.

He boarded the flight and went on to take his seat, which luckily was an aisle seat. He took two snaps again and packed his camera in his backpack, stowing it away in the overhead compartment.

As he sat in the seat, he saw the man with the limp enter. Funnily enough, his face now didn't seem so familiar! *What was happening to him?* It was probably the lack of sleep that was catching up. He strained to see if it was a mistaken identity. No, it was the same guy, wearing the same Khakhi pants, with a limp, and North Indian features! *Hmmm... time to forget this chap!*

He stretched a little and had an irresistible urge to rub his eyes again... but this time, it was not because of the itching.

He wanted to make sure his eyes were not fooling him!

One of the passengers, who had just entered the flight and was proceeding to the allotted seat, was none other than...his newfound crush!

Chapter 10

After the boarding gate incident, Sanjay Sharan had been pretty much jobless. He just moved around meeting his colleagues and got back. He had had his lunch in a leisurely manner. Well, this was one of his coolest mornings definitely. Only one incident needed to be sorted out the entire morning; cool indeed.

He felt a little sleepy as he had no work to do. Instead of just sitting idle in his counter, he decided to get a cup of coffee. Although there was a staff lounge at the far end of the terminal, he preferred the coffee shop right next to where a set of escalators brought passengers from the security hold below to this floor. He didn't mind paying some extra bucks here.

The coffee shop owner recognized him. "Rather early today, Mr Sanjay?" he spoke in his rather strong Arabic dialect.

"Yes! A cool day so far, not much action. Hoping it to be this way till 5:00 pm!"

"Lucky you! No action at all today?"

Sanjay thought about whether he should mention the Manikam incident. He decided to skip it. "Nope, none whatsoever!"

The owner smiled as he himself prepared the coffee for Sanjay. Sanjay thanked him, took the coffee and walked back to his counter. Just as he took the first sip of coffee, his phone rang. *Roshan! What has this bloke gotten into?*

"Hello, Roshan."

"Sir, this is kind of an emergency. I need you here immediately."

"Where, boss?"

"Gate C22."

Sanjay wanted to know what happened now, and why he couldn't handle it himself. *These kids needed to grow up!* But yes, it had been a boring day, so any action was welcome. He headed to the gate.

As he approached the gate, he saw the sign that the gate was already closed. The destination read Chennai, and yes, as per the timing, the flight should be ready to leave in a minute or so. *So why was Roshan calling now?*

A couple of possibilities ran in his mind. Maybe a passenger, or worse still, a group of passengers had not made it on time and were held up elsewhere… probably at the security hold and were creating a ruckus for having to miss this flight. This situation was not uncommon, but the logistics team could not hold up the flight any longer. They would have to accommodate these passengers on some other flight. The other possibility was some software malfunction, which did not allow Roshan to give clearance to the flight team that boarding was complete. This hadn't happened in the recent past. The software was pretty robust.

"Yes, Roshan?"

"Sir, there seems to be a problem here!" Roshan blurted out.

Give me a break from this sentence. Surely you guys don't call me to share any good news. Get on with it! "Yes, tell me…"

"The Chennai flight has received clearance for pushback… but suddenly I get a call from the pilot that we need to evacuate two passengers."

Drunken riot? Racist comments? Misbehaving with the cabin crew? "Why on earth?"

"The captain received a call from the security it seems!"

"About what?"

"The security team has noticed on the CCTV camera placed on the aerobridge that two passengers onboard have conjunctivitis. They need to be disembarked immediately to prevent people from catching it."

Something was definitely amiss here, in fact, quite a few things were amiss. Sanjay's mind was quickly racked up with a number of things that were strange, but he didn't want to analyse them now. He had to act quickly as the plane was cleared for pushback and disembarking two passengers would have to be done quickly.

"Mr Roshan!" Sanjay wanted to say, '*You bloody idiot*' but decided not to do so at the moment. "Why the hell were you or your colleagues not able to pick up the same?"

"Sir, most passengers would have red eyes coming from long connecting flights! I didn't notice, sorry!"

Sorry, my foot! If a CCTV camera could catch it, how could this dick miss it from such close quarters? No wonder people detested this guy so much! "What's the status with the passengers?"

"They are being informed now sir, and surely they will create a huge commotion, that's why I called you, sir!"

"Hmmm…" Was Roshan right in anticipating trouble and calling him here, or was he doing the wrong thing by chickening out of the responsibility? It was difficult to tell. One thing was for sure, Sanjay's relatively cool day could really turn into a nightmare even if these two passengers were inherently cool people. They would in all possibilities blow their heads off. *Brace for it!*

Chapter 11

Gabriela had just settled in her seat after returning from the washroom. The captain was announcing that the flight was ready for pushback. As usual, they were instructed to sit back, relax and enjoy the flight.

She once again gazed at her phone to see if Steve had replied to her message and photo that she had sent on WhatsApp just before entering the flight. To be fair, it would be close to 5:00 am in New Jersey, and she didn't expect him to have seen the phone. Well, he hadn't. She decided to call him once she reached Chennai. *He surely would be pleased!*

In the washroom, she had checked her eyes again. Yes, the left eye was bright red. It was surely some infection because it just was worsening over the last few hours, instead of clearing.

She could have sworn it was the Indian guy, who seemed to follow her everywhere, was the source of this infection. Or rather, it was she who was following him everywhere. It was, after all, she who reached the resting lounge after him and then the restaurant, and now, to top it all, she had followed him into the same flight! *Whatever!* It was clear that this dude had a similar eye problem and surely she got it from him. She had looked at him in the eye multiple times by now. The virus must have transmitted from him. *Damn him!*

It was rather strange as she knew that the virus couldn't spread just by looking at him. Maybe he had used the same resting chair that she had just before she arrived there. *Yes, that was definitely possible!*

She adjusted her seatbelt. She could swear that the flight attendants were chatting with each other while intermittently looking at her. They had probably noticed her eye.

Sure enough, one lady, who happened to look like the senior cabin attendant, approached her, "Miss Gabriela Fabregas?"

"Yes?"

"I am Shirley, the lead cabin attendant. I hate to be the one breaking the news, but we have been instructed to ask you to deplane from this flight." One could hear the discomfort in her voice.

"What? Why?" Gabriela asked, although she already knew the answer.

"I'm afraid you have highly contagious conjunctivitis, which will be disastrous for all the people on board. You know this is a highly pressurized closed environment and we risk everyone here."

"No! I don't want to deplane. I have important work in Chennai!"

"I know how you must be feeling. I understand that bad feeling, but it is only in the safety interest of all the other passengers and the crew that you must leave!"

Gabriela didn't know what to do. Her instinct was to look at the Indian chap, and she could see that a male attendant was breaking the news of the same fate to him. He too was clearly agitated. Well, she had to attend to herself first. "Why can't I just wear my sunglasses and sleep? Or maybe eye covers on top of those and sleep?"

"No madam, please try to understand, it spreads mainly by touch…"

"Just tie my hands up damn it…but let me go!" Gabriela screamed but cooled down immediately. Her expression turned to one of pleading, "Please! Please let me go!"

"I'm sorry, madam. Please try to understand!"

The people around her all started to give her dirty looks, and a man next to her also requested, "Please lady! Please leave!" A mother of two children looked at her pleadingly.

She had no choice, she guessed! *Damn that guy! Wish I had never seen him!* She picked up her bag from the overhead cabin. She gave one final try… "Can I sit in first class: in a suite? I'll pay the difference!"

"No madam! That too won't be allowed. Besides, the flight is full."

"Can I sit in the alleyway? Somewhere?"

"No madam." Shirley was adamant.

She could see the equally ruffled Indian chap also being escorted out of the flight.

The two angered and irritated persons were escorted until the aerobridge, after which one of the ground staff ushered them off.

The South Indian guy looked requally bewildered, said, "I could have sworn I was totally alright until I reached the part where we rested in the airport!"

Gabriela was taken aback. *Was he trying to blame her?* "And I'm sure *I* was totally alright until then too!"

"And it is unlikely that this virus I have got is from the icy, frozen New York. Where have you flown in from?"

"Hong Kong." *Really? Was it possible that it was she who actually had the infection and she had passed it on to him?*

"Sir and madam," the person who accompanied them, spoke for the first time. "I know a little medicine! I used to work in a hospital and I know for sure that conjunctivitis does not spread from one person to another, and manifest itself immediately. It's just a coincidence. Must be in the air. You must have acquired it at least twelve hours before meeting each other!"

The three didn't speak further. Yes, what this other guy had said was right, perhaps. It was too premature of her to assume that she had acquired the infection from the tall guy. *Surely, he too was thinking the same about her!*

They reached the boarding gates where two other people, one of whom had scanned their boarding passes, greeted them.

The person, who looked senior, addressed them. "Hello, madam. Hello, sir. I am Sanjay Sharan, the terminal in-charge today, and this is Roshan, my colleague."

Like shit, I want to know your names! I just want to go to Chennai! Gabriela wanted to scream loudly. She didn't hide her irritation. She just said curtly, "What now?"

"May I have a look at your boarding passes?" Sanjay said.

"Why? You don't want to get conjunctivitis. I have touched it all over!" the Indian guy said.

Gabriela realised the truth in the statement, and she could not help but chuckle when she saw Sanjay biting his lip when he realised the same!

But Roshan was up to it. He immediately pulled out a pair of blue gloves from his pocket: frisking gloves. He wore them quickly and asked, "Please pass them now!"

They reluctantly handed them over.

Roshan read out their names as if they were in line entering a prison, "Miss Gabriela Fabregas. Mr Rajesh Rajesh; did I get that right? Your name and family are the same?"

The tall South Indian nodded.

"Mr Sanjay, you have to help us and get us back on the flight. Immediately!" Rajesh said.

"I'm sorry, the flight has already left as we speak."

"What!" the two of them roared in unison.

Chapter 12

Well, well. This was never going to be easy.

As expected, the two passengers threw a fit of rage. They both spoke simultaneously.

Rajesh was trying to explain how he needed to report to work the same night.

Gabriela was screaming how important tomorrow morning's meeting was, and they had no idea how much money was involved.

Here, Sanjay had to be a cool cucumber. If he lost his cool, the situation would escalate like crazy, especially because the guy next to him, Roshan, could only make the matters worse and not improve them in any way. "I hate to be the one breaking the news. Please realise that I am only a messenger on behalf of the Health Authorities and Airport security."

"This is the second time I am hearing this shit excuse!" Gabriela said, "If all of you are only messengers, I need to talk to the person in authority here!"

"Yes, of course, madam. To leave the airport and reach a safe place, we need the health authority's clearance and immigration and security clearance."

"We need to leave the airport?" Rajesh screamed, "Why can't we just take the next flight?"

"Because sir, the condition of your eye is unlikely to improve any time so soon," Sanjay said calmly. He felt sorry for the two actually.

"What shit! Why can't we just be accommodated somewhere in the airport? The doctors can check us and give us some medicines and send us on our way by the evening flight!"

"We cannot allow you to be at the airport, please. It is an equal health hazard in this very crowded airport!"

"Why can't I have a doctor see me here? This is my civil right!" Gabriela shouted now.

"Civil rights are alright madam, but we have civil responsibilities as well. We need to protect other people too, don't we?"

"Why can't we be put up in the airport hotel until the doctor sees us?"

"We tried that madam, to be very honest. But all the rooms are booked here. There has been another flight delayed near the A gates."

Rajesh looked at Gabriela and said, "I don't see the point arguing with these two here. We need to speak to the authorities."

Gabriela didn't want to budge, but sadly, she saw the sense in the point that Rajesh was making. This conversation with the two was getting them nowhere.

They looked at each other and just shrugged.

"Okay, take us to the Health Authorities," Gabriela said.

They followed Sanjay and Roshan reluctantly walking past all the gates and going down the elevators to the ground floor. They then proceeded to the security hold where Sanjay had a long chat with the security officer. The Security officer seemed upset, but he let the four pass in the opposite direction.

Gabriela had been to this airport so many times before, but this was the first time she was walking in the opposite direction. She lost her orientation for a while. They went past the sign that said 'Way to immigration and baggage collection.'

They were taken to a room, which read Dubai Airport Health Authority. The next twenty-five minutes or so, everything they said seemed futile. A doctor certified them as having conjunctivitis, prescribed them antibiotic eye drops that were not available at the airport anyway, and recommended that they be quarantined outside the airport. All the pleas of the two passengers fell on deaf ears. The doctor told them that they needed a fresh check-up from a hospital the next day to see whether they were fit to travel. He gave them the address of the hospital they needed to visit to get the certificate. Until the day they produced the certificate, they wouldn't be allowed on a flight out of Dubai. He was pretty clear and stern about that.

They went to a counter where they were issued a hotel pass for two nights, a complimentary chauffeur drive to the hotel and a pass that would guide them through immigration. Sanjay and Roshan were still with them as they passed through immigration like two police officers that were posted just to guard them.

To their surprise, the immigration officers didn't ask a word, and their passports were stamped to enter the United Arab Emirates. The duo was literally being thrown out of the airport into the wild world!

After immigration, Sanjay told them, "I will now guide you to the Emirates Chauffeur Service, who have decided to help Eastern Airlines today, and they will make sure you reach your hotel Radan. I'm sorry, madam, and Sir... this is the protocol!"

Protocol my ass! Gabriela thought.

Something else troubled Rajesh though. He could have sworn that he saw the familiar-looking Maharashtrian/Gujarati limping his way out of the airport as well. A member of the airlines was accompanying him too...

But... there was something strange... the deplaned passenger also seemed to be in the uniform of Eastern Airlines staff. *Why did that happen?* He was going crazy. He had first seen this guy scanning his passport at the gate of the flight. Then he saw someone similar in the flight, but he was almost sure that there was something amiss; the faces did not match. Now he saw someone similar again, however, this time the faces matched but the dresses did not! *What was happening? Or was it just his imagination that was driving him wild?*

He snapped back to reality as Gabriela said firmly and loud, "Wait a minute. I need to collect my checked-in bags! Where do I collect them?"

"Me too!" Rajesh said in agreement.

What Sanjay said next really made them fume.

"Since it was not a major safety issue, we could not unload your baggage from the flight. The luggage compartment had already been closed and the paperwork was already complete. So if we had ordered that we remove your baggage from the flight, it would have involved reopening the luggage compartment, searching your baggage, unloading them and completing the papers all over again. It would have delayed the flight by nearly an hour. Again, as I said before, it was not a major security or safety issue so we are not allowed to delay the flight. I am sorry to say, your baggage has gone to Chennai and will be collected there by the staff. Meanwhile, the airlines will ensure all basic amenities are taken care of..."

CHAPTER 13

Rajesh and Gabriela were fuming. Gabriela gave a huge scream of disgust. "This is a torture of the first grade! I need to go to the American Embassy. You people have jailed me here for no reason!"

"The American and the Indian embassies have already been emailed, madam," Roshan said.

Sadist!

Just then, they reached the exit and Sanjay guided them to the right, while most of the public headed left. It was the way to the Emirates chauffeur service.

Rajesh had one mind to run to the left and away from this pack, but he weighed his options carefully. He just decided to follow the others.

"Why couldn't you remove my baggage? What will I wear for two days?" Gabriela asked.

Just as if to answer her question, a huge burly man approached them. His looks were intimidating, to say the least. So was his voice, "Miss Gabriela Fabregas and Mr Rajesh Rajesh... hey wait a minute, your first name and family name are same...?"

"Yes!"

"Okay, here are your amenity bags. These contain certain toiletries, a pair of underclothes and also a T-shirt and jeans for the Gent, and a T-shirt and pants for the lady. Hope we picked the right size for you, judged from the CCTV footage."

"What CCTV footage?" Rajesh asked.

Again Sanjay had the unpleasant task of explaining how they were actually identified to have conjunctivitis in the first place.

"Okay, you dude! Better wash your hands with all the fucking soap available at the airport as you might just get the shit from us!" Rajesh was clearly exasperated.

"Sir, please mind your language. I am just doing my duty. All this is just not my fault!"

Rajesh regained his composure quickly.

They were guided to the cab counter; they gave their names again, and then they were taken to the place where the cars were. They were all made to sit in a BMW SUV, and the driver was instructed to take them to the hotel Radan.

Gabriela and Rajesh took the backseat.

There followed a short period of uneasy silence. Gabriela decided to break the silence with an awkward but extremely common question, "Your name and family name are the same? Why?"

Rajesh had been asked this question a zillion times before. He grinned, something that he had not done for some time now. "Blame it on my beloved maternal grandmother, who prayed at a certain *Sheetaladevi* temple in Pune, the place where I was born. She asked the temple priest as to what he suggested was a good name to her newly born grandson. He had asked her to name him the same as the doctor who had treated her husband when he had had a heart problem recently. And what was the doctor's name? The same name as her son-in-law's!"

Gabriela also laughed, but it was apparent that she was awaiting further clarification.

Rajesh continued, "Now, we are Tamilians...are you familiar with the states of India?"

"Yes, quite a bit, quite a bit. I work for Infosys and travel often to India."

"Wow, really?"

"Yes, really... now complete your story first!" Gabriela was easing into a conversation with Rajesh. Rajesh too was happy for it seemed to be the sensible thing to do. They both were in the same boat; the same wretched boat.

"Well, in our state, we usually don't have family names. All our second names are actually our father's names. If my father's name had been Raman, my name would have been Rajesh Raman. But thanks to the temple priest who was so clear in his thoughts, I came to be known as Rajesh Rajesh!"

"Great! What do you do, Mr Rajesh?"

"I am a reporter, and guess what? I was supposed to cover the maiden flight of Eastern Airlines! And guess where I am? Wheeled out of the maiden flight!" Rajesh laughed.

Gabriela smiled too.

Oh, her sweet smile! "What about you, Miss Gabriela?" Rajesh asked.

"As I said, I work for Infosys. I am a software business consultant. I travel frequently to India."

"Interesting!"

"And guess what? I too was supposed to be especially excited to be in the maiden flight!"

"Really, why do you say so?"

"My fiancé is the major investor in this airline! Although this is not the official launch of the airlines, I wanted to surprise him by being part of the first flight!"

Oh Shit! She is already engaged! By what she says, her fiancé is the billionaire from New Jersey that he had come to hear about, what's his name…?

The driver of the car interrupted his thoughts, "We are here!"

It was hardly six or seven minutes that they had been in the car. The hotel was really close, and it was majestic, similar to all the structures in Dubai.

Gabriela and Rajesh thanked the driver, went up to the reception and presented their vouchers. The check-in process took unusually long. As they stood, Rajesh looked at Gabriela. She looked gorgeous, even after all that she had been through.

His mind then wandered to the guy with the limp… he had seen him somewhere. Why was he in the airline uniform? Where had he seen him before? Was he his batch-mate in engineering? Or maybe in school?

Somehow he felt he had seen him somewhere, sometime. Something was amiss here.

Chapter 14

Sanjay and Roshan were walking the long road back. They knew that to re-enter the airport they had to walk in through the departures again, which was a circuitous route. Sanjay was actually feeling sorry for the individuals he had to escort out. He could imagine how irritating it could be to be holed up in a foreign land, especially when the two looked to be young professionals who had to report to work. Moreover, they were to stay here without their luggage, which was on its way to Chennai. He sure hoped his colleagues would take good care of them.

Gabriela and Rajesh must be absolutely distraught at this prospect, he presumed. But this was a risk he could not take. He could not expose the fellow passengers and the cabin crew to a highly contagious disease such as conjunctivitis. Not only it was dangerous, but such an incident would also have brought the airlines and airport into disrepute.

He looked at Roshan and asked, "Kid, why were you not able to spot such an obvious problem when they were presenting the boarding passes?"

"I don't know, Sir! To tell you the truth, maybe I was irritated. The airlines have made me run around since morning as they missed many small things in their operations systems. I have been working since breakfast without a single break! Maybe that's why I missed it. I am sorry, sir!"

"You haven't had your lunch until now either?"

"No, sir."

"Okay, come on. I'll accompany you for lunch once we get into the main terminal building. The treat is on me." *Why on Earth did I just say that? I hate this guy! Maybe not… maybe I am really sorry for all this guy has been through since morning. He was just being sincere at work. Well, whatever, I have had enough action for today I guess… I too could do with some coffee!*

"Thanks, sir!"

They crossed the security hold and passed into the terminal. Sanjay looked at his watch. It was quarter-to-four. Another one hour and fifteen minutes, and he could drive back home and take a cool shower. *Oh, how he longed for one now!*

"I guess it has been quite hectic for you too, today, sir!" Roshan said.

Sanjay was actually beginning to like this guy. "Yeah. I think I'll just put my walkie-talkie and mobile phone off!" Funnily, just as he was picking up his mobile phone to do the same, it rang. It was somewhere from the airport, he guessed by looking at the number.

"Hello?"

"Mr Sanjay Sharan. I am Irfan Mohammed, the deputy security officer in-charge today. I need you and the Eastern Airlines staff member Mr Roshan to visit the security headquarters immediately!"

"Okay. Why? … Okay, no, we shall come!"

"Good!" Officer Irfan just hung up abruptly.

So much for the uneventful day that Sanjay was pleased about until lunchtime! What the hell was this now? He explained the same to Roshan but advised him to grab a quick sandwich before he joined him there. He would go ahead.

Roshan growled loudly. But he knew he couldn't oppose one bit.

The boy was having a tough day! Sanjay felt sorrier for him than he had just a moment ago. He just patted him on his back and set to the security headquarters.

He wondered. *Why did they want him and Roshan and him?* It was obvious that it had something to do with the passengers they had escorted outside. That was the only possible connection between Roshan and he, which was of any significance today. However, Sanjay was sure that he had adhered to all set protocols of escorting the passengers out. Nothing was out of the ordinary. *Were they worried that they too may have conjunctivitis and send them home for a small paid vacation? Hmmm…*

He entered the Security office where he immediately recognized Officer Irfan. His six-feet-three-inches frame and broad shoulders were not to be missed. He had a worried look on his face.

"Hi Sanjay, come!" he said.

Sanjay was sure it was not some cordial meet. Irfan looked dead serious. "Hello, officer!"

"Sanjay, we have to be quick…"

What happened? Why Roshan and he? Instead of racking his brains too much, he just decided to listen, and when he heard what the officer said next, the reason why Roshan was summoned with him became clear… And it was not pleasing to the ear at all.

"The Chennai flight that had taken off half an hour back has a security issue. It is returning. The passengers will be evacuated immediately. I want you and the manager, who was posted there, Mr Roshan, to be back at the gate to handle them. I am sending two officers here…" He pointed at two other officers "… with you, just in case. Please feel free to ask them any questions once you get there. But you have to leave now, and now means now!"

Chapter 15

Rajesh and Gabriela were allotted rooms next to each other on the second floor. Rajesh entered his room and headed straight to the bathroom to check his eyes. Yes. The left eye was really red. No wonder they had removed him from the flight.

He washed his face and neatly towelled it, being careful not to irritate his eyes much.

He looked at his cell phone. It was still in flight mode. He slid the flight phone mode off and logged on to the Wi-Fi. Instantaneously, all his apps buzzed. He first proceeded to WhatsApp. There were around seven messages waiting, mostly jokes from his pals. One number was unrecognized though.

He opened the message. It just said, 'Rajesh, you are in deep shit. Message me a number where I can call to explain. Captain."

At first, Rajesh's instincts told him to just ignore the message. But considering how strange the day had been, he wanted to be sure that whoever this guy was not fooling around.

He thought for a while and decided his day could not get any shittier than it already was. He also concluded that it would be unsafe to give his hotel number and room number to this guy, whoever he was.

He messaged back, "Call me on WhatsApp now."

His message was read almost immediately.

"No WhatsApp calls allowed in Dubai. Please let me know if you have international roaming on your cell. Or give me some other number."

Oh yes, that was true; it wasn't allowed. This guy was serious, whoever he was.

He had international roaming on, so he could receive phone calls. He only preferred to keep his cell carrier disconnected at most times as he was on leave and checked his missed phone calls only once in a while. Whoever this guy was, he already knew his cell number, and so it was wiser to just put it on and ask him to call. He switched on his carrier and chose Etisalat.

He then messaged the person on WhatsApp, "You can call me on my cell now. But be sure this is very important as receiving calls is very expensive for me."

"It sure is. It sure is."

"Okay," Rajesh replied and waited.

An Indian number rang.

"Hello," Rajesh said carefully.

A lady spoke in Tamil, "Sir, we are calling from Annapurna developers. We have some open plots for sale near the East Coast Road. Will you be interested?"

Rajesh wanted to blast the lady on the phone and dish out some abuses, but that would only increase his phone bill. He just said a quick no and cut the phone. *Bloodsuckers!*

Another phone rang. This time it was a UK number, starting with +44. Hope this was not a promotional number. Rajesh picked the phone up.

"Hello?"

"Hello, Mr Rajesh Rajesh, I am the one who messaged you now." The man was perhaps no older than him. His accent was similar to some Indian who had just moved to the US or UK.

"Who are you? The message I got was from an Indian number!"

"Yes, I use that number for sending WhatsApp messages." The man read out the number so that Rajesh could double-check, which he did by putting the call on hold. He had to be sure that no one was playing a fool with him.

"Okay, who are you? From where are you calling? What do you want from me?"

"You ask a lot of questions, Rajesh. At the moment, you can just call me Captain."

"Okay, Captain. Please tell me."

"Well, let me tell you first, I am your absolute well-wisher."

"Okay?"

"You must listen to me. In less than probably thirty minutes, you will be in danger of being one of the most wanted men in Dubai..." The Captain said flatly.

The tone was so flat that Rajesh did not take him seriously at first. However, here was a guy who was taking exceptional measures in calling him. It was unlikely that he was just a fraud caller. "What do you mean?"

"I mean just that. Gabriela and you have been deplaned on purpose. The flight you were on has a bomb in it. The terrorist organization wanted you both deplaned so that all the attention is diverted to you!"

"What?" Just as he heard that, he heard a commotion outside his room. He was sure that policemen were outside. "What are you saying?"

"I meant what I said!"

As the Captain said that, the commotion outside grew louder. "I'll call you right back!" *Rajesh said and cut the call. Had the Captain spoken the truth? Was it the police already?*

Chapter 16

Rajesh decided to take the bold step. *Anyway, there was no option either!* He decided to open the door. As he did, he was surprised to see no one outside his room. The sounds he had heard now emanated two rooms away from his. He decided to have a peek. He went out of his room, being careful to pull out the key card. The last thing he wanted now was to be locked outside the room. He went to room number 208, and it was open. He took the liberty to just stop right outside the door. *Oh My God!* He was stunned at what he saw.

There were four people in the room. Two were members of the hotel security, one was a policeman and the fourth person was the shocker… it was the Indian guy with the limp, again. *He seemed to follow him everywhere! It took him some more time to realise that this guy had actually checked in to the room next to his. Who the hell was he? Was he also deplaned from the flight? Why? His eyes looked normal! Even if he was deplaned, why didn't he come with them? Why was he being treated differently? Besides, he appeared to wear formals when entering the flight, when he came out of the flight he was dressed in some airport uniform, and now he was in informal clothing!*

Who on earth was this guy? And where had he seen him before?

The security personnel and the policeman were going through his baggage, and the mysterious man hardly seemed to protest. The policeman pulled out a revolver from his bag. *What! This was getting more and more dangerous! This guy was carrying a gun!*

"Now, what about this Mr Kabir Dravid?" the policeman asked.

Kabir Dravid? I have never heard this name before! It just doesn't ring a bell! Yet, with each passing moment, Rajesh was certain that he had seen Kabir sometime before and also possibly interacted with him.

"That's my gun. Purchased in June 2014." He pulled out two papers from his bag. "Here is the bill and the license of the gun. It's a UAE license."

Kabir's accent seemed typical of a Maharashtrian. Rajesh had stayed long enough in Pune to realise that. Kabir was around five-feet-nine-inches tall and had green eyes, which were also typical of Brahmins from the Konkan area of Maharashtra. His surname suggested the same origin too. However, his name sounded more cosmopolitan; a name that was common to both the Hindus and the Muslims. *But where had he seen him before?* He still failed to recollect.

"But you stay in India."

"Yes, but I am a senior manager in Magna Builders. I am based in Mumbai. We have a project here in Dubai. That's why I am here. I have some valid reasons to hold a gun, which I presented to get this gun and the license."

The hotel security said, "I am sorry sir, as per our rules, guests are not allowed to hold firearms in this hotel."

"But I hold a license, right? Officer?"

"Yes, technically he can have it," the policeman said.

The security officer was not however convinced, "No, sir." He paused. "Okay, I will be taking your gun into safe custody for an hour. I would hand it over to you once the hotel management has sorted it out with the police. Please understand, sir, the security of the hotel is my only job!"

"Okay," the police officer said, "Do what he says, Mr Kabir."

"Really? That's absurd!"

"That's fair enough!"

"But my papers are in order!"

"Whether or not it complies with the hotel policies is the only concern. Frankly speaking, I don't have much clarity on this issue, either. We will return the gun if and when it is feasible, as quickly as possible."

"Okay, do I get a receipt?" Kabir asked.

That was enough for Rajesh. He headed back to his room

He introspected for a short while.

Many things were strange here.

There was a bomb on the flight! Or at least, that's what the Captain had said. Oh my God! His mind had to make the choice of thinking further of the implications of the same for the passengers on board and their families. But his mind decided to shift to another topic.

Gabriela and he had been deplaned on purpose! Both were made to get conjunctivitis by the terrorist organization! And now everyone would believe that they had to do something with the bomb on board! Holy shit!

Then, it was indeed strange that Kabir Dravid had also boarded the flight. It was also strange how he had changed clothes so many times. He also had been deplaned for reasons unknown. Airport staff apparently did also escort him. He too was given a room at the Radan. He had a gun, but with a valid license. So Kabir was a fellow passenger deplaned. But somehow there was something strange.

He paused. Kabir had walked out directly from a flight that he had boarded. That means...

Yes! Of course! How could Kabir possibly have a gun with him now in Dubai? The only luggage they had with them is what they had carried onto the flight, and it was impossible to carry a gun on to a flight! That means Kabir had received the gun from someone else after landing. He was no ordinary person like Gabriela and him. If there was a bomb on the flight, he had something to do with it! And Kabir, in all probability, was after Gabriela and him with some ulterior motive!

CHAPTER 17

Officer Irfan Mohammad recapitulated what had just happened to the security in-chief, Shahid Aziz, who was on leave today. Shahid had to rush to the airport immediately. Irfan had been brief, "Sir, wherever, whatever. Please report to the airport immediately."

Luckily, Shahid was just relaxing at home after a hectic morning drive to Sharjah and back, to meet his aunt-in-law. His house was only three kilometres away and he could make it here in fifteen minutes. Irfan had sounded quite worried on the phone.

Twenty minutes back, Irfan had just settled on his desk with a cup of coffee. His landline rung. "Hello…" he had said in a bored tone.

"Hello, officer Irfan, this is exchange. There seems to be a person calling from the United Kingdom. He has a very specific request saying that he has to talk to you and it is a matter of supreme urgency."

"Must be some nut trying to play a prank."

"No sir, I don't think so. His number begins with plus four-four. He says it's about avoiding a great disaster. He sounded confident and composed. We must listen to him, I feel."

Irfan was not convinced one bit. He received hoax calls at least once a month, and it often ended in a wild goose chase. He had sighed, "Okay, connect me."

The call got connected. A voice with a distinct Indian accent spoke on the phone, "Hello, Officer Irfan?"

"Yes, sir. Who is this?"

"You can call me 'Captain.'"

Irfan smirked. Hoaxers had progressed in life. "Yes, Captain, tell me!"

"Don't ask me too many questions. Just listen to what I say carefully. The flight EA001: Eastern Airlines flight from Dubai to Chennai. It has a bomb on board."

"Really, ha?"

"Yes, absolutely serious. It is a scientifically advanced bomb; the chemistry and physics of which will be beyond your comprehension right now. This flight will be blasted to smithereens and all passengers will be dead."

Irfan was astonished at the level of confidence this voice had. It didn't seem like any ordinary hoaxer's usually shaky voice. As he listened, he clicked on the computer screen to check the flight status. It had just taken off.

Well, it hadn't happened since he had joined this post. Hoaxers usually spoke of bombs in different parts of the airport, or flights that were yet to take off. He had heard instances where the hoax was about a flight that had already taken off in other airports, but not here. It was usually by someone who wanted the flight to land back, usually by a jilted lover or someone who had repented fighting his or her spouse.

"Okay, Captain… how do you know about this? Why will anyone in the UK know about it? What is the connection? What is the ransom?"

"Don't ask questions. This is not about some ransom. Let's put it this way – At this moment, I am a well-wisher. We will get to the nitty-gritty later. Now we have more than 250 passengers about to die. Take care of them first."

"Look… Mr Captain or whatever; we have advanced security systems in place. No bomb can enter the airport, leave alone a flight."

"As I told you, this bomb is too advanced. Not many people know the science behind it yet. It will never be detected in your systems. But I can tell you, it can blow everything in a one-mile radius. So hang up now and take some serious steps to avoid the blast. If I am right, the bomb is set to go off around five forty-five to six-fifteen, local time. And I'll give you one piece of solid advice. Don't try to find the bomb with a bomb squad. Even if you remove the plane of all the checked-in baggage, you will never be able to detect it whatsoever. Don't involve them at all and waste precious time. Bye."

The Captain had hung up abruptly, but his tone had left a lasting impact on officer Irfan. He had to act extremely swiftly.

Now it was five minutes to four pm and a remarkably cool Shahid Aziz sat in front of him. Shahid was a cool and composed leader, a quality that most people admired. He almost never showed emotions suggesting panic or tension. Many people jokingly referred to him as Mahinder Singh Dhoni, the name of the erstwhile captain of the Indian Cricket team, who was supposed to have the same leadership qualities. Although Irfan hated cricket, he had heard enough of this comparison before by his colleagues.

He spoke. His emotions were in check, but his voice was authoritative. "I can think of four possible problems here. One is how to handle passengers. They have to be deplaned quickly. But I guess we have Sanjay from operations and two of our best officers on that job. So it should be smooth. However, we must have one team member constantly monitoring the evacuation.

"Second, if the informant is correct about the complexities of the bomb, how can we be sure it is not in the carry-on baggage of a terrorist on board? We must have one of our brightest officers to create and execute a plan regarding the collection and transfer of the hand baggage to a remote area at least four kilometres away from any inhabited areas before five forty-five. In fact, I suggest that you take charge of this. It will save us much more time than explaining and giving instructions to another chap. It is possible. The baggage can be returned once things are clear. Okay?"

"Okay, sir!" Irfan said. It didn't seem a great responsibility, but it seemed a very important one. Irfan had to admit to himself that he had not even considered this possibility! His boss was smart.

"But I have a hunch that the bomb isn't actually there in that baggage," Shahid said. It deflated Irfan's feeling of importance a little bit.

His boss continued, "Third, should we really involve the ground staff to remove all the checked-in luggage and move it to a remote place too? I don't see how we can do that in time. The bomb could be anywhere on the flight as well. How do we get our bomb squad to go through an entire Boeing 747 in such a short time? Besides, the informant is extremely clear that they will be of no help whatsoever.

"Fourth and the most important plausible option. We need to remove the flight from the airport almost immediately after the passengers come out. There is an isolated airstrip two hundred kilometres south of Sharjah. We need to get clearance from the Sharjah monarchy, from our air traffic control and monarchy. I take the responsibility of doing this. The most difficult part is to find a brave pilot to fly the plane there, as it would really be a touch-and-go situation. Assuming we have it all smooth at Dubai airport after getting the requisite permissions and if the flight leaves and reaches the designated place, the pilot would still require to be removed quickly and taken to a place which is at least two kilometres away from the plane for his own safety. All this has to happen before five forty-five and that's gonna be an enormous challenge."

Irfan had to take a few seconds to admire his senior's great analytical skills. There was hardly any time he had taken to calculate all this. No wonder he was called the cool leader. But one thing was clear, he had to execute his plans immediately. "I agree, Sir. I will now ensure Hassan takes care of task one – that is monitoring the rapid evacuation. I will assemble a small team and carry out task two immediately. As I understand, you will take care of sending off of the plane to Sharjah's isolated airstrip. I will allot five officers on duty to you right away. Okay, Sir?"

"Absolutely, Irfan. Best of luck to all of us! This will be a do or die mission. By the way, ask Hassan to find out more and do a background check on whoever this Captain guy is."

CHAPTER 18

Rajesh was stunned.

Is Kabir the terrorist? Was he a don of some sort? Just why was he provided with a gun? And when? Did he plan to murder someone? Did he plan to shoot Rajesh and Gabriela?

He decided to call the Captain.

"Now listen coolly. I can tell you one thing for sure. You are in deeper shit than you think you are," the Captain said.

That he had guessed!

"You are in multiple levels of trouble my friend. I can tell you the worse is yet to come. The flight you were supposed to board took off an hour back, but is now returning to Dubai!"

"What! How?"

"Most probably some Intelligence input has warned them of a bomb threat. We still don't know how, but we know one thing for sure – the flight is coming back and Dubai police will now be on the lookout for anyone remotely connected with the security threat."

Rajesh gulped.

"As per the initial sequence of events, the bomb was supposed to go off much later..."

How did the Captain know that? Was he the terrorist? Or was he himself from Dubai police?

The Captain continued, "Now as things stand, Dubai police are already aware of the bomb and be sure they will get to your doorstep in no longer than half an hour."

"What? Who are you? How can I believe you anyway?"

"You should, and you will survive. Yes, I said it right. You will live only if you believe me. If you don't, there are two possibilities, either you will be dead for real, or near dead rotting in jail throughout life!"

"What! What! What!" Rajesh was going crazy. This entire scenario was too difficult to digest. "Already, Kabir has checked-in to the room next to mine. I am trapped!"

"Kabir?" The Captain's voice definitely spelt surprise, even though he didn't try to make it obvious. The Captain did not know who Kabir was!

"You don't know who Kabir is?"

"No!"

"He is a guy who had checked into the flight with me. I am sure. But mysteriously enough, he too is off the plane and has been put up in the room next to mine!" Rajesh did not offer more details.

The Captain paused. "This, my boy, I too am not aware of! So, Mr Kabir is probably from the terrorist organization! Or maybe he is from the Intelligence agency. Either way, you are fucked, I guess!"

"What do I do now?" Rajesh fretted.

"My boy, the time has come to act swiftly! The time is 4:00 pm. Gabriela and you have thirty minutes to meet Mark at the concierge. We have a tight schedule to be followed. You may come with your hand luggage, but make sure your phones are left behind. Your phones will be tapped very soon. You will be provided with new phones and new SIMs by Mark. He will then guide you to safety. No more questions. Choose to live, that's my advice! Bye."

"Wait!" Rajesh said, but the Captain's phone went dead.

He dialled back, not once, but thrice. Each time, he got an 'engaged' tone after the first ring. It meant only one thing. The Captain had blocked his number.

Choose to live...

CHAPTER 19

The two officers who accompanied Sanjay and a bewildered Roshan back to gate C22, gave an impressive briefing of what Officer Irfan had told them. The message was crystal clear. The Chennai flight had a bomb. The passengers needed to be evacuated, and all of them needed to be seated in the C22 boarding lounge only. They were not allowed to leave that area.

Sanjay was horrified at the prospect. *Wow! How pleasant a task it was going to be to take care of all of them!*

As they reached the gate, both officers got phone calls, and both were busy on the phone for a minute. Sanjay looked at Roshan, and he could see the lad too was terrified and frustrated at the same time. This day was even worse for him, Sanjay guessed. He looked at the watch. 4:00 pm.

The taller officer hung up first and waited for his colleague to complete his call. He spoke to the team first. "Irfan Sir just called. He has a specific task for which he will require help from all of us."

Now what?

"The passengers have to be deplaned, but every person's hand baggage has to be collected in exchange for a voucher. The voucher book is being delivered to us. Eight other guys will join us. The hand baggage has to be packed onto a series of buggies, which will also reach the gate soon."

"Why does he want to do that?"

"He was crisp. He simply said that the bomb could be in one of those bags and they will transport them away. Where, when and how?

That was not divulged. Our job is cut off. Our *fucking* job! It is to handle the irate passengers who may get violent."

Sanjay imagined what a scene it could be. Taking away the handbags from the passengers was going to increase the temperatures of all people to the boiling point. Passengers would become violent, scream, post his photos on Facebook, Twitter and Instagram and also break some furniture for sure... a nightmare come true for any operations manager and security.

"And guess what? It has to be completed before four-thirty at any cost!"

"What! When will the flight reach the gate?"

The second officer spoke. "It has already reached the gate. I spoke to chief stewardess, Shirley. She has already spoken to all the passengers. She has told them directly about the bomb on the plane, which is scheduled to go off at five forty-five to six-fifteen pm. She has urged them to deplane quickly and cooperate with the ground staff."

"And the passengers must be crazy already I presume?" Roshan spoke for the first time.

"She did mention about them being a mixed bag. Some were shouting angrily, but most were shit scared."

"Don't know about the passengers, but I am shit scared!" Roshan said loudly.

Sanjay almost smiled at what he said, but he saw that this joke didn't go down well with the officers, who were about to give him a piece of their mind.

Luckily, there was a distraction. The aerobridge in-charge came onto the walkie-talkie. Doors open. "The first passenger came out almost immediately."

All four tensed up.

Welcome to the jungle...

Chapter 20

Rajesh wanted to sit and ponder about the clue that Captain had given him and try to make sense out of it. But it was clear that he had to be quick in taking action.

It was a fight or flight scenario. *Choose to live.*

He immediately dialled Gabriela's room. After 10 agonizing rings, she picked up the phone. Her voice echoed, "Hello!"

Rajesh very well realised that she was in the shower, but was in no mood to fantasize how she may be looking now. "Gabriela, I need to speak to you. Now! In-person!"

"Why? What is so urgent?" It was evident that she had realised the panic in his voice and chose not to get irritated.

"It's terribly urgent!"

"Okay, give me five minutes. It better be urgent. Meet me in the lobby."

"Okay, not five, but ten minutes. But be completely ready to possibly vacate the room."

"What!" Gabriela was not sure whether to blast this guy now. *What was he saying?*

"Just listen to what I say, I beg you!"

"Okay!"

Rajesh quickly undressed and in a matter of three minutes took a shower. He dried himself in two minutes, dressed up and ensured all his stuff was packed. *Damn it, he himself had taken twelve minutes!* He pulled out the key card, picked his bag and went to the lobby. Gabriela was still not there. He had the irresistible urge to go and bang at her door, his heart racing.

Luckily for him, she appeared. Her hair was uncombed and wet. She was dressed in the same jeans but had worn the new blue shirt provided by the Emirates staff. It fit her perfectly. She was in no mood to smile at him, "Yes, Mr Rajesh? What the hell happened?"

Rajesh ranted off all the things that had happened word by word. He mentioned the Captain's message, his first conversation with him, the finding of the gun in a certain Kabir's bag (he told her he would tell Kabir's story later), its possible implications, the fact that the Chennai flight had a bomb scare and was returning back, and most importantly, the Captain's specific instructions to her and him that they should evacuate, leaving their phones behind, or else they were sure to die or rot in jail.

Gabriela's expression changed in these five minutes from one of amusement to disbelief to anger to panic. She took just another fifteen extra seconds to make her decision. She had to go with what this Indian was saying. "But to hell, I am going to leave my phone in the room!"

"I thought as much. Look, I'm racing down to the concierge to meet whoever this Mark fellow is. You get your bag, lock your room and find out about a locker system at the reception. We could lock in our phones for a while."

Gabriela thought it was a good idea. At least only they would know the passwords and would prevent miscreants from using their phone easily. She just said, "Okay!", and raced off towards her room.

Luckily enough, the elevator was at his floor. Rajesh took the lift down. As he proceeded towards the concierge, his mind started throwing doubts. *Am I right in believing this Captain? Was someone trying to play a mean trick on me? Was I part of a foliage plan of some secret terrorist organization, which was trying to bomb a plane?*

But the Captain had left them with a very eerie alternative. He was insistent that they either listen to him or die. It was not an option where he was willing to take a chance. He had to follow the Captain. Why the hell did he decide to come to this trip to meet Manish? He could have been happily nestled in his South Chennai home by now.

Well, his mind had to stop. He was at the concierge. A lady stood there. *What?* "Well, I need to meet Mark."

"Well, Mark is off duty, sir. How may I help you?" the lady said.

Rajesh's mind was spinning. *It was a hoax after all.* But suddenly the expression of the lady in front of him turned to that of surprise as she looked over Rajesh.

"Well, speak of the devil. Mark is here."

Rajesh didn't know what to feel; relieved or further anxious. He turned back to see a neatly dressed man, in a three-piece suit. Mark was also the same height as he, but well-built. He probably spent hours at the gym. He had blond and wavy hair.

"Mr Rajesh. Hello, I am Mark. Are you ready to leave?" his voice had a distinct American accent.

"Well, yes. Do I have any other choice?"

"The one the Captain would have already given you." He grinned. "Well, we must be quick. Where is the lady?"

Rajesh looked towards the reception. Gabriela was there. She was in conversation with the lady there. "Just give us another minute or so, Mark."

"I give you four. I am bringing my car up from the parking. Black Merc. The number is 131. I will be at the portico, waiting for you. Don't be a minute late!"

Well, are these guys serious or what? This seems to be well set up! Where am I being taken? Am I doing the correct thing? Choose to live!

By the time he was at the reception, Gabriela was swiping her card. She was paying up for the locker services. "Quick, you fill up these forms, I will keep my phone in the locker and then send you."

Rajesh started filling the form. Gabriela was ushered by the lady to the locker room and she appeared an agonizing two minutes later. She then ushered Rajesh into the room and he chose a locker and quickly keyed in a password and stored his cell in there. He was careful to leave it on, hoping that he could retrieve all SMSs and missed calls if and when he got back. As he shut the locker, he felt severe separation anxiety. His phone was probably his best friend; in fact, the phone is probably the best friend of most humans now. He rushed towards the hotel lobby. He had a timeline to meet. He beckoned Gabriela to just follow him.

Gabriela followed him and they both reached the portico. Mark was already there, playing a beat on the steering wheel with his fingers; clearly impatient.

Both Gabriela and Rajesh got into the rear seat. It didn't seem to upset Mark one bit. He just wanted to leave. The car started moving almost instantaneously as they got in.

A journey that was a pure trust in their instincts.

Rajesh looked towards the hotel and he dreaded what he saw. Kabir had reached the door and had a look of disdain as the car passed the portico and out of the gate. Kabir now knew that they were leaving the building, and one thing was sure, he was not at all pleased with that!

God be with them, Rajesh prayed.

CHAPTER 21

The flight evacuation had been swift, but as expected, the time limiting-factor was the handing over of the hand baggage.

"What the... this is a basic violation of human rights!" "I understand ma'am, but this is a dire emergency. We have a receipt for you and it will be handed over safely!"

"I have my valuables in there, understand!" "It will be perfectly safe, sir!"

"At least let me have my laptop for Christ's sake!"

"I am NOT giving you my bag, understand?" "All others will be intimidated sir, please understand!"

"My asthma medicines! Let me have them, please!" "Madam, we have highly qualified doctors here and we will ensure that all medicines will be provided free..."

"You bloody airlines! What shit security do you have!"

"I have a meeting to attend in Chennai this night, please send me home!"

"Are we all going to die?"

Luckily for Sanjay and team, no passenger had got violent, but almost all were irritated with the fact that their handbags were taken away. As time passed, it was evident that all of them would start complaining and start screaming. The Security team better be up to it.

As promised, the extra reinforcement in the security arrived. With remarkable speed, they transferred the handbags onto ten buggies that were all lined up outside the gate. Sanjay was surprised at the speed with which all this was organized. Many times he struggled to get even one or two when the operations team needed them. As soon as the buggies were loaded, they left immediately, and they left at a speed they were seldom allowed to travel, close to 40 kmph. And miraculously, as far as Sanjay could see, they moved without any hindrance. That meant the traffic of passengers who could have been in their way had also been systematically cleared. Someone in clear authority was behind this.

He suspected it could be Irfan; and Hassan, the officer who was monitoring the situation on the walkie-talkie from the control room, soon confirmed it. Sanjay was initially irritated that someone from the security team was actually supervising them when they should have been allowed to do their duty swiftly. However, he soon realised that it was a hugely coordinated event, where passenger evacuation was only one part.

Sanjay presumed that it was Irfan's duty to take this baggage far away so that the bomb squad could be with them. And he also expected the flight to have moved away to a place where another bomb squad would be combing it thoroughly.

Well, his job was cut out, he had to take care of the passengers until a solution was in sight. They were all holed up in the boarding gate seating area. Now, he had to arrange for their refreshments. He had to ensure the washrooms were clean. He had to ensure drinking water. Newspapers and magazines had to be brought in. And most importantly, tempers had to be pacified.

Almost until just after lunchtime, this day was one of his dullest in his duty as a Deputy Operations Manager.

After that, however, it was quickly changing to be one of the most hectic days. There was no near end of this duty day in sight. He had to hang around until all the passengers were safely sent off to Chennai.

But this was only complicated by the fact that their hand baggage was going to somewhere in Dubai, and their checked-in baggage was going somewhere else... and it was possible, that they may never be able to see them again, should the bomb really go off...

Well, if any day he needed litres of coffee for himself, it was going to be today.

He looked at his watch; it was four-thirty.

He went back to the gate; Roshan was standing there, waiting for him...

"Sir, the trouble is far from over. The plane has not moved from the gate yet... I hope there is some plan to move it away from here, otherwise, if the bomb blows, we are all going to die!" He was shivering.

What! The plane has not been moved! What was all the hurry in getting the passengers out then? It should have been moved immediately after evacuation, which his team had neatly carried out!

He switched on his walkie-talkie and connected to Hassan. He asked point-blank. "Why on earth has the plane not moved away? You know it has to be taken far away and bomb squad requires good time for their work!"

"There seems to be a genuine problem here, Mr Sanjay. It is a genuine problem!"

Chapter 22

Shahid Aziz had got his first half of the plan pleasantly wrong. He had calculated that it would take him close to half an hour to get the diplomatic work done, even though it was a matter of urgency.

But to his utter surprise, the swiftness at which the Dubai monarch had acted was incredible.

He had managed to speak to the aviation minister directly in three minutes flat. It took him five minutes on the phone to brief him. The honourable minister had understood the seriousness of the problem. "Shahid, you now coordinate with the Air traffic control. I will speak to Sharjah and get back to you."

Yes! That was a much better approach rather than he himself speaking to the ministry in Sharjah. "Sir, please get back in fifteen minutes or so!"

"As soon as possible, Shahid!"

He hoped that the minister got back soon.

He looked up to see three officers standing in front of him. He realised that as he spoke on the phone, Irfan had assembled them to help him. They saluted him.

"Mohammad and Noor," Shahid said, looking at their name badges, "I want you both to speak to the pilots on board. The pilots have to be ready to take off as soon as I give clearance. The exact runway and the coordinates of the place where they would be landing will be instructed to them soon. But prepare them that they would have to leave the flight after landing and move away from the flight for at least two kilometres. We believe this may be some sort of advanced nuclear bomb. We would arrange their transport. They have to do a great job. They will be rewarded handsomely."

Mohammad and Noor again saluted him and said, "Yes sir!" in unison.

Shahid then called up the Air traffic control. It took him seven minutes, seven precious minutes to explain to them the situation. They finally understood the seriousness and asked him to give them a ten-minute leeway time. They would clear the emergency runway for a quick take-off.

Luckily they said that it was a quiet period. Dubai airport had three busy periods in the day when many flights would land first, and then they would all take off. This ensured the easy connectivity of all passengers to different parts of the world, without having to spend long hours at the airport.

Shahid was pleased with this. However, what pleased him, even more, was that the phone rang almost immediately as he cut the previous call. The Aviation minister was on the line. "Good news, Shahid. Sharjah has agreed to cooperate with us fully during this time of need. You have their clearance for landing on the Al Khair airstrip, south of Sharjah, as you demanded. They have also ensured that the vehicle would be ready for the pilots. The only thing they say is that the vehicle will be parked there without a driver. Nonetheless, the key would be there. It would be the responsibility of the pilots to drive the car away. This also means that there would be no staff to help the pilots come out of the flight. They would have to come out through the emergency exit with the inflatable ladders."

"Sounds fair enough. They cannot risk the lives of their civilians. Thank you, sir, thanks a lot!"

Shahid looked at his watch. 4:20 pm; and the work was done! The time-limiting factor here would be Hassan's work. Evacuating the passengers! He was sure that Irfan would take the handbags as far away as he possibly could.

He genuinely hoped that this was a hoax. No airline would like one of its prime flight to be damaged badly… but at least his team had ensured that no human life would be lost if this bomb really blows up. He felt proud of himself but was wary that until everything was taken care of, he could not relax.

He looked up at Hassan who was at the far end of the room. Hassan looked back at him and gave him a big thumbs-up. "Evacuation complete. Flight ready to move. Sanjay and his team will finish loading the buggies in ten minutes. Buggies will be leaving immediately after that!"

Shahid smiled. It was obvious that the terrorist or hoaxer had put his system to a very, very tight examination. But he was passing the exam with flying colours. He would ensure that no life was lost, should the bomb really go off. The loss of the Boeing had to be the sacrifice.

Had he smiled too soon?

Mohammad and Noor came back to him. They were shit scared. Their expression didn't look good; *not good at all!*

"What happened?"

"Both pilots have deserted. They will not fly the flight and risk their lives. Even if it means they lose their job and credibility. Their life is not what they are ready to gamble with at all."

Shit!

"Now this is going to be a challenge." Shahid's voice and expression just did not give away one bit of the crunching feeling he was having in his stomach. However, he believed in one dictum mainly; don't ever express panic as a leader. It would just percolate the ranks quickly. "We, of course, need to do our best in trying to find another pilot. The whole thing is not going to be easy. Noor and Mohammed, call the best pilots we have who are now stationed in Dubai and ask them point-blank whether they are willing to fly a plane with a bomb on it to a place of safety. Ask them to ask questions only if they are actually considering it in their minds. Explain in one line that urgency in making a decision is a must and there is no punishment for saying no. Just start your job immediately.

"Salim!" he looked at the third officer, "Please somehow reach the air force headquarters and explain the situation to them to see if anyone will be of help. It will take a lot of time, but we should use all our cards now."

"Before doing that, please connect me with the pilots on this flight, I'll try to convince them."

Salim did the needful.

"Hello, this is the Security in Chief, Dubai International Airport; Shahid Aziz on the line." He went on to explain the safety arrangements he had made for them and also the time advantage they had now that all the diplomatic work had been completed in quicker time than anticipated.

But it was clear that it was futile. They had not joined Eastern Airlines to embark on such a mission. They were commercial pilots and they had joined for money. Although it was not international law, the ethics demanded that they should not abandon the flight before the onboard passengers were first taken care of. However, this was a totally different scenario. The on-board passengers were now all safe; so were the cabin staff. So it no longer became their moral duty. Their lives were equally precious as the thousands they were trying to save. *And who was to argue with them?*

Shahid was trying to plead with them now, realising that time was ticking. It was 4:30 pm. He decided to abruptly hang up.

He looked up at Hassan, who was now explaining to the men at the gate on the walkie-talkie.

He now spent a moment to analyse what he could do next. He seemed to have reached a moment where he could not think any further. He had to wait for some pilot to put his hand up.

An air force pilot seemed to be the best guess, but it would take enormous time to mobilize the whole thing. An air force pilot would be ready for the supreme sacrifice too, but that would be a defeat, a definite defeat for him and his team.

The second guess would be some brave stationed pilot. He certainly hoped that one such pilot could also be mobilized quickly.

He was staring at defeat.

Hassan, however, seemed to show some excitement.

"Really?" he was shouting.

There was someone speaking on the other side, but from where he was sitting, Shahid was not able to hear the complete conversation.

Hassan's smile widened for a moment. Shahid sensed a ray of hope. *Had the bomb been found? Had the caller been found? Was it a hoax? Did he find a pilot?*

However, suddenly, his face became serious again as the sounds were heard over the walkie-talkie. "Oh…okay, let me touch base with the boss now. I'll get back. Over and out."

Shahid had already walked up to him.

"Sir, we have a volunteer for the pilot."

"Wow!" Shahid wondered as to who Hassan was in contact with here. *Had the Captain arranged for a pilot too? No... I don't think Hassan would have been in contact with the Captain yet. He had hit his forehead as he heard the answer. But of course. Why hadn't he thought about asking him before?*

"Sanjay Sharan. He is a retired senior pilot from Emirates airlines. Now Deputy Operations Manager; taking care at the gate, this very moment."

Of course, Shahid knew Sanjay. They had met in many a meeting. He was a likeable guy. He was sincere. And what he was about to do now underlined his concern for fellow humans and the airline's reputation. May Allah be with him!

"But he says that this flight will most definitely require a co-pilot for take-off. It requires only someone with some basic knowledge."

"Oh..." Shahid's reaction was similar to what his colleague's had been just a moment ago. *Could this task be easier anyway?*

It was.

Noor, the six-feet-two-inch tall officer, spoke like an angel on earth. "I have basic training to be a pilot. I have been in a Boeing cockpit before, should be able to help more than a bit."

Shahid could not conceal his emotions here. He had been enormously relieved. He just hugged his junior tightly.

CHAPTER 23

To any onlooker, this would be a common scene in Dubai. A black E class Mercedes sped at 100 kmph on the E11 highway towards Sharjah.

However, Rajesh felt rather uncomfortable. The signboards said that they were headed towards Sharjah. He was travelling at speeds that were alien to him. *What on earth was happening?*

He looked up at Gabriela, who seemed equally lost and anxious. He then looked up at Mark, who was driving coolly, with sunglasses on.

"Care to explain what is going on, Mark?" Rajesh said. His voice was, well, a mix of anxiety and sarcasm.

"Hmm… Okay, Mr Rajesh, I will…"

Both Rajesh and Gabriela sat upright. They didn't expect him to answer in the affirmative. They both jolly well wanted to know what was happening.

"I am Mark Andrews. I will be your official escort out of this country…"

"What! We are leaving Dubai? Why?" Gabriela asked.

"Not Dubai; the United Arab Emirates!"

"Okay… whatever!"

"Because here, my friends, you guys are in an amazing soup!"

"Why?"

"The Captain must have already told you, didn't he?"

"Yes, a little bit. But that was a hurried conversation, can you help us understand it a bit better?" Rajesh asked.

"Okay. By now you must have guessed that you have been deplaned on purpose."

"Yes! But why Gabriela and me in particular?"

"Well, someone needed to take the blame, didn't they?"

Gabriela asked, "How did we both get conjunctivitis? Did someone infect us on purpose?"

Mark shrugged, "I guess it must not be an infection, but some irritant must have been sprayed on your eyes!"

Gabriela looked at Rajesh, and Rajesh was looking at her eyes. Both noticed their eyes were still red.

"Why did the Captain decide to rescue us? Who is he?" Rajesh asked

"Well, he is someone important, as you may have presumed. At the moment, let's say he is just a well-wisher."

"Someone important? He knew we were going to be deplaned?"

"Yes, he sure did! He painstakingly is planning your exit from the UAE, before the police fry your ass!"

Gabriela and Rajesh felt shivers going down their spines.

Mark continued, "Although I must admit, the Captain is hurrying me too. I had thought there would have been more time for us to escape, but the flight has come back soon, and the police already know about the bomb. Hence, we are escaping quickly."

"The Captain placed the bomb?" Gabriela asked.

Rajesh was wondering the same. *Were they on the wrong side of the law?*

"Nope. Mostly it's the Captain who has informed the airport as well about the bomb! He has to evacuate you guys before you get falsely prosecuted!"

"I still can't imagine why he would do that!" Gabriela said.

"Well, you know you both are not involved in the flight bombing, I know it. The Captain knows it. If you get into the hands of the Dubai police, they will arrest you and torture you, without fail. He wants the real terrorists caught and you two will help in that; very specifically."

Both Rajesh and Gabriela registered the second statement, but they were really scared when they heard the first statement itself. Gabriela blurted out, "Why will they torture us? Everyone knows that we have been deplaned against our wishes, don't they?"

"*Why* would they torture you? Madam, you must realise that this is a major bomb that we are talking about! Had it gone off, many people would have died… It would be considered an act of aggression against the UAE. I am sure the investigating teams with special powers are already on the job. They will arrest anyone they suspect and not release them unless the correct answer has been found.

"Now, let's answer the second part of your question. This can easily be assumed to be good acting skills. Two terrorists board the plane. Their checked-in bags have already reached the plane. Conveniently, they both are deplaned! But their baggage remains on the flight! The baggage contains the most advanced bomb known to humankind yet, one that has escaped detection at the Dubai security. How convenient! You are the number one suspects!"

"Oh God! What bad luck!" Gabriela cried, "I am screwed. I was on my way to an important meeting in Chennai. That should have been it! Instead, look at me now! I will be branded as an international terrorist! At least for a while. Life sucks!"

Rajesh was at a loss for words, so Mark intervened. "What has happened was for your good. What is happening now is also for your good, I shall explain later…"

"How could it have been good? I should be reaching Chennai tonight, ideally! Instead, I'm going towards an unknown location!"

"Well, let's put it this way. You were seated on a flight with a bomb. All passengers on board, including you, would have blown down to smithereens. You would have never landed anywhere alive, ever!"

"But all passengers are now safe, at least!"

"That's just luck. You would have died if no one had intimated the airport staff and security! Luckily for you, they took the informer seriously as well!"

Gabriela considered what he had just said. *The Captain had informed the airport? Who the hell was he?* Mark was right. Even if the Captain or any Tom Dick or Harry had called up the Dubai airport, they could have thought he was just trying to pull off a prank. But this was something serious. The plane in all possibilities had a bomb and there was a definite possibility that she would have died if she were on the plane.

"And believe me, lady; the passengers are not safe yet. They are still in close proximity to a huge, believe me when I say, huge bomb blast! You are in the safest position right now!"

CHAPTER 24

Shahid had not calculated this time. It took Noor, Hassan and he almost fifteen minutes to get to the gate. Dubai was a huge airport and this was at their disadvantage now.

On the way, Shahid checked with Irfan, who was already in the process of loading the hand baggage of the passengers onto a truck at the parking. Shahid had full trust in Irfan. He would do his job neatly.

They reached the gate at 5:00 pm. This was going to be really tight. As per the Captain, the bomb could go off in the next forty-five minutes. If the pilots had agreed to take off with the flight, they probably would have already wheeled the flight to safety. Now, this was going to have dire consequences if they could not make the flight take off on time. It was going to be touch-and-go, especially for the two makeshift pilots. They may be able to land the flight on time, but they themselves had to escape to safety!

Sanjay was already on the flight. He was a Godsend.

"Hassan, please escort Noor onto the flight. Noor, my boy, best of luck!" The boss hugged him again. "I will stay back and coordinate with Air traffic control. Tell me when you are ready for pushback. It must be very quick."

Noor saluted him and rushed towards the aerobridge; Hassan barely being able to catch up with him. Noor entered the flight. He gulped. He had never seen an empty flight before; he was always used to seeing at least a few cabin crew on board. However, this Boeing 747 was completely devoid of life in the passenger cabins. It looked very eerie.

He rushed towards the cockpit where he saw Sanjay Sharan all set at the Captain's seat.

"Hello, Captain Sanjay," Noor said, panting. He quickly took the seat next to him.

Sanjay smiled at him. "Hello, officer."

"You can call me, Noor. I am much younger to you!"

"Okay, Noor. Have you flown this flight before?"

"Never."

"Okay, then I am going to need a full five minutes to brief you about the controls here before we give the thumbs up for pushback."

Just then Hassan entered the cockpit. "All ready, guys?"

"What are you doing here?" Sanjay blurted.

"Boss had asked me to escort Noor."

Sanjay wanted to blast him. *Was Noor a kid?* This chap was wasting precious time, but he had to keep his cool. "Okay, officer. You must leave immediately. Make sure the aerobridge has disengaged from the flight"

"Okay." Hassan proceeded to hug him and then Noor as well. "Allah be with both of you!" More precious time wasted, but thankfully, he was out after that.

Just then, a voice on the radio crackled. It was Air traffic control. "Please inform when ready for pushback. All landings and take-offs have been put on hold for another fifteen minutes."

"Okay, sir!" Noor replied.

Sanjay started explaining the cockpit to Noor when again the radio crackled. This time it was Shahid. "All ready guys?"

"I am giving a quick briefing to Noor about this flight. Sorry Officer, but I should not be disturbed at all for the next four minutes."

Shahid was quick to understand. "Got it, over and out."

Luckily, there were no more interruptions. Sanjay went over the cockpit details swiftly and clearly. Noor was smart and picked up instantaneously.

"Okay, ready to leave?" Sanjay asked.

Noor gave the thumbs up and a huge sigh.

Sanjay spoke on the radio, "Ready for pushback."

As soon as he spoke, the flight started moving backwards. It was a superfast response by all means. Shahid had got things arranged perfectly.

Sanjay had not flown a flight now for more than three years. He realised this when he saw that he had ignored an alarm all along, "Oh Shit!"

"What happened?" Noor panicked a bit.

"All the flight doors are disarmed. The crew had disarmed them after they landed and we have to arm all of them before take-off."

The voice on the radio crackled. "Pushback complete. You may proceed to emergency runway one immediately."

"We need an extra five minutes! All doors on the flight are disarmed. We need to close them immediately."

Shahid's voice was cool at the other end. "Do it then!"

It took an entirety of eight minutes for both of them to reach each and every door of this huge and deserted Boeing flight and arm them. They then reached the cockpit and quickly buckled on. Noor looked at the watch. The time was five-twenty now.

Sanjay was about to speak on the radio when Noor interrupted. "Sir, do you realise that we may not make it alive?"

Sanjay feared the worst. "Yes, my boy."

"Do you think we should at least message our near and dear?"

Sanjay waited a few seconds. *Shit, what Noor had said was true. They might die. He must inform Myra at least. He needed to message her.* He nodded. "Let's do it very quickly."

He started messaging Myra, as the voice again crackled. This time Shahid was sounding a bit impatient. "Time to get a move on. Quick."

"Ready in sixty seconds," Sanjay said calmly. He knew that more precious time was being wasted. Although the flight will be taken off to a safe place, if the bomb did go off at five forty-five, it was almost certain that Noor and he would not be alive after that.

He had to message Myra. It would be 7:30 am in Boston. He swallowed hard as he turned his phone on flight mode immediately after he typed the message out.

'Hi, Myra. Going on a daring mission. Be rest assured, if you don't hear from me anymore, you would still be very proud of your dad."

Chapter 25

Rajesh noticed that the traffic had thinned down significantly. It was clear that they were no longer on the main highway towards Sharjah. The road on either side of them had desert stretched for miles. The colour of the sand had changed from yellow to red.

Gabriela was still in a state of shock. She was refusing to believe that this was a better fate than being on the flight to Chennai.

"Kabir Dravid is most likely the terrorist, isn't he?" Rajesh asked Mark.

Mark was silent for a while. He then replied, "I can only guess so! The truth is, I don't know!"

"What! You must know! You said that the Captain is a very important man. I guess he must know who the terrorist is, especially because he is taking extraordinary efforts in destroying this plan. More so ever, he is also helping us escape so that we may be of help... that's what you said?"

"Well, yes. The Captain is helping you escape punishment in Dubai. In return, he is sure that you can help him nail the real terrorist. It may be Kabir Dravid, logically."

"What do you mean by 'maybe'?"

"Well, the truth is, I only follow orders from the Captain. He has not told me who the terrorist is and I didn't ask him. I can only guess."

Rajesh and Gabriela looked at each other. *Was this guy speaking the truth? Was he only an intermediary or was he lying?*

Rajesh decided to test him, "And why do you 'guess' it's Kabir?" He had not told Mark or the Captain about the gun that Kabir possessed. Gabriela knew.

"You apparently told the Captain about Kabir. He briefed me the same and asked my team to run a check on him. By the time you met me, my team had come up with a little bit of information on him. More information is forthcoming. Apparently, he too had checked into the same flight. We are still to receive information as to why and when he was deplaned. He was also housed at the Radan; we are still to find out how he got there. His checked-in bag too was on the flight. The bomb could very well be in his bag!

"But what I heard last from my colleagues was a shocker. Two of the security staff of Radan have confirmed that he was in possession of a gun! Now think of this, Mr Rajesh, if he had been moved out of the flight directly, how did he have a gun? That means that someone has handed over the gun to him after he was deplaned!"

That was enough to convince Rajesh. He voiced his conclusions loudly. "Yes, I know he possessed a gun! That is because I peeked into his room when the security was with him! And yes, I agree that I too had the same thought! Someone has handed over the gun to him!"

Gabriela continued, "He must be the terrorist then! He seems to be very well-connected!"

"I am sure that the Captain knows that *he* is the terrorist then!" Rajesh said, "Do you agree, Mark?"

"Hmmm…"

"Wait a minute, something is odd here. If Kabir were the terrorist, why would he come to the Radan? It will only raise suspicion and he will be caught soon! He could have escaped anywhere in Dubai!"

"I can think of some reasons…" Mark said. "They may be far-fetched… I will let you know in a moment. Now, ladies and gentlemen, hold on to your seats tight! Don't ask questions."

Mark suddenly pressed the brakes hard, bringing the Merc to a powerful stop. Both Gabriela and Rajesh were caught unawares, in spite of being warned. Luckily, Gabriela had her seatbelt on, but Rajesh was thrown out of his seat and banged into the seat in front of him. Fortunately, the little bit of prior warning prevented serious head injury, but he was bruised and his whole body hurt. However, his excited mind did not concentrate on the pain. It was wondering what the hell Mark was up to.

As the car screeched to a complete halt, Rajesh looked out to see where they were. The stretch of the road was isolated, except for two cars. One was a car that was at least a kilometre away, driving away from them, not possibly significant. Another was a Hummer that was parked just before their Mercedes, which was now pulled up to the right side of the road.

"Why the hell did you have to brake so suddenly?" Gabriela demanded. She was in more shock than what she was in the moment before.

"As I said lady, no questions now. I will clear all your doubts. For now, just get down from this car!"

"But this is the middle of the desert!"

"Yes, I know, don't waste time whatsoever!"

Rajesh was too stunned and too much in pain to protest. He just decided to give up on his fate. His instincts told him to trust Mark, and he quietly got off the car. Although it was five-fifteen in the evening, the wind that blew across the desert had become cooler. He got down and moved to the side of the road to await further instructions. Gabriela reluctantly joined him.

"Okay guys, time to move on…" Mark said after ensuring that the doors of the Mercedes were locked.

Where are we headed now?

To their surprise, Mark led them to the Hummer that was parked in front of them and unlocked it. He instructed them to enter that vehicle now. "After you…"

It was obvious that Gabriela was thinking the same as he was. *Why the hell were they being made to shift cars? What on earth was happening?*

They both got into the backseat again. Mark, as expected, got into the driver's seat. He started driving the car immediately. It was extraordinarily hot inside the car. It was obvious that it had been parked there at least for a few hours. *Why? This was some amazingly planned sinister operation. They were some VIPs! What was happening???*

The powerful air conditioning in the Hummer cooled the vehicle in a minute or so.

"Yes, Mark… care to share something?" Gabriela asked.

"Okay, let me tell you what I think… Kabir probably intends to kill you both. He is a shrewd terrorist."

Both Rajesh and Gabriela shuddered.

Mark continued, "According to his plan, the bomb would have gone off, killing everyone on board. After that, the suspect number one and two will be both of you."

"Then he should not kill us!" Rajesh said. "The police will arrest us!"

"Oh no! Now, the Dubai police would continue looking for other suspects after catching you both. Eventually, they will find out that you are innocent, after investigation!"

"So?"

"But if he eliminates you and disposes off your bodies where no one can find you... guess what?"

Rajesh was lost, but Gabriela took the cue, "The police will never be able to prove our innocence. They will forever be lost in a wild goose chase trying to find out our whereabouts and also carry the investigations in India and the US! Assuming that no one else would know that Kabir had deplaned if the bomb had gone off, Kabir himself would have made the great escape!"

<h1 align="center">Chapter 26</h1>

Shahid stood at the gate looking outward as he saw the plane moving forward finally. It was five twenty-two in his watch. The Captain had given a time frame. He had said that the bomb would go off between five forty-five and 6:15 pm. He was hoping that it was a hoax. Or if it were true, he was hoping that it was in the latter part of the estimated time. Only then the two brave gentlemen on board the plane would ever make it alive.

He wondered what the bomb could be.

'More advanced than what the current technology could detect.' That's what the Captain had said. Did it contain a miniature nuclear reactor or something like that?

The flight wheeled away from his sight. He then connected to Mohammad, Noor's partner, who by now had made his way to the Air traffic control tower.

"Yes sir, the flight has made its way to the emergency runway one. The ATC is guiding them. They will be cleared for immediate take-off. They will be flying at thirteen thousand feet only so as to facilitate an easy landing at the Al Khair strip. Once the flight takes off, it will take twenty-five minutes to touch down again."

Twenty-five minutes to touch down! Well, one thing was sure. By five forty-five, the flight would be flying over desert land, almost ensuring that there will be no civil casualties should the bomb go off at that time. Hopefully, there would be time for Sanjay and Noor to get off the flight and drive away to safety. *Allah! This was really tense now!*

"Flight cleared for take-off, sir. It has already started accelerating."

"Okay, just don't cut the phone until it takes off!"

"Sure," Mohammad said and in twenty seconds he announced, "Taken off, sir!"

"Thanks!" Shahid said. He looked around. He sensed that the deplaned passengers had also come to know that the plane had moved away, although he was sure that they all thought that it was taken away to a place where a bomb squad was attending to it. They had started to feel safe.

Hassan had now taken up the responsibility to help Roshan manage the crowd. As an Operations' Executive, Roshan was more capable of handling the crowd. He had quickly made arrangements for some refreshments. Drinking water bottles had already arrived. Hassan and the security officers who were already at the gate mainly took up the responsibility of answering questions.

Are we safe now? Yes, madam.

Is this a hoax or a real bomb? (How the fuck will I know?) We don't know yet, sir, but we have to keep people safe at all times.

Will we ever get to Chennai? (Of course, you dimwit!) Yes, sir, already there is another team ready to mobilize a new flight.

I want my handbag! When will it come? Soon, madam, as soon as possible!

My checked-in luggage, it had all my original certificates! What will I do now! (You are lucky to be alive, bugger!) I understand, sir, but this was a must to save so many lives!

Shahid was proud of this team on the ground. They were doing a good job until now. He rang up Irfan.

"Things as per plan, sir, we have laid down the hand baggage on the dunes. We are now making our way back to the cars and should be back on the main road by five-thirty, which is almost five kilometres away from where we have kept them. We have ensured a complete lockdown of all the desert safari vehicles today. No vehicles on the dunes for miles!"

"Bravo!" Again Shahid was happy that if the bomb was in the hand baggage and did go off, it would not harm any humans. The terrorists would have to find another day and occasion. Nothing was going to happen to the common man in his territory. However, he only feared what would happen to Sanjay and Noor.

Mohammad called, "The flight has crossed over to Sharjah. Sharjah ATC is now taking over. In five minutes the taking over will be completed. The flight will commence its descent after that!"

There was nothing Shahid could do now, except pray, which he did with all his heart.

Chapter 27

The driver of the SUV, in which Irfan sat, drove it as fast as he could. Easily, he was clocking close to eighty kmph, which was a really high speed considering that they were riding a roller coaster-like ride over the red dunes of Sharjah. Although the hand baggage was stored in the dunes of Dubai, Irfan calculated that riding over to Sharjah would offer them the maximum distance that they could drive away. Not a soul was visible for long distances, but soon he would hit the highway. Irfan calculated that the highway was a good distance away from the place where the hand baggage was stored.

He had heard it from the boss that the flight had taken off. He knew that it would roughly go over them in just a bit. He looked at the watch. It was, in fact, nearing five twenty-five. He said a silent prayer for the guys on board.

As they got closer to the highway, they saw two parked vehicles. One was a Mercedes E class car and one was a Hummer. It was always funny as to why tourists liked to stop on the road to take photos. Many of the tourists did that. For them, being in the desert was something like a novel experience. Anyway, he had to warn them about the impending danger; he could not explain what, but they had to vacate.

Would he be right in telling them the truth? Would it not raise panic among the common public? Hadn't he already calculated that the 'possible' bomb in the hand baggage would not harm anyone on the road?

As he thought all this, he could see the Hummer leaving the place. It just re-joined the road and moved away further into Sharjah.

His SUV joined the road now. Irfan thought that they too should park near the Mercedes and wait. They had to wait for clearance from the team at the airport. They then would have to go fetch the hand baggage again.

When would the clearance come? Four possibilities.

One: The bomb would have been found.

Two: The bomb would have blasted the flight into pieces.

Three: The Captain's identity would have been identified and he would be a prankster.

Four: The predicted time would be over. The Captain had warned the bomb would go off before six-fifteen. But if nothing happened until, say, seven-fifteen, the mission would be called off as a hoax. This was the most possible outcome according to him.

He asked the driver of the car to park beside the Mercedes. Two other officers were with him. They chatted a little for ten minutes. Then, Irfan asked them to be seated in the car while he stretched his legs outside. More than doing that, he thought he would be able to get a glimpse of the low flying aeroplane.

The weather had cooled down nicely by now. He walked up to the Mercedes to see if anyone was there. To his surprise, the car was empty. He only hoped that the occupants of the car were not wandering somewhere close to the baggage now. Unlikely. No one would walk three miles in the desert having parked his or her Mercedes in the middle of nowhere. *Hmmm... it was certainly odd.*

The time was now five thirty-eight. The countdown would begin soon.

He heard a car coming towards them from Dubai. The car suddenly braked as if the driver realised something that was dangerous. The car screeched to a halt some twenty metres away. It just stood there for a minute. *Why? What was wrong?*

It suddenly started moving again. *Why did tourists prefer this particular spot?* The car moved slowly and then again slowed down right in front of him. An Indian was driving the car.

"Excuse me, officer, can you help me with something?"

"Yes?"

"Where are the occupants of this car?"

Just as he said that, Irfan sighted the flight. It was unmistakably the Eastern Airlines flight, its bright red colour visible! All other flights were barred from taking off or landing or flying at low heights at this time! Yes, it was the Boeing 747, with Sanjay and Noor on board.

"Sir?" the guy in the car asked.

He had to get rid of him immediately, "I don't know. I saw some people leaving in a Hummer just now, towards Sharjah. Don't know if that is useful information for you, but I have not seen anyone come to this car in the last fifteen minutes or so."

"Okay sir, thanks," the driver said and started driving off.

Oh boy, look at how low this flight is flying! This is the flight with the bomb! Irfan prayed for the well-being of the pilots.

Kabir also noted the low flying flight as he drove away from the police officer. *Shit!* On two accounts: *One, this was the flight with the bomb being flown away! And second, now it was a Hummer with an unknown number that he had to trace to get to Rajesh and the girl...*

CHAPTER 28

S hahid kept looking at his watch. Five forty now.

He received a call from Mohammad, "Sir, bullshit luck. We are running into some problem. We last heard from Sanjay as we handed over to Sharjah ATC, but Sharjah ATC has not yet been able to detect the flight."

What! Shahid feared the worst. *The flight had already exploded!* "Have we contacted the flight again?"

"Yes, but we too are not able to make contact!"

"Shit! That means the flight might have exploded already!"

"We did not get any distress call, sir. Even if a bomb did burst somewhere in the flight, the pilots would have enough time to send a distress call."

Enough said! The bomb could have been in the cockpit! Unlikely. But the Captain had said that the bomb was an extremely powerful one. Even if it had burst anywhere in the flight, it could have ripped apart the flight in seconds! He hoped that it was a temporary radio-disconnect and that's all. He hoped he would hear from Mohammad that they had re-established contact.

"Sir?" Mohammad spoke. It was clear from his tone that he too was scared.

"Just hang on, Mohammad, don't disconnect the phone until you've heard something from Sanjay and Noor."

"OK, sir!"

Just as he said that, Shahid heard a faint beeping sound. Someone was trying to call. He pulled the phone a little further away to see who it was. It was his wife. He had to put her on hold. This was far too important. He again prayed and put the phone close to his ear.

The beeping stopped. That meant his wife had given up. He pulled the phone again away from him and confirmed the same. He put on the speaker now so that he could keep the phone a little away from himself. However, all he could hear was the distant muffled sounds of panicked officers at the ATC, as they were trying to get to Sanjay.

"Dubai ATC to Sanjay Sharan. Dubai ATC to Sanjay Sharan. Please come in."

Usually, the ATC would use flight numbers and not names. But this was an exception. The flight had no number and the only flight they were trying to contact was this one, the other flights were just circling the airport now.

Again, the screen changed. Someone else was calling. It was Irfan. *Well, Irfan too had to wait. This was important.*

What on earth had happened? Shahid was just not able to think of any other alternatives... he prayed again.

As soon as Irfan's incoming call stopped, the screen changed again for another call. *Irfan again!*

He marched to the officer who was with Roshan. As he walked from where he was, he wondered what Irfan was calling for. *Had the bomb been found in the hand baggage? Or was he just trying to find out about the flight?* Whatever it was, he had to wait. He had to hear about the flight first.

"Officer, please call Officer Irfan. He seems to be desperate to talk to me."

He strode over to the nearest chair and put his phone to rest near him. He didn't want to look at it, but he had to make sure that he heard what Mohammad had to say. Mohammad was dead silent. Only the desperate distant voices of the ATC officers were heard.

That's it. The bomb had exploded. Shahid had the sinking feeling. But again, his mind contradicted his thinking. If the bomb had indeed exploded, there would have been a huge fireball over Sharjah by now. Surely, many phones would have started coming in from there. No phone call had come to anyone yet, so it was unlikely. He heaved a sigh of relief.

"Mohammad?"

"Yes, sir?"

"Any news?"

"No, sir." Mohammad was to the point. His tone was also defeated.

Shahid again looked at his watch. It was now five forty-seven. The flight had lost contact around eight minutes back. But then again, someone from Sharjah would have sighted the explosion.

But... no one except a select few in Sharjah knew that an Eastern Airlines flight was making its way to the Al Khair airstrip. Even the ATC at Sharjah was situated far away from where the flight could have been. It meant that anyone who would have seen the explosion could not have made such rapid calculations, assumed that it was a flight outbound from Dubai and ring up Dubai airport. Anyone in Sharjah at the place where the flight had exploded would have been too stunned to assume and report anything, even to the Fire Safety authorities. *Shit!*

Then, he suddenly remembered.

He looked up at the officer who was trying to contact Irfan.

The officer shrugged. "His phone is continuously engaged, sir!"

Shahid looked at his phone. Irfan was still trying to contact him! *Of course! What a fool he had been. Irfan was very close to where the flight would have been!*

He picked up the phone. The phone asked him whether he wanted to end the call with Mohammed. He had no choice. He ended it.

"Irfan?"

"Sir, I have been trying to call you since..."

"Doesn't matter! What happened? Tell me quick!"

"Something extraordinary!"

"What? Did you see the flight?"

"Yes!"

"Okay?" Shahid's voice boomed with impatience.

"Something extraordinary. The flight just passed above our head. Within a few seconds of passing us, mind you, right in front of our eyes, it just vanished into thin air! Just vanished! It's a clear sky. There was no explosion, no sound, no light. It just disappeared, in probably less than a second! Nothing falling of the sky, no debris, no explosion."

CHAPTER 29

There was a sudden jolt again. Rajesh and Gabriela were flung onto the right side of the Hummer as Mark made an abrupt sharp left turn.

"God! Why are you doing this, Mark?" Gabriela screamed.

"Yeah, I had to make this turn before anyone saw us on the road."

"Right!" Gabriela said sarcastically. As she said, she realised that the SUV had slowed down drastically. "Now, why did you slow down then?"

"Look outside!"

Gabriela and Rajesh looked outside. They were astonished to see that Mark had driven right into the desert, which was filled with red and soft sand. The Hummer struggled just a little bit now. After going a short distance, Mark stopped the vehicle.

"Now, what?"

"Give me a moment, guys!" Mark jumped off the driver's seat.

"What is it; a pee break?" Gabriela said, and for the first time after a while, both she and Rajesh smiled.

Rajesh too jumped off the car. His leg was still aching. He looked around. He saw nothing but sand in all directions. Even the road from which they had just exited was not visible. Mark was making sure they were not seen at all!

He looked at Mark. Mark was not taking this break to relive himself. He was furiously at work with the front right tyre. "What is it? Is it flat?"

Mark chose to ignore him. He moved from the front right tyre to the front left one. He seemed to follow some sort of routine with that one too, and he repeated the same with the two back tyres. "Get in!" his voice was commanding, and Rajesh thought it was wise to follow him for the moment.

As soon as Mark was confident that Rajesh had got in, he put the foot on the accelerator. The Hummer now eased over the desert, contrary to what had happened just before Mark had done something to the tyres.

"If you deflate the tyres a bit, the car will run faster in the desert," Mark explained, putting an end to the petite suspense he had created.

"Why are we running through the desert? Wouldn't it be easier to drive on the highway?"

"Guys, guys! Don't underestimate the UAE police, please. They are very shrewd. Once they get the instructions that they have to go after you, they will trace the road you have taken very quickly. It would be easy for them to realise that you have left in a Mercedes, went on the highway towards Sharjah, taken a detour towards the dunes. Very soon, they will realise that you have changed cars, and very soon they would also realise that it is a Hummer. We are trying our best to confuse them. We will only succeed if we make quick changes to our cars as well as directions."

"Makes sense!" Gabriela said, although it still didn't make any sense to her why she was in the midst of all this in the first place.

"And let's not possibly underestimate our immediate possible threat, Kabir. If he is on our tail, he would have found our Mercedes on the road by now and would be using his sources to find out which vehicle we are on now. He must have great contacts in the UAE, maybe even more reliable contacts than the police themselves."

Rajesh gulped. *What the heck was wrong with Kabir? He wanted to blow a flight with three hundred-odd passengers. He wanted Gabriela and him to be deplaned. Now he was possibly out on a mission to kill them! Were they right in assuming him to be the terrorist? Well, if not him, then who else? He seemed the most logical person! And yes, where had he seen him before?*

A massive sinking feeling interrupted his thoughts. Mark plunged the Hummer up a huge sand dune.

"It's just the beginning, hang on folks!"

Gabriela and Rajesh wanted to protest, but they saw no sense in doing that. They just held on to the handgrips near them.

Mark took the SUV up the sand dune and took them down immediately, giving a sickening feeling in the tummy. It was similar to a ride on a roller coaster.

However, as Mark said, it was just the beginning. The sand dunes were getting bigger and bigger. The SUV made its way up the sand dunes that were almost as high as six to seven storeys, again bringing them down quickly. Many a time, he was also running the car sideways on an incline, which meant that they were not only going downwards, the car itself was inclined sideways, just like the popular roller coasters. Rajesh wanted to puke, and he saw that Gabriela also wanted to do the same.

Again, Rajesh thought of the same. He should have been relaxing in his apartment now, after a day's work. Instead, he decided to take this Godforsaken trip to meet Manish in New York; and now he was completely screwed. He was in Dubai. Three parties were now potentially controlling him.

One, the Dubai police; they would surely be after him. The flight from which he was evicted forcefully, had a bomb in it. Funnily enough, although it was a forceful deplaning, he would be one of the prime suspects of planting the bomb!

Two, it was Kabir Dravid and some idiosyncratic thought in his mind. He was supposedly out to harm him, maybe even kill him.

And three, he decided to trust the third party. It was Captain and Mark. Was he right in trusting them?

Well, he was stuck between the devil and the deep sea.

Chapter 30

The instructions from the command were clear.

The Dubai monarchy had just been informed about what all had just happened. It hadn't taken them much time to make a decision.

Officer Shahid Aziz would now lead a task force, to be active with immediate effect.

Four senior officers from the Dubai City Police would report to him, and so would Irfan from the Dubai airport security.

He could assemble a team of any number of policemen he wished.

However, the tasks were cut out.

First, they were to find the plane or its debris at any cost.

Second, they were to hunt the terrorists down. They could arrest anyone they suspected.

Third, they were to find the prime motive behind targeting the new Airlines bound on its first trip from Dubai.

Fourth, they needed to submit a report on what possibly the bomb could be, and how it escaped the robust security system of the Dubai Airport. If at all, any security personnel was found guilty of being bought out by the terrorist organization, he would be executed.

Even before the four Dubai city police officers got to him, Shahid issued his first orders.

The two officers who accompanied Irfan to isolate the hand baggage were to remain where they were, await further instructions as to when they could retrieve the baggage, collect them, and make sure they were returned to the passengers stranded at the airport.

Officer Mohammed was to sit at Dubai ATC, which should resume the normal air traffic. However, they also had to post someone specifically to try and restore communication with the two pilots. As he spoke to Mohammed and them, he realised the prospects were getting bleaker and bleaker. It was now six-thirty pm; fifty minutes past the time they had lost contact with the flight. Nevertheless, he hoped against hope.

The officers at the gate, where the Chennai passengers were, had to detain them there for a while for questioning. The questioning had to be done by one of the seniors coming in from the city. The operations manager, Roshan, had to take charge now in the absence of his brave senior, Sanjay. *God bless Sanjay!* Roshan had to take care of the hospitality part, which was going to be one of the toughest jobs, he guessed.

Irfan had to report to Sharjah police. Shahid had already contacted them and they were well abreast of the need for utmost cooperation now. He would need their help for two main reasons. They had to help to find the plane or more likely its debris, in Sharjah. Second, they had to help in the combing of the terrorists. Irfan was now well aware of his new responsibility. He would wait at his present location until a police vehicle coming in from Sharjah picked him up.

As he finished the last of his phone calls for the moment, he saw Roshan standing a small distance from him. Well, this was the moment the manager needed to step in. It was well past his regular working hours, but he needed to go on and on tonight. It would be the same for his entire team too.

Oh boy! He had to call his wife! He was supposed to be on holiday today, but this was an exceptional circumstance. He didn't see himself going home, at least for the night.

He signalled Roshan to allow him a minute as he called his wife and explained the situation to her. Of course, she was shocked, but she had been a good wife here. She wished him best of luck and said she would pray for the two on the flight to be alive somewhere.

He hung up after four minutes. He looked up and saw Roshan pacing up and down impatiently. *I hope he doesn't oppose what I have asked him to do. It was well within his rights to do so, but he didn't want any of this now!* He asked him to come over. "Yes, my boy?"

"Sir, I have a hunch for a long time. Can I share it with you?"

"Really?" Shahid was genuinely amused. *He hadn't expected Roshan to have a hunch*! "Go ahead!"

"Sir, I don't know if you were aware of what had happened earlier with the same flight."

"No, what?" Shahid listened more keenly now.

"Two passengers were evicted from the flight after they had already boarded and the flight was ready for pushback…"

"What!"

Roshan went on to explain the situation in brief.

Well, well, well… this changed the complexion of the story completely. The two passengers had their luggage checked in but were conveniently, forcefully evicted from the flight at the very last moment. This ensured that they were safe, while their baggage had gone with the flight… How convenient, how fucking convenient!

He had to trace and arrest these two people immediately: Gabriela Fabregas and Rajesh Rajesh.

CHAPTER 31

Kabir too was astonished at the sight. Well, he knew for sure that this was going to happen, but didn't expect such a spectacle!

The Eastern Airlines Boeing flight flying over him just vanished within a second. There were no flames, no sound. The flight just disappeared into thin air. The professor had told him that something similar would happen, but this was extraordinary.

Although he was awestruck, he tried to check for glitches.

Was he seeing a mirage? A mirage would disappear as he got closer. Unlikely. The officer on the road also had been distracted by the plane.

Could he just have missed seeing the flight fly away from his line of vision? Again, this was unlikely. He was keenly following the progress of the flight when it suddenly disappeared.

Could it be bad weather that contributed to him losing the sight of the plane? No. It was crystal clear.

Again, he reminded himself that he knew this was going to happen. However, this sudden disappearance still shocked him!

Nonetheless, he had to focus on the work at hand. He had to chase down Rajesh and that chick to achieve what he had set out to achieve. Should the Dubai police trap them, he would not achieve what he wanted. He had to get them.

It was funny. His aide, Fardeen, who was at a location twenty kilometres ahead of him, had not yet spotted a Hummer go past. So these guys had changed cars again on the way! He had to find out. One thing he had calculated in his mind. There were no exits out of this road from where he was till where Fardeen was. That means the

Hummer must be parked somewhere on the road. If he did find an abandoned Hummer, he would now need to find which car they took for the journey ahead. Luckily, he had instructed Fardeen to photograph every vehicle that went past him.

He was thinking of other possibilities. From the corner of his eye, he caught tyre tracks moving into the desert from the road. But this was a common sight on this road. Many tourist vehicles exited the main road for the 'Dune Bashing', a popular experience in this part of the country. It was unlikely that these chaps would use this road, as it would slow down the progress considerably. The only person that they were running away from presently was probably him. They still didn't know what his personal motive to get them was. They would not try to play the fool now. They would rather escape as fast as they could, and not go over the dunes. He rode past.

But once he had seen that, he noticed something rather odd...

There were just no more car tracks entering the sand. This was odd. This was a popular tourist time of the year. He had expected to see many more such tracks. And what more? Just before sunset and just after it was the most popular time of this sport.

He just continued to observe the same for another three minutes on the road... no car tracks whatsoever.

He immediately called Fardeen and explained what he saw.

"Just give me a minute, boss, I'll get right back."

Hmmm... now what?

Ninety seconds later, Fardeen called back. "Boss, it seems the Dubai and the Sharjah police have suspended all 'Dune Bashing' activities for the day for 'security reasons'..."

That's enough! The guys ahead of him had yet again given him the slip. Someone was most probably tipping them off. He had to think hard to get to them.

"Fardeen, I want you to stay put where you are. Also, I want one of your pals to come down the road towards Dubai to see if they can see an abandoned Hummer somewhere on the road. Meanwhile, I have no other choice. I am going into the dunes chasing the tyre tracks I had seen... I will definitely catch up with the smarty pants."

CHAPTER 32

They had spent almost half an hour on the sand dunes. This was more of a joy ride for tourists, but it was no fun for Gabriela and Rajesh. A group that was trying to protect them was almost holding them hostage.

Rajesh looked at his watch; it was 6:30 pm. He wondered how long they would be on the dunes. He wondered if this drive was ever going to end.

As he looked up, he saw something different. Finally, he saw some tents on the sand. And Mark seemed to be heading right towards them. *Who were in these tents? The Captain? Was it someone from the Indian embassy? Or was it someone who was the mastermind of a mega-prank?* He certainly hoped it was the latter!

As they neared the tents, it was obvious that there were occupants there. The lights were on and there was a Land Rover parked right in front of them.

Mark drove right up to the tents and brought the Hummer to a stop.

"Where are we now?" Gabriela asked, her voice half as loud as it had been when she was excited. She was visibly exhausted and most probably had given up to her fate.

"This, madam, is our rest house for five minutes. There is a restroom, which you both must use now as we don't know when our next stop will be. Also, there are packed dinners for all three of us along with some soft drinks and water. We must take them along with us."

"What! I don't want to follow any of these orders!" Gabriela protested again, meekly.

"I suggest you don't be stupid. I can tell you, either Kabir or the Dubai police or both by now would be hot on our trails already. Just do as I say."

Rajesh had already made his way into the tent that had a male symbol attached to it. He relieved himself in the makeshift toilet. He then washed his face at the basin and stretched. His leg ached a bit but had reduced since the injury. He only prayed to God that he had made the right choice by following the orders of the Captain. He looked at the mirror. To his astonishment, there was no sign of any conjunctivitis now. His eye had cleared completely. *Thugs!*

He had one mind that told him to escape to Abu Dhabi and take the Etihad flight back to Chennai by booking a fresh ticket. He felt the bag that hung around his neck. It lodged his passport. It also had two hundred US dollars in it. His wallet had another two hundred. If he did escape, this money would not be enough to get him a ticket. He could use his credit card. *That he could do!*

He considered where and when he could escape. *He was in the middle of the desert, damn it!* Right now he had to head back out of the tent and follow Mark's orders.

He walked out where he saw Mark eating a sandwich and drinking Pepsi. He pointed to a neatly packed zipper-lock bag that probably contained his food. "Pick it up, pal. You will need it. Do me one favour, just hold on to my food until I pee too!"

Mark disappeared into the tent. As Gabriela came out of the ladies' tent, Rajesh pointed to the food bag.

"Where is this guy?" she asked Rajesh.

"In the restroom."

They both looked at each other and Gabriela read off exactly what was in Rajesh's mind, "Shall we make an escape in the Hummer now?"

Rajesh actually considered it for a moment longer than he usually would, but then laughed it out. He laughed at their destiny. They were right in the middle of the desert. It was now almost pitch dark. The natural light was almost disappearing as they spoke and the only light was from the bulbs outside the tents.

Gabriela also broke into laughter. She looked better after she had combed her hair. She looked beautiful. A damsel in distress. "We are basically screwed, aren't we? We can't escape in the dark, starting from the middle of nowhere. And guess what? We don't have our phones to guide us too. Those fuckers made sure they took them away!"

Right! Rajesh hadn't considered this aspect. *How true she was*! They were screwed. Somehow he hoped that later in the night, they would reach a civilized space and they could somehow escape.

Mark, who came out of the tent, had something to say about it all though.

"Hmmm... as expected, guys! I have just received news from the Captain. The Dubai police have locked down the passports of the two of you. Soon they will begin the pursuit. Better move our asses immediately!"

Chapter 33

"We have received the following information from the Hotel Radan." City Officer 1 reported to Shahid. Shahid had met too many people today to remember the names of each one of them, so he decided to call his colleagues – City Officers 1, 2, 3 and 4. None seemed to mind as they imagined what the senior officer might be going through.

City Officer 1 was informed about the 'deplaning' of the two individuals, even as he was still on the way to the airport. Shahid had introduced the topic, and then Roshan had taken over. He explained to the Officer how Sanjay and he had escorted two passengers, who were visibly suffering from conjunctivitis, out of the airport, through immigration and to the Emirates Chauffeur service. He also told him as to where they were headed.

Officer 1 had quickly deployed one of his juniors go to the Radan immediately. Meanwhile, he had made his way to the boardroom in Dubai airport, where he met with Shahid, the team leader and the other three officers. Also, there was a junior officer called Hassan, who worked at the airport.

The four officers had been briefed about the whole situation. Officer 1 was to follow the lead of the mysterious duo of Gabriela and Rajesh to see if he could unearth any connection between them and the bomb in the flight.

Officer 2 was to be in-charge of recording the statement from each and every passenger from the ill-fated flight, who were stranded at the airport. He was to do it quickly and allow them to fly off in the makeshift flight before their being held captive became an international media issue. He had to coordinate with the two officers who were stranded with the hand baggage of all the passengers and make sure they started back soon.

Officer 3 was in-charge of finding out as to who the 'Captain' could be. Officer Hassan who had been in the thick of the action when the Captain had called the airport was to help him in his mission. Getting the 'Captain' could make the investigation much easier as he seemed to know a lot.

Officer 4 was to be in-charge of helping the Dubai police comb the area and help find the whereabouts of the plane or its debris. Irfan and the Sharjah police would do their part in Sharjah.

As already decided, Officer Mohammad would be at the Dubai ATC.

Shahid himself would be taking note of all intelligence information on all terrorist organizations and countries that were potentially anti-UAE in the recent past, and see what the information could do to help in the case. He would also be the one-point contact with the royalty and the investigating team, and also with the media.

Almost simultaneously as he had finished assigning the duties, Officer 1 had excused himself as he was getting a call from his staff at the Radan. He attended to the phone call and returned to the room in less than five minutes. Only Shahid was there now, the other officers had left for their tasks swiftly.

"It seems that the two people in question, Rajesh and Gabriela had checked into the Radan. Then funny events followed.

"One. There was a man named Kabir Dravid who also checked into the hotel around the same time with them. He is a disabled man, a man with a limp. Now, you may ask why this is important, but listen to me completely, sir! He was found in possession of a gun; a gun with a valid license.

"Two. Someone had tipped the hotel security that he was carrying a gun. Who was that? Why did that person do that?

"Three. Hotel CCTV camera shows Rajesh snooping outside Kabir's room at the same time when Kabir was being grilled by the hotel security and a police officer. He looked surprised and astonished, stood as if he was overhearing the conversation and then rushed into his room. It seemed pretty obvious that he too had been tipped off by someone to see what was happening in Kabir's room at *that* very right moment.

"Four. Rajesh and Gabriela meet at the lounge on the second floor of the hotel after ten minutes. He tells her something and she appears astonished. She then rushes back to her room while Rajesh leaves to the ground floor. Gabriela too reaches the ground floor. They meet an American concierge guy employed in the hotel. His name is Mark. They then go to the lockers and lock something up, one after the other. What did they lock up?"

"Five. Mark drives in a black Mercedes; the number is EH 131 to the portico. Rajesh and Gabriela hurriedly get in and the car moves off.

"Six. Kabir reaches the portico in time to see them leave. He makes a phone call, possibly one or two, as he heads back to his room, comes out with his bag and heads to the basement. Astonishingly, He gets into a parked car, an Audi and leaves the hotel.

"Whatever, boss! There is something fishy about the three of them. I think we are on the right track by tracing them!"

Shahid spoke. "Hmmm... Kabir Dravid. Interesting. Do we have anyone trailing them?"

"As we speak, we have contacted the traffic police to help us find the whereabouts of the two cars. They are tracing the direction of the car's movements with the help of camera footage."

"Did we look into what they have stored in the lockers?"

"Should we? This would be a gross deviation from the trust that millions of tourists are promised when they lock their stuff in the hotel. It could be sensational news to the media."

"Open the lockers. This is an investigation with special powers."

"Okay, sir!" Officer 1 said and marched off.

Of the four city officers, Officer 1 probably had the most important job. Shahid had a gut feeling that nabbing Gabriela or Rajesh, or possibly this Kabir fellow too would be an important step in the investigation. Officer 3 had the toughest job: to trace the Captain. If he did that, the investigation would speed up. But it was going to be tough. Whoever the Captain was, he must be a seasoned player.

Officer 4 had the heart-wrenching job of finding the plane's debris. It was a very important step here. Probably, the easiest but most annoying job would be that of Officer 2. He had to record statements of the passengers, who would be a mixed bag of emotions now. He probably would not contribute anything to the investigation at all.

He was wrong. Just as he thought that, Officer 2 came back with some information.

<h1 style="text-align:center">CHAPTER 34</h1>

Rajesh and Gabriela were stunned with what they just heard. This was it. They were completely cornered.

However, Mark didn't give them much time to introspect at that very moment. He quickly motioned them to leave. "Pick up your dinner packets, for Christ's sake!"

He led them to the Land Rover now. Rajesh realised that this was no ordinary rescue mission. This was something top-class. The Captain knew exactly what he was doing. Mark and he had planned every move carefully.

They got into the Land Rover, which was warm, but not as hot as the Hummer, probably because the weather around them had drastically become chillier. Mark turned the AC on, nevertheless.

"What a soup we have all landed ourselves in!" Gabriela told Rajesh. Her face was white with fear ever since she had heard what Mark had said just some time back. "Here we are, stuck in a foreign country, with a terrorist possibly at our heels. Why he is behind us, we don't know…

"But to top it, the police think that we may be the terrorists ourselves! So we have the police behind us too!

"And further, we don't have our phones with us to contact anyone, and our passports are blocked and there is no escape. Wow!"

Mark interrupted, "Madam, you forgot one thing! You have the Captain on your side! He will make sure, he will try his best to get you safely out of here!"

Each statement Mark was making was adding new dimensions to the complexity.

Rajesh too listed the problems and added a few. "One. Blocked passport. Two. Kabir, the possible maverick terrorist, is behind us. Why he saved us in the first place and then wants to get us now, remains a mystery. Three. Dubai police are behind us, as they suspect that we may have something to do with a possible bomb on the flight..."

"I would want to add something on that," Mark interrupted, "but you go on for now..."

Whenever Mark wanted to add something else, Rajesh knew it was not good news that was coming. He continued nevertheless. "Four. No phones. We can't reach out for help. The Captain made sure we don't have our phones, why? And now five and six; Mark has made it very clear that the Captain wants to get us out of here! That means we are going to be in another foreign land, that too as illegal immigrants! We are fucked further now!

"Sixth: We don't know whether to trust the Captain! Who is he? Maybe he is the terrorist! Maybe Gabriela, you know, you and I should turn ourselves to the police!"

"Yes, we should!" Gabriela said.

"No, you shouldn't!" Mark said firmly

"Why not?" Rajesh asked. "At least a fair trial will begin!"

Mark laughed loudly, much to their irritation. "Okay guys, time to know a few things.

"Firstly, the Captain has to be trusted because he and only he can get you out of this soup.

"Secondly, your phones had to be taken, as any call from or to your phone, will give our location away immediately!"

Yes, of course, it would! How stupid of us!

"Thirdly, my dears, the flight in which you were supposed to be safely flown to Chennai, to put it bluntly, no longer exists. Luckily, all the passengers have been safely deplaned! Two pilots flew the plane away from the airport, is what I heard. But the most powerful bomb known to humankind has probably ripped the flight apart. This is the biggest emergency the country has ever faced, believe me! You guys won't be dealt with any hospitality if you turn yourselves in. You will rot in jail forever!"

Chapter 35

Officer 2 had come with two other cops accompanying yet another handcuffed man.

"Who is this, now?" Shahid asked although he knew Officer 2 was dying to tell him the same.

"This guy is Ramprakash. He is employed as cleaning staff in Eastern Airlines. He himself has surrendered. He will tell his own story."

Shahid pushed a stool for Ramprakash to sit and ordered him to sit. "Shoot..."

"Sir?" Ramprakash asked.

"Tell me all you have to tell..." Shahid spoke softly to him and also beckoned the three cops to be seated.

Ramprakash shuddered. "Please don't hit me or kill me. I have a wife and two small children to take care of. Please!"

Shahid wanted to slap him across his face for wasting time, but he decided against the same. "You have surrendered. We will try our best to give you full justice because you did so. Now tell me..."

"I was employed in this airline only one week back. As it was a new airline with only one flight, only another person and I were employed as cleaning staff. So it was sure that I would be at the gate during the take-off of the first flight. I knew that, but so did the man who approached me five days back. I remember him clearly. That man of a similar build as me. He had a limp and he had a strange request.

"He asked me first to 'acquire' a limp. He asked me to forge a story about an accident and told me to 'get' a limp similar to his.

"He said that he would check into the first flight, have his passport scanned and would enter the flight. After this, he would make his way to the toilet where he would change into a uniform similar to what I was wearing. At the same time, I was to enter the toilet right opposite where he entered. I had to change into the clothes, which I was carrying in my tool bag. The clothes were absolutely similar to what he was wearing when he boarded the flight.

"Even if any flight attendant had seen us, she would probably only nod her head in confusion and let the matter pass. I was supposed to fly to Chennai using his passport and he was supposed to move away from the flight when the ground staff would ask to deplane, with my ID card around his neck.

"In return, I was not supposed to ask what he was up to. I would be paid handsomely in cash; two hundred thousand dirhams worth of Indian Rupees would reach my 'new' home in Chennai the moment he managed to get out of the security area, he said. Also, he would take care that my family reaches Chennai a day before I do. They did. That is too much money for me. I had to give in! Please understand, sir! Please don't throw me in jail, please! I am not a terrorist! I am just an imbecile who fell for the money offered! Please, sir, please!"

Shahid asked Officer 2, although he already knew the answer, "Whose passport is he travelling with?" This guy had to be the same person Officer 1 was referring to, the 'differentially abled' Kabir.

"A guy with an Indian Passport. His name is Kabir Dravid."

Shahid spoke coolly to Ramprakash. "You must have realised by now that Kabir is probably the terrorist who has tried to bomb the flight. Your wife and children would probably be awarded for the 'sacrifice' you have made to achieve terrorist ideologies!"

"Sir! Please, sir, please!"

Shahid had stopped listening to him. *Who was this Kabir Dravid? He had never in the recent past heard of an Indian terrorist outfit. Was Kabir his real name? Was he travelling with forged papers?*

Shahid presumed the following. Kabir could well be the person they were all looking for. He was the terrorist. He had checked into the Chennai-bound flight. His checked-in baggage had contained the advanced bomb and was sent to the flight. The bomb was so advanced that the Dubai security system could not pick up anything abnormal; they let it pass. He could have escaped immediately, but he chose not to do so, as it would have raised an alarm. Had he not boarded the flight, his luggage would have been deplaned immediately due to security reasons. He had to get into the flight, and he did so and got out with a master plan.

In every flight, the flight attendants do a headcount before taking off. In this case, the cabin crew counted the right number of people because Ramprakash sat in Kabir's seat.

To avoid suspicion, he had to deplane another two passengers, in this case, Rajesh and Gabriela. He had to do so to minimize suspicion. He moved to the Radan thereafter and checked in as a normal guest. He possibly wanted to get rid of Rajesh and Gabriela as well, either by killing them and then disposing off them, far away or by taking them hostage. This way, the Dubai police could never find them and could never prove their innocence. They would be the 'terrorists' once and for all in the records! *Fucking genius!*

Thereafter, some things didn't go as planned.

The Captain informed them that the plane had a bomb and the flight was brought back to Dubai. The passengers had deplaned and then Sanjay and Noor had set off with it. It presumably blew up over the deserts in Sharjah and the plans for widespread destruction, as desired by the terrorist organization, failed miserably.

Somehow, Rajesh and Gabriela came to possess some information about Kabir that they were not supposed to know. Hence, they fled the hotel.

Kabir knew that Gabriela and Rajesh had escaped, and is now hot on pursuit.

Whatever, it meant some simple things.

They needed to catch Kabir, the presumed 'terrorist' and/or Gabriela and Rajesh, as they had vital information.

This had to be done fast, really fast. The country's security had never seen a bigger security threat than this before. Ever.

Officer 1 arrived.

"News. Our men have broken into the lockers. They contain phones. Both iPhones. Both are locked by fingerprint and number lock. There is no way of accessing the data as iPhones have extremely high security. We need to approach Apple and ask them for help to unlock the data. And believe me, it is more tedious than finding these chaps and making them open the phones. The former could take a month!"

Shahid remembered a similar case in Europe, a few months back. It took the authorities a long time to get in terms with Apple's privacy policies and a long period of discussions before any breakthrough was made. Officer 1 was right.

"Where are the cars? Any idea?"

"Both cars had headed over to Sharjah. Not on the highway but through the desert."

That's where his trusted aide, Irfan was posted!

"Tell me, what are the two cars again?"

"Mercedes and Audi."

"Numbers? Series?"

"Mercedes E class, 131 and Audi A6, number 322."

Shahid immediately picked up the phone and dialled Irfan to explain the situation.

"What! Please give me a moment, sir, I will call you back in a minute!" Irfan said and hung up.

What had the lad seen?

As promised, Irfan called in exactly one minute. "Sir, I just spoke to my colleagues stationed by the hand baggage. They are, in fact, right beside the Mercedes E class 131. The occupants had changed over to a Hummer right where we were stationed and headed onward. After that, the Audi A6 pulled in beside me. The driver, an Indian, had asked me about the occupants of the Mercedes! After I had informed him, he set out in pursuit of the Hummer! I believe, sir, it's the people we are after!"

"Where are you now?" Shahid asked.

"On my way to Sharjah, to report to the police there!"

"Are you travelling in the same direction as the cars?"

"Yes, sir!"

"Did you cross any intersections, yet?"

"None, sir!"

"I am sure you know what to do. Your role has changed, Irfan. You are now to be in pursuit of Rajesh, Gabriela and Kabir." Shahid looked at Officer 1 as he still spoke on the phone. Officer 1 was visibly upset that he was being moved away from the most important mission in the whole investigation. However, he had to follow his senior's orders. "The officer here will call you after I hang up and brief you about the developments thus far, as far as this part of the mission is concerned. He will now take over your mission. He will report to Sharjah to help them find the plane's debris. You chase the buggers down and bring them to me." Shahid added after a cool pause. "Alive!"

Chapter 36

Three things slowed Kabir down tremendously.

Firstly, his Audi A6 was not made to run on sand, even with the tyres mildly deflated.

Secondly, he had to carefully follow the tyre tracks of the Hummer. The Hummer had used extraordinary angles to go over and down the sand dunes, which for obvious reasons, he could not follow. The guys responsible for driving the chaps before him were obviously professionals and had a plan in mind. He cursed under his breath each time he had to deviate from his path substantially just to maintain the balance of his car. He was losing precious time.

What made matters worse was that it was now dark. 7:00 pm. Although his Audi had powerful headlights, being right in the middle of an isolated desert did little to help him.

However, he had no choice. He had to get them.

After a gruelling fifty-five minutes on the dunes, which he was sure the Hummer would have covered in half an hour, he saw it.

The Hummer was there. It was parked near some tents, which were lit by bright lights.

Kabir knew he had to be careful. The driver, Gabriela and Rajesh would be there. There could be more people. And those people could be armed.

He parked his Audi a good hundred metres away from the tents and switched off the engine immediately. He picked up his pistol. (Thank God that the Dubai police had not found this one, hidden in the car!). He walked towards the tent.

The sudden chill took him by surprise. Weather in January at night in the middle of the desert was not kind. *Well, he had a job in hand and could not complain about the weather, could he?*

He sneaked up to the backside of the tents. The lights inside the tents were on, but there seemed to be little activity; almost as if no one was there.

He slowly moved to the front side. No movement or noise, yet. The guys were sleeping, or crouching for an attack. He better be careful. He removed the safety lock of his gun.

He reached the front of one tent. The door showed the symbol of a ladies' toilet. He thought for a moment and decided to crash in. A ladies' toilet was probably the best place to hide, he guessed.

He crashed through the door, the gun held firmly at arm's length. There was no one there.

He had to be extra careful as the noise he had made would have alerted people in the other tents. He ran quickly to the other tent, which understandably was a gents' toilet. He immediately crashed in again. No one.

No one in the tents! The lights had been left on as a decoy!!!

That means the guys were still in the car or hiding beside the dunes.

He rushed to the parked Hummer with his gun held high. He knew this was a risky move, but he didn't expect to be shot by Rajesh or Gabriela! Nonetheless, the people guiding them could be dangerous...

He reached the Hummer and flashed the torchlight of his cell phone.

There was no one in the car too. *These guys must be around! They can't be far away! What the hell!*

He quickly searched for some clue. He had to keep guard as well. The least he wanted was to get shot in the desert.

He went around the car. No clue. He kept the torchlight on and wandered a little away from the car in each direction...

On the left side of the Hummer, after wandering a bit, he found his clue.

The fuckers had fooled him again. Thoroughly. It was surely the work of some mastermind.

They had left the place on yet another large vehicle; the third car change. Someone clearly didn't want him to achieve what he had set out to achieve.

CHAPTER 37

"Who is the Captain? How does he know so much about us? Why does he want to save us?" Gabriela asked. "You must realise that we have given up. We have no choice but to come with you and do whatever you say, Mark. So at least we deserve to know something."

"That you will know soon, won't you? He for sure is your well-wisher!"

"Who is he?"

"I am not permitted to reveal his identity to you until we actually meet him!"

"And when is that going to happen?" Gabriela asked. As she said, Mark swung the car onto a tar road. This was almost after an hour on the sand dunes. Now the car eased on to the road and the ride seemed much less bumpy.

"I guess we will be meeting him as early as tomorrow afternoon."

"What?" Rajesh intervened. "What are we going to do until then? Be running around from place to place in this car?"

"Hmmm… you shall see. At the moment, we need a way to get out of the clutches of the Dubai police."

"Many puzzles need to be solved here!" Rajesh realised, "Number one. Is Kabir the terrorist? Number two. Why did he deplane both of us specifically? Number three. Now that he did save us, why is he after us? Number four. Who is the Captain? How did he know about the plan of the bomb? Number five. How did he know that we would not be on the flight? Number six. Why is he interested in saving us at all? What have we done to deserve this?"

Mark chuckled. "Let's put it this way, some part of it is a mystery for me too. Okay, let me tell you some things; some that may be permissible."

Gabriela smiled, "We are all ears!"

"The first. It's obvious that Kabir is the terrorist, isn't it? He got the advanced bomb into the flight. The bomb was so advanced that even Dubai security couldn't detect it. Now, he could have just walked off from the airport after checking in his luggage, couldn't he? No, he couldn't. As per security norms in all airports, if a passenger does not board the flight after checking in, his luggage would be automatically unloaded from the flight. So he had to make sure he had entered the flight.

"He had to deplane two passengers from the flight. How he himself got out still remains a mystery, but it is for sure that he deplaned the two of you on purpose. He had to do it for pinning the suspicion on to you guys."

"Jesus Christ!" Gabriela said.

"But there is apparently some other reason why he chose to deplane you two, in particular, something which even the Captain doesn't know. You two could just be incidentally selected, but the Captain feels that one of you has been selected on purpose; the other one is incidental. Most probably Rajesh was selected, and Gabriela was the incidental casualty or vice versa."

"Nonsense! I have no probable relation with Kabir!" Gabriela said, and then she looked at Rajesh, "You have mentioned that you know Kabir somehow!"

"I didn't say I know him!" Rajesh snapped. "However, yes. He does look familiar. I must have interacted with him sometime in the recent past. But surely I don't remember him to be a significant person in my life! Definitely not significant enough for him to be pulling me out of a plane with a bomb on it!"

"Come on, there must be some connection! It is strange, isn't it? You seem to know Kabir. We don't know for sure that Kabir is the terrorist, of course. But he is definitely up to something very strange. He had apparently gotten into the flight and then got out of it. Now, has he been escorted, just like us, by the airport staff to the Radan hotel? Unlikely! Because he would have accompanied us then!" Gabriela said.

Rajesh continued, "To think of it, I saw him walking in an Airline staff uniform out of the flight. I am dead sure it was he who walked out of the flight; it surely was not a case of a mistaken identity. Also, I am sure that the man in the flight who appeared in his clothes was not he! He definitely exchanged dresses with a similar-looking airline staff member and came out of the flight!"

Gabriela paused. This guy sure was spooky. "It all the more underlines the thought that he actually may be the person who checked in the advanced explosive into the flight!"

"Yeah!" Rajesh said, and Mark also seemed to nod in the affirmative. It was clear that he too didn't know much about Kabir. He probably was not lying when he said that he didn't know who the terrorist actually was.

Gabriela continued, "Not only that, he was found with a gun, which he could have only acquired after deplaning. Also, he checked into a room next to ours. Why? He probably wanted to harm us too. Now… Now…just think! Is there a connection between you knowing him and what he is doing to us?"

"I don't know! I just can't remember where and when I saw him before!"

"Think about it Rajesh, don't you remember any guy with a limp when you were a student or early in your career? In your school, college or at your workplace?"

Rajesh remembered only one plump guy in his glass, who had lost his right leg unfortunately in an accident. Kabir was only limping and certainly, his limb was intact. It was as if he had been injured badly. He must have had a fracture that did not heal properly. It was probably an accident or…

Rajesh went limp for a moment. To Gabriela, his face was almost paralyzed.

He suddenly came back to life and said in an agonizing tone, "Oh fuck, now I remember where I have seen this chap before! His name is not Kabir. It is clearly him, Sachin Karad."

Chapter 38

Rakhee Bora was stunned. What she had just heard was crazy.
She had joined this special twelveth-grade classes a month back:
Sudeep's classes. Right on Tilak Road. The twelveth-grade final exams
were next year, in March 1997, but the classes had begun last month;
April 1996.

The class easily had two hundred students, half of them girls. She
was sure of one thing; if today there was an opinion poll as to who the
best looking girls in the class were, her name would not figure in the
top ten...

So, it was indeed surprising what she had just heard.

Her friends, who should have been giggling when they told her the
news, seemed to have a terrified look on their faces.

Three guys in the class apparently liked her, and they liked her crazy.

One was Wasim Shaikh: an extremely thin but a smart-looking
fellow. He seemed like a fun-loving guy, until today.

The second was Sachin Karad, a typical son of a local politician.
He sported a full beard and rode on his Royal Enfield. Many girls she
knew liked him, but she felt he was a show-off. However, it surprised
her to know that he too seriously liked her, when he could have liked
any of the better-looking 'babes'!

Well, she was no 'babe' by the day. She loved to party in the evenings,
but none of the three guys had ever seen that aspect of her in real-
time, although they must be knowing that already. In the class, she
was a simple girl. She was dressed up mainly in salwar kameez and
sometimes in shirts and pants. She was five-feet-five in height, and she

never wore heels to class. She was of the firm belief – work when you work and party when you party. This aspect of hers mainly attracted maximum guys as per her friends.

The third guy was more of the bookworm types. Although he had a good sense of humour and often joked with his pals, the south Indian Rajesh was no Wasim or Sachin. The latter two were more outgoing.

Therein was the problem. None of the three had ever conveyed their liking to her. However, today, Sachin and Wasim were prepared for a showdown. For obvious reasons, both hated each other, but their dislike had slowly reached to violence and immense cuss words. Jostling and pushing each other had become a norm, but Wasim had gone a step too far. He had broken the headlights of Sachin's Royal Enfield.

Sachin entered the class with a chain of a bicycle. Today, after class, he was going to teach Wasim the lesson of his life.

Wasim had anticipated violence. He entered with a hockey stick, prepared.

Rajesh was looking petrified according to her friends. Little would he have anticipated that his competitors would reach such a level. He would surely give up on her.

Rajesh and Wasim knew each other and were friends: not close ones, but friends, nevertheless. However, Rakhee knew that Rajesh, and for the matter of fact, any close friend of Wasim, would not stand up for him today, for Sachin was the son of a local politician.

The news had spread, and no one knew what to do to prevent the fight. Nothing happened in the class. The first jostling began in the parking lot. Sachin backed up his Royal Enfield onto Wasim's path.

Wasim immediately knew what was going to happen next. The people next to him tried to cool Sachin down, who obviously was not going to. He parked his bike, pulled out the chain from his bag. Wasim pulled the hockey stick close to him.

He wielded the hockey stick menacingly towards Sachin. Sachin took a step back; Wasim took a few steps forward. Sachin kept moving backwards, his face showed some fear, and Wasim was managing to scare him.

Apparently.

In a planned move, the hitherto backward stepping Sachin, suddenly lunged forward and grabbed the hockey stick hard and shoved it towards Wasim. Wasim tumbled backwards, losing his footing, and landed in a seated position onto the ground. That was enough. The clearly more powerful Sachin overpowered him. Wasim lost grip on the hockey stick.

Sachin gave him very serious blows with his hand that didn't have the chain tied to it, his right hand. As Wasim's nose bled and eyes started swelling, the bystanders stared in horror. Among them, was an overwhelmingly horrified Rajesh and Rakhee, a girl, who was beginning to hate Sachin more with every passing second.

After Sachin had knocked Wasim into a position where he could no longer respond, he prepared for landing the real blow, with his left hand, which was made into a fist with the bicycle chain surrounding the fingers. It would be enough to disfigure Wasim's face permanently besides dolling out excruciating pain now.

The people around him stared in absolute terror.

None moved an inch for the first second.

In the next second, a possessed person made the move. Rajesh didn't know what came into him, as he moved in a flash, picked up the hockey stick nearby and gave a telling powerful blow on Sachin's right shin. The cracking sound of Sachin's shinbones was heard loud and clear. He let out a loud scream of agony before collapsing in a heap on the floor.

<h1 style="text-align:center">CHAPTER 39</h1>

It took another quarter of an hour more to figure out, but as soon as he did, Irfan became only the third person to drive on the sand dunes that night. He was sure that he should follow the marks of the narrow tyres, which was probably the Audi being driven by Kabir.

Officer 1 had sounded him on the developments.

His intuitions were in place.

Kabir was the terrorist, probably the most wanted person in the entire country. He was riding an Audi A6. He even remembered how he looked.

Ahead of him were Rajesh and Gabriela, being driven by Mark, in a Hummer. He remembered how the vehicle looked like. They perhaps possessed some information, which was important for the police, but dangerous for Kabir. Or perhaps they possessed no information and were only trying to run away from Kabir, who was trying to kill them or kidnap them.

He had alerted all the police posts on the parallel desert road where probably these tyre tracks were headed. They were to stop any black Hummer that passed or any Audi A6.

The route was tedious, having to follow the tyre tracks in pitch darkness. Luckily, the headlights of his Nissan were strong.

After half an hour on the dunes, he came to the tents.

However, it took him only another five minutes to gauge what could have happened. The trio had escaped in yet another SUV, and the Audi was still in pursuit.

Now, this was a difficult situation.

He didn't know which car the trio was using. He only knew that Kabir was still in his Audi A6, with a known license plate number.

If the police ahead managed to stop Kabir, they would have achieved something significant. But what if… what if Kabir was not the guy they were after? What if the people of significance were actually in the first car? By stopping Kabir, who was possibly in hot pursuit of the trio, they would completely lose them. The main problem lay in the fact that he didn't know which car they were in.

Just as he thought that, the radio crackled. "Officer Irfan, come in please."

"Officer Irfan, salaam aleikum."

"Walekum Salaam, one of our patrol cars has traced the Audi A6, number 322. He is on his way back to the city of Dubai. We are about to intercept him."

"No! Don't intercept. Just tail him."

"What?"

"Yes, do as I say! And ask the patrol cars much ahead of him to check for any large SUV, perhaps a Fortuner, Hummer or Range Rover, with moderately deflated tyres!"

"Okay! But how much ahead?"

"Anything between five to twenty kilometres ahead!" Irfan had just guessed the numbers.

"That, officer, is half the city of Dubai!"

"Well, officer! This is for the pride of the country. It is a war and even if we need to mobilize all our forces to catch these people, we must!"

CHAPTER 40

The Professor got in touch with him again. All when he thought his chase was ending.

"You are now to follow a Land Rover, which is on the Shaikh al Zayad road, racing from one side of Dubai to the other, probably on its way towards Abu Dhabi is what I guess."

"How did you know this?"

"No magic, my friend! My guys are posted in all the tollbooths entering Dubai and Sharjah. We spotted them with ease!"

"Why didn't you stop them?"

"You should know the reason by now, my boy!"

Yeah, he knew a few reasons, but one main reason would be not to alert the Dubai police or else, they were done for!

"The bad news is that they are at least half an hour ahead of you. Just keep driving down the Shaikh al Zayad road. You will have to make a stop when I tell you. A brand new car will be awaiting you there. You need to change your car too. If there is any deviation in their route, I shall keep you posted."

Surely, Kabir was the most sought after person in Dubai today. Yet, he himself was following directions given by someone else; a person more powerful than him. The Professor.

Kabir had no other work but to drive on. He could not risk overspeeding and getting caught. He had to maintain a low profile. One thing surprised him. He was let to go past the tollgate without being stopped. That meant the Dubai police, although they knew they had to get him, had yet not figured out in which car he was in.

He turned on the music. It played old Hindi songs, but little did he listen to them.

His thoughts went back to the fateful day in 1996.

He was Sachin Karad then. He was the son of Samar Karad, a local MP. He enjoyed being the son of an MP. His friends used to adore him. He had many friends: only a few foes, but they were all shit scared of him; except that prick Wasim.

Although he was impressed by many a girl before, there was something different about Rakhee. She was ideal. She was good looking. She was simple and studious by the day, but she was a party animal at night. Perfect blend; something that he really liked.

People always viewed him as being pushy and arrogant, but he was willing to change himself for her; if she agreed with him.

Wasim was going to be the thorn in the flesh. He liked Rakhee too. *Okay, he could like her!* She was of course likeable. Even that nerd Rajesh liked her. But Wasim was going a few steps too forward. He viewed Sachin as a villain. He had started jostling and pushing him now, and in a fit of rage had smashed the headlights of his bike. He needed to be put in place.

The day at the parking.

Sachin was sure that he would overpower Wasim. He would give him some telling blows on his face. He had carried the bicycle chain just to intimidate Wasim. He was going to swing his hand that was wrapped with the chain close to his face and then back off. He, of course, didn't plan to really hit him with the chain; for that would be disastrous. In the worst case, he might have killed him if a little extra force was used. Nonetheless, surely, it would at least cause a grievous injury, for which he could be jailed. His father's reputation would take a beating. The chain was meant to intimidate; and nothing else.

Just that one second before he actually executed the final step of his plan, it fell apart. In a senseless fit of anxiety, Rajesh had picked up that hockey stick and struck an extremely hard blow on his right shin. It was the most agonizing moment of his life until date.

Both his shinbones were fractured; in fact, they were split through and through. He had to undergo three surgeries in the next six months, but the bones had mal-aligned and he had been left with a permanent limp; a permanent disability.

He could have exacted his revenge on Rajesh. He wanted to do it, but couldn't. The reason was the photo. *Who on earth took the photo?*

A photo of him wielding the chain was enough to make his father mad at him. His father had to trade. The photo, whose negatives were in Rajesh's possession, now, was never to get to the media. In return, no act of revenge would be dolled on Rajesh, and no police case would be filed for inflicting grievous injury, which could land Rajesh behind bars.

Rajesh had fucked his life forever.

Chapter 41

Gabriela was angry; very angry.

"Kabir Dravid hates you." She pointed a stern finger at Rajesh, who momentarily was engulfed in guilt. "For that purpose, he pulls you out of the flight. He wants to take revenge on you personally. He wants to break your leg or kill you or whatever…

"But what have I done? I have been dragged out of my flight to Chennai, where I needed to be for a simple business trip. I am an incidental, an 'also deplaned'! Now, where am I? Travelling on Shaikh Al Zayad road to 'God knows where'! With whom? Two unknown men! Who is on my tail? Some crazy terrorist and an entire police force! My life is screwed for no fault of mine!"

"Lady! Lady!" Mark interrupted. "Let me get myself clear! You were deplaned from a flight that had a bomb on it! There was a good chance that you wouldn't be alive now! Had the flight not been recalled, all the passengers on the flight would have been dead! That includes you too, if not deplaned."

"But no! The people are safe! No one died!"

"That's lucky for them!" "What was in it for me?"

Rajesh burst in, "You were in a much better position. You were always going to live. Kabir would not have harmed you, would he have?"

"Then whom am I fleeing from?"

Mark replied to that, "You are fleeing the Dubai police. Perhaps now Kabir too wants to get you, but that's less likely."

Gabriela fell silent for a while. She thought of all possibilities. Yes, had she been on the flight, it could have been death. Had she turned herself in to the police, as Mark said earlier, she would rot in jail for years until the interrogation was over. This situation was bad, but probably the better of the three.

Rajesh's feeling of guilt was disappearing, "Besides, if it is Kabir who is trying to get me... then who is this Captain who is trying to save me? I am not such an important soul. The person who is making us flee the situation might be trying to protect you and not me. I cannot see anyone pulling out such a major coup for my sake!"

Gabriela was taken aback. Maybe there was some truth in what Rajesh was trying to infer. She thought of her billionaire boyfriend Steve Mehrotra. But she dismissed that thought immediately. She had planned to speak to him after taking a shower at the Radan hotel. However, things had moved so fast that she was unable to do so. Steve would have probably read her WhatsApp messages by now and would have tried calling her.

Surely, he would have heard the news about the bomb on the flight and would be trying to contact her. *Oh, God! He must be shit scared!* She had not informed him prior that she would be boarding this flight. Now he must be trying to get in touch with the Airline staff to find out where she was! He might have found out about her deplaning and probably would also have come to know that she had fled. As she thought that, she had a glimmer of hope. *Maybe Steve would find a way out of this mess. But whatever he had to do, he had to do it quickly!*

She asked Mark, "Well, Mark? Does the Captain know me?"

"No comments. I am not allowed to comment!"

"What the hell! What's going on?" Gabriela shouted.

"You are being towed away to safety. That is going on!" Mark said coolly.

There was no point in getting further anxious, she guessed. She took a few deep breaths. She could see Rajesh doing the same.

"Okay, dude! Tell me why were you not arrested for breaking Kabir's leg? Is it common for people in India to just escape after breaking someone's leg?"

"I was not arrested as there was no case registered. Luckily for me, one of the students had captured a photo where Sachin *aka* Kabir was about to smash the head of Wasim with a chain. He offered me the negatives of the photo. Not many people liked Sachin, you see. I made several copies of the same.

"Sachin's father was a respected politician. If this photo got to the media, it would mean severe defamation and possible loss in the next elections. He just subdued the matter with no case but got me to promise that I too would not rake up this issue anymore.

"I never saw Sachin again. He probably had shifted cities; probably forced to do so.

"What would have rubbed salt into his wound, had he been around in Pune longer, was the fact that Rakhee and I dated for one year after that. She was the only girlfriend I ever had..."

"What an asshole of a Romeo..." Gabriela said, and couldn't help but smile finally.

CHAPTER 42

Shahid had to give his first media briefing at 9:00 pm.
However, first, he had to get to know what all the officers under him were up to, first.

Officer 1 was presently in-charge of helping the Sharjah police. He was still on his way to Sharjah, but last he had heard from the Sharjah police was that they had not found the debris of the plane.

Nor had Officer 4 who was in-charge of the combing operations in Dubai. Malaysia airlines 370 in 2014 had a similar fate. It just disappeared. As things stood now in 2018, still no one had a clue about what happened to that flight. Was this going to be a similar story? At least, in this case, Shahid had a clue that it was a bomb. Also, he had made sure that the passengers were safe. However, he had lost two of his brave men. One was a citizen of the UAE and one was a respected professional working in this country for a decade or so. He breathed heavily as he remembered the faces of Sanjay Sharan and Officer Noor.

Officer 3 and Officer Hassan had made some inroads. They were to find out the identity of the Captain. He had made a call from a UK number. However, as they investigated further, they found out that the number belonged to the Matrix Company and the caller was making the call from France. However, that was all that they had got to know until now, but at least it was some progress!

Officer 2 had provided the greatest inroads, but after that, he had to get back to the torrid job of taking the statements from all the passengers. Understandably, they were agitated, angry and frustrated.

None of the passengers could add much to the investigation, although at least ten of them suggested the obvious. The terrorist was most likely one or both of the members that were deplaned moments before the pushback.

The good thing was Officer 2 had summoned for the handbags and they were to reach the passengers in fifteen minutes. The makeshift flight was to take off at 11:00 pm and reach Chennai by 4:00 am IST, eight hours behind schedule. But at least they would make it safe, thanks to the Almighty!

Officer Irfan had made significant progress, although he could not share it with the media. He had sighted Kabir's vehicle and had already put two cars on his tail, as Kabir re-entered Dubai. Kabir himself was in hot pursuit of Gabriela and Rajesh, although he was yet to understand the correct motive. But yes, the assumption was that he was the man they wanted.

Shahid, for the first time, shuddered. The officer next to him had just told him what he did not want to hear... "The Press conference is ready. You need to be at the podium now!"

As he walked towards the makeshift media room in Terminal One, a large number of cameras flashed. He felt more uncomfortable. He had given many press interviews in the past, but this was by far the one that disturbed him the most.

He got to the podium.

"Ladies and gentlemen, this is the first press notice of many to come. It is a matter of national security, hence, I will not be in a position to give too much information..." He went on to tell the people about the information received by the airport police, the calling back of the Chennai flight, the deplaning of the passengers, the flight being flown away by Sanjay and Noor, the disappearance of the flight, the investigations being carried out by the officers (he was careful not to mention about Rajesh, Gabriela, Kabir and Officer Irfan's role), and the safety of the passengers. He said he had the full support of the royalty to carry out the investigation and they would go to any level to catch the culprits.

However, the terrorist had already partially succeeded in what he was trying to achieve. The media were going to create panic in the mind of every UAE resident. Shahid had the moral responsibility of getting to the bottom of this investigation as fast as he could...

CHAPTER 43

Mark kept on speaking for a while like a tourist guide. "That, my friends, is a view of the Burj Al Arab; we are now entering the Abu Dhabi highway; that is the Yas Marina; that is the Ferrari world; do you know about it?"

Gabriela was lulled into a semi-sleep, having given up to her fate.

Of course, Rajesh had heard of the Ferrari World, Yas Marina etc... but this was hardly the time for any sightseeing. All he knew was that they had now crossed yet another princely state and they were in Abu Dhabi, wondering how long they would go on, on the road. *Were they being taken to Saudi Arabia by any chance?*

Seeing that the passengers were bored, Mark turned on the radio. The radio played Aerosmith's Dream on. Hardly an appropriate song at the moment, but he let it play on. It was a rock show and was followed by 'We Are the Champions' by Queen and 'Wish you were here' by Pink Floyd.

At 9:15 pm, the song was abruptly interrupted by an important news piece.

The Head of the Police at Dubai Airport had issued a statement. Rajesh woke Gabriela up, who was stunned for a moment but was all ears after that momentary lapse.

They listened clearly. This problem was huge; really huge. A happening of this magnitude would shake the whole country: in fact, the whole world would be shaken!

But what was surprising was that there was no mention of the three passengers that had been deplaned earlier. The emotion passed from one of a surprise to that of a little comfort; before it turned to fear again...

Mark just said the obvious aloud, "Don't you relax folks. The police are hot on our trails. They are not going to tell the people of the UAE about us. They would be enough scared anyway. It would scare them more if they knew that the police were chasing three suspected terrorists who are zipping from Sharjah, through Dubai and now are in Abu Dhabi."

They bypassed Abu Dhabi, however, and were hurtling further southwest. Mark was just not giving away anything.

After an hour and half of further driving, at 10:45 pm, Rajesh finally saw Mark enter a town: Al Hamra. He raced the Land Rover through the relatively empty streets, which was expected at this time. After another ten minutes on the road, he finally pulled the car on to the sand.

"Yet another desert now? Oh boy! When are we going to stop?"

Mark grinned. "Right here! But our night still goes on further!"

"That I guessed!" Gabriela said. Rajesh and she expected yet another desert camp, and yet another car change.

Mark screeched the car into a halt. "Let's get down!" he said in a voice that was commanding.

Rajesh and Gabriela didn't resist. They could use some fresh air now.

As they got down, they heard a distinct sound: not something that would be expected in a desert.

Then they realised their folly. They were on a beach and the sound was that of the sea water.

Mark was leading them towards the water, where a dim light was moving up and down; as if someone was showing a torch and signalling them to come there.

As they approached the light, they realised what it was: yet another illusion from far. It was a ferry's headlight. It was black in colour; hence it was just not visible from a distance.

Rajesh was expecting someone to be there. *Was it the Captain? Was he called a Captain because he was a Captain of a ferry? Possible!*

But soon they were to realise that there was just no one on the ferry. It was just like the previous two occasions. On the first occasion, the Hummer was parked for them. On the second occasion, a Land Rover was parked. Now it was a ferry: and for sure it was going to be driven by the one and only...Mark!

And for sure, he was not going to tell them where he was going to take them!

CHAPTER 44

The time was 11:30 pm: five hours and forty-five minutes since the flight was last spotted by anyone. Perhaps the last person who saw it was, in fact, Officer Irfan. It was strange; the flight had disappeared into thin air. It was not intercepted by anyone else: and its debris had not yet been found.

Shahid pondered.

Malaysia Airlines 370 in 2014 had met a somewhat similar fate. It was en route from Kuala Lumpur to Beijing. The crew of the Boeing 777-200ER aircraft last communicated with air traffic control around 38 minutes after take-off when the flight was over the South China Sea. The aircraft was lost from ATC radar screens minutes later but was tracked by military radar for another hour, deviating westwards from its planned flight path, crossing the Malay Peninsula and the Andaman Sea. After that, no one till date knows what had happened to it. In spite of a large multinational rescue operation, which involved billions of dollars being spent, the wreckage of the flight was never found.

It was no doubt that the next day's newspapers would be full of this comparison, but there were significant differences here.

One. There were 239 people on board on that flight. There were only two here.

Two. That flight was lost over unknown terrain and was not under scrutiny until much after it disappeared. Here, it was different. They were actively tracking the flight's progress and there was little chance that it could have deviated from its path majorly without being traced. It had, in fact, in Irfan's words, vanished in thin air!

Three. No one had a clue as to what might have led to the disappearance of the Malaysia Airlines flight. Was it a bomb? Was it an accident? Was it hijacking? Was it an alien invasion? Here, in this case, there was a clear mention of a bomb that was extremely powerful... yet the odd part was the debris of the flight was still not found.

Officer 1 was with the Sharjah police and Officer 4 was with the Dubai police and yet no news about the plane's wreckage was forthcoming. He knew that the search was going on; even at night.

The report from Officer 2 was that the hand baggage of all the passengers was handed over to them. There were a few people who grumbled about loss of their checked-in baggage, but the majority of them were relieved with the fact that they were, in fact, alive and not blown to smithereens. Most were relieved to know that they were going to board a new flight shortly and get to their destination. So the agitation had cooled down. Roshan ensured that they had been good hosts. They had provided each passenger with a good dinner pack and soft drinks.

Officer 3 and Hassan were making some inroads, however. Shahid had no idea how they managed to do that, but they had traced the Captain's call to an area near the Eiffel Tower. The number belonged to a Mr Amarinder Chauhan, who was at this moment in a town called Kurukshetra in Haryana, India. He had reported a loss of his mobile phone and sim card; both of which he had rented from the Matrix company when he had travelled to London a month back. The Matrix Company had not de-activated the number as the Indian Cyber Crime Department had instructed them to pick up any usage of the number. It had never been used thus far until today.

The bad news was that it was never used again either. It was used to make only one phone call: that was to the Dubai police. In all probability, the call was made from near the Eiffel tower and the mobile phone was dumped somewhere nearby. The Interpol with the help of the IMEI number of the stolen phone would soon lay a hand on it, but Shahid assumed that it would be of little significance now.

Irfan had made the maximum progress.

His team had successfully tailed Kabir. Kabir had made a car change. He himself was now in a Hyundai Accent car: unfortunately for him; it was less of a decoy as Irfan's team had very nicely followed him. Irfan himself made a helicopter ride from Dubai to Abu Dhabi, which enabled him to catch up with his team and he too was very close in pursuit of Kabir.

Irfan and his team had followed Kabir up to Al Hamra, where they found Kabir standing hopelessly beside the Land Rover at the beach.

It had taken Irfan not much time to realise what had happened.

Mark, Gabriela and Rajesh had escaped into the sea. From here, the destination was more or less obvious. It was to another country: a country, which, given the current political scenario, would just not help at all. They had in all probability escaped to Qatar. *Shit!*

There was only one option left now, and Irfan had called Shahid just moments ago to take his permission. After that, he had proceeded to carry out what was the logical next step.

With all guns raised, the Dubai police had caught and arrested Mr Kabir Dravid; the suspect number one in today's crime; a crime that had threatened the sovereignty of their beloved country and almost thrown the world into pandemonium. Kabir was being brought back to Dubai after the arrest. Today was going to be a long night...

CHAPTER 45

It was 1:30 am. The Great Guru Amar was finding it difficult to sleep and had put on his Times of India app on his IPad.

The first news item was indeed disturbing. A flight from Dubai to Chennai (Eastern Airlines flight, apparently its maiden flight) had been called back as there was a bomb scare. The passengers were deplaned and then the flight took off again, most probably to protect the airport. However, what happened after that was bad. The flight lost contact with the Dubai ATC after a short while and was never traced again. Its debris was never found and no one had reported spotting the flight or picking up its whereabouts. It was presumed that it was a very powerful bomb; a powerful terrorist act. The reporters also suggested a high-level conspiracy, the motive of which was still just a guess.

But that did not bother him as much as the article number two on that page since evening.

It read boldly "Scientists challenge religion."

A Scientist group based in Europe had recently challenged the concept of religion. This itself was not new, was it?

But the scientists had promised that they had hard-core proof. They had proof of the Big Bang. They had proof that the world as we know it was a by-product of this great moment in time. No God had created the world by saying, "Let there be Light!"

Well, again, this was not quite new. The Scientists at the European Organization for Nuclear Research or CERN were set to prove it. There was the discovery of the God particle or Higg's boson/antimatter in 2013, which was sounded loudly as the victory of science over religion.

However, still far from it, the CERN had failed to provide further meaningful insight as to how the Universe was created on its own. God *had* to be there!

In 2014, the Pope had given a statement that the Big Bang was definitely possible, but God had orchestrated it. Many experts believed this to be the first crumble of religion; the acceptance of the Big Bang.

For centuries and more, humans believed there is God; the ultimate superpower who created him and all the species on Earth. He created the entire universe as it stands now. Also, He controlled the destiny of all. He punished people who did evil actions and helped those who were good.

As scientists like Galileo, Newton, Copernicus, Aryabhatta, Darwin, Einstein and Hawking started to make remarkable discoveries, many of the religious assumptions had fallen flat on the ground. However, the truth remained that man was still not able to find out the ultimate answers. *Who created the Universe? Was it God or was it some vague mathematical equation?*

Well, none of those bothered the Great Guru now. This question would arise again and again.

The thing that bothered him was this particular 'Scientist group'.

They had chosen to target only two people; the Pope and the Great Guru!

Well, they could have chosen any other person of religious importance; it could have been famous Maulas from the Arab world, it could have been more famous Gurus from India, it could have been the ISIS, damn it! But they had specifically decided to include him...

The Scientist group had sounded a strict warning to the Pope and the Great Guru Amar that they would be the first people to witness the proof they had and they would force them to beg forgiveness from the people for misguiding them all these years!

It was his internet presence that had probably made the Great Guru a target, he presumed.

Whatever it was, it was not going to be a great feeling. He had to represent religion and God's faith against this devilish group. Rama had to kill Ravana once again...

Chapter 46

It was quite chilly. Mark had his suit on, so he suffered less. Gabriela and Rajesh were in informal clothing and shivered. They had the option to sit inside the room, but they decided to sit in the pilot's room with Mark.

"Rajesh, just hold on to the steering for a while, will you?" Mark asked.

"What? I don't know anything about manoeuvring a ferry!"

"You don't need to do anything at the moment. Just hold the wheel. It's a problem only if a big ship is in our way, which we won't know as I have switched off the radar. Or maybe if we run into an iceberg, which, believe me, is not at all a possibility in this sea!" Mark laughed, but the shivering Rajesh and Gabriela were not up for a joke. "Let me use the washroom, dude!"

Rajesh took over reluctantly.

Mark went into the ferry, leaving Gabriela and Rajesh by themselves for the second time only after they had got onto the journey with Mark.

Rajesh smirked. "This guy makes sure he leaves us for a while only when we are in a hopeless situation. The first instance he left us was in the middle of the desert, now he leaves us in the middle of the sea at midnight!"

"Should we jump off the boat and swim to land?" Gabriela laughed nervously.

"Well, I guess it's a choice we need to make. Either we trust this chap and go where he wants us to, or get caught by the Dubai police, or be eaten by sharks of the Persian Gulf!" Rajesh too laughed, and this time Gabriela laughed more open-heartedly.

However, it was difficult. Both of them were in the middle of nowhere; in a place that had no relation with their individual lives. They only had to live with their instincts. Their instincts presently guided them to follow Mark's instructions. Only time would tell whether they were right.

Rajesh continued. "We just headed off perpendicular to the beach. That means most probably we must be on our way to Iran, I guess."

Gabriela shuddered. As a US citizen, it was time to fear Iran. Relations between Tehran and Washington were at an all-time low. "But of course, we won't know how many times Mark has steered the ferry. At this time of the night, it is difficult for us to guess!"

"Yeah, I guess you are right. We are at the mercy of this guy!"

"Let's hope we made the right decision by trusting him! Jesus Christ will surely guide us the right way!" Gabriela said as she made a cross with her fingers and looked up to the sky.

"Do you believe in God, Gabriela?" Rajesh asked.

"Given the situation that we are in, it doesn't seem like an inappropriate question. But I am surprised you ask me the question. Of course, I do. Don't you?"

"Well, yes and no"

"What do you mean yes and no?"

"Well, let's put it this way – I believe in God, but somehow I do not believe in too many religious customs. God is someone who created the universe and probably controls it. So, I worship Him directly. However, I don't believe in like... you know, praying to God in temples or churches... building these huge monuments for God. Well, we could make the world a better place if we don't believe and preach religion, or fight for it!"

"Makes sense! But I believe religion is one way of reaching out to God! Hindus pray in temples, we pray in churches, Muslims in mosques, but the ultimate aim is to talk to Him!"

"I believe that God is powerful enough to hear us from wherever we are. Just because we are in the Persian Gulf and not in a temple does not mean that God won't hear me if I pray to him!"

"Point! Point. Why this discussion suddenly anyway?" Gabriela smiled.

"Sorry... sorry! I just kind of... you know... related to what you said about Christ saving us now and a story that I was working on before I left India for the US."

"What was that?"

"There is this religious Guru in our country... he is driving everyone nuts now."

"The Great Guru Amar?"

Rajesh was taken aback. He hadn't expected Gabriela to know him. "Wow! Thanks to the internet! A US citizen knows about the Great Guru Amar! What propaganda!"

"Yeah, I heard about him alright! Even some of Steve's friends talk about him in New Jersey!"

"Hmm... well, whatever! I was doing the media coverage for my TV channel when he was touring Coimbatore and Chennai recently. Some of the things he preached were atrocious according to me. He insisted that every Hindu visit Rameshwaram, Tirupati, Haridwar, Yamunotri, Gangotri, Dwarka, Konark and Kashi. Not only we must do that, but we must also get a ritual known as *Aarti* done on our name and our family's name. Only then we would have achieved the right to be seen as good humans in the eyes of God!"

"Hmmm..."

"And guess what? There were so many followers of his in both cities, and they seemed to be in complete agreement with him!"

"Yeah, I can see why you feel what you feel now! It's absurd!"

"But then came the best part. The Guru was in Pune for a sermon, when a fifteen-year-old girl, Deepti Iyengar, stood up publically and challenged all his beliefs. What she said made perfect sense. She was recorded on video and the video was uploaded on YouTube. It has close to a billion views already. I further had to cover this part of the story, hence, I was a little involved in this discussion, so sorry, Gabriela..."

Before Gabriela could acknowledge his apology, Mark reappeared. "Good job, pal! You would pass your sea driving test soon!" He tossed two blankets towards the duo.

They accepted them happily. Mark had taken care of everything.

"Both of you go into the cabin now. I have heated up coffee and put it in a flask kept on the table next to two cups. Either take a short nap or stay awake by drinking coffee. We should reach our destination in an hour or so!"

"What is our destination?" Gabriela tried.

"Wait and watch..."

"Okay." She sighed heavily as she prepared to leave the Pilot's cabin towards the main cabin.

"Oh, by the way... I got some news on my satellite phone!"

Both Gabriela and Rajesh stopped.

"Our friend Kabir has been captured by the Dubai police and is being driven back to Dubai! Imagine this, he had reached Al Hamra, right next to the place we got onto the ferry. He is quite a connected chap I must imagine! He tracked us in spite of our changing cars twice!"

Both Gabriela and Rajesh shuddered.

Rajesh was the first one to speak up, "That means...that means... they will catch us soon too!"

"Nope, they can't!"

"Why can't they? It only proves that the Dubai police is no mug either. They too had reached Al Hamra and must be on our pursuit now!"

"No, they can't do a thing now!"

"Why?"

"Because, my dears, we have entered international waters at least thirty minutes back. They have no right to do anything to us here!"

Chapter 47

The Nissan came to a screeching halt on the service road that ran between the Al Hamra sea-side to the main roadway that led back to Dubai.

What Irfan saw was unmistakable. Three men, dressed in all black, held a person at gunpoint in the middle of the road.

Irfan had captured Kabir Dravid thirty minutes back. There was questioning in the car and he was to bring him back to Dubai for further interrogation.

However, he was naïve to assume that an international terrorist such as Kabir would surrender so meekly. Terrorists usually kill themselves if they don't see an alternate plan of escaping. Kabir did not attempt suicide whatsoever. He readily accepted the fact that he would be arrested.

That initial move itself surprised Irfan – giving in without resistance.

Surely Kabir would know that his life would become miserable now. Even if he were not guilty, he surely would be tortured without an end by the Dubai police. After all, this was a matter of national security. It would be at least two to three years in jail before he would be released.

So, there was only one possibility; and he almost guessed it then itself. He had a sure-shot way of escaping; being a person of such assumed importance.

Irfan had to act fast. He made the call to Shahid and explained the situation.

Shahid took a long pause at the other end. "Do what they say. We have to protect this dignitary at all costs; even if it means trading the terrorist with him. Bloody assholes. Allah will get them and burn them alive."

It was a super simple trade-off for Kabir. He was released and walked past the police with all pomp and glory to the men in black. As he did that, the men kept their promise, and let go of the person in their possession, who walked to the Dubai police. He had a bomb tightly strapped and sutured at places onto his torso, which would be triggered off by the remote in the one of the men's hand.

The deal was clear. Kabir and his men would have to escape and the police should not move until the next ten minutes, otherwise, the bomb could still go off. There was no need to explain as to how they would keep an eye on the police even after they left the place.

Kabir waved bye to Irfan as he got on to the Jeep parked for them.

Irfan could do nothing but smile. All his continuous non-stop effort since afternoon just went down the drain.

Chapter 48

"Surely, we cannot float in the Persian sea forever..." Gabriela said. "Surely we can't!" Mark smiled.

"That means we will enter some nation soon. This must already be an international operation. All the countries in the neighbourhood are friendly to the UAE!" Gabriela said.

"Really?"

Rajesh intervened, "We are going to Qatar or Iran, aren't we?"

"That's spoken like a truly well-informed journalist! We, as we speak, have just entered Qatar's waters."

The Qatar diplomatic crisis began in June 2017, when Saudi Arabia and the United Arab Emirates along with several other countries in the neighbourhood, severed diplomatic relations with Qatar and banned Qatar aeroplanes and ships from entering their airspace and sea routes along with Saudi Arabia blocking the only land crossing.

The Saudi-led coalition cited Qatar's alleged support for terrorism as the main reason for their actions, insisting that Qatar has violated a 2014 agreement with the members of the Gulf Cooperation Council. Saudi Arabia and other countries had criticized Al Jazeera and Qatar's relations with Iran.

Many students and workers from Qatar who resided in the UAE and Saudi were sent back overnight to Qatar.

But this meant that the reverse was also true. UAE could not expect any cooperation from Qatar now. Certainly, it was not going to be easy to extradite Mark, Gabriela and Rajesh back to the UAE.

Suddenly, a blinding light from nowhere hit their eyes. He didn't know why, but Rajesh shuddered. *Was this the beginning of the end?*

Mark was unperturbed as if he was expecting this to happen.

It was a Qatari coast guard ferry that was pulling up to them.

"Rajesh, hold on, I will be back."

Mark went down once again as the coast guard boat pulled over beside their boat. The coast guards, heavily armed reached close to their ferry.

Mark greeted them and spoke with them. The guns were still cocked up; some phone calls were made. Whatever was spoken on the phone was something significant, as the coast guards lowered their guns and then shook hands with Mark.

Mark looked up to Gabriela and Rajesh and smiled. Whoever this Captain was, he had made immaculate plans. He had even managed to convince the Qatari government to allow them in, or had he just simply bought the authorities?

Whatever! The coast guard ferry backed off, and Mark was back in to the pilot room.

"The road is clear, folks!"

"The road to where?" Gabriela asked.

"To Qatar!" Mark said triumphantly.

"Without our passports or phones! Welcome to one jail from the other!" Rajesh added.

Just as he said that, Mark opened a drawer and handed over two envelopes. The envelopes read 'lady' and 'gentleman'. "Check these out. It's for you guys."

Rajesh collected them with a small look of surprise. He handed over the envelope marked 'lady' to Gabriela.

He felt the envelope. It was clear what was in it. It was a passport. *Wow! What's this now?*

He opened it in a hurry. It was a British passport. *Whose passport was this? Why is it being handed over to me?*

He opened the name page and to his surprise, he saw whom it belonged to. The photo was very familiar!

Mark said, "Don't worry. This passport is perfectly valid anywhere in the world. The Captain has taken care of that!"

The passport name read out 'Rajesh Rajesh', born in Liverpool in 1979. A citizen of the United Kingdom…

CHAPTER 49

After another fifteen minutes in the sea, the boat finally approached a jetty. There stood a man there. It was clear that he was expecting them. He stood six-feet-two in height, had blond hair and was very muscular. He must have been around forty-five years of age or so, by the look on his face.

"Hi, Captain!" Mark shouted as he manoeuvred the ferry parallel to the jetty.

So it was him! The Captain: the person who was the mastermind behind this whole operation!

The last ten hours of Rajesh's life flashed before his eyes now. It was around quarter to four in the afternoon when he had received the message from this guy. 'Rajesh, you are in deep shit. Message me a number where I can call to explain. Captain.'

How much life had changed since then!

They had changed from Rajesh Rajesh, from Chennai and Gabriela Fabregas, a US citizen to Rajesh from Liverpool and Gabriela from Manchester. The two of them, with their new phoney identities as UK citizens, had reached the shores of Qatar, and were finally with the man himself; the Captain!

Rajesh looked at Gabriela to see if she could recognize the Captain. She looked equally lost in her own flashback and showed no sign of recognition.

If he was not someone of importance in his life or Gabriela's, then who the hell was he? Why was he so interested in protecting them from the Dubai police? What did he want from them? Were they being used as some international bait or as some prisoners of war or something like that? These questions raced in his mind as Gabriela and he made their way inside the main cabin and onto the main deck from where they would have to hop off onto the jetty.

Mark introduced them.

"Captain, meet Mr Rajesh and Ms Gabriela Fabregas."

"Glad to meet you guys!" the Captain boomed.

"Hello, Captain!" Rajesh said.

"Who are you? Have we met before? Why did you save us?' These were Gabriela's first few questions.

"Not a nice way to greet your saviour, right madam?" The Captain laughed loudly, "You will come to know soon! Right now, we have a schedule to maintain. We better be quick! Come on Mark!" He set off inland.

Gabriela was lost in thoughts. Rajesh was sure that she was contemplating whether to shout at them or just follow them. She chose the latter.

But Rajesh also had something else in mind. Before he came to a conclusion, he stretched his memory back to the afternoon.

He spoke to Gabriela, but it was loud enough for Mark, who was just in front of them, to hear. "This man is *not* the Captain!"

"What? What makes you say that? Mark is addressing him as Captain and he is acknowledging!"

"The person who spoke to me had an accent that was typical of a first-generation Indian settled in the US. This guy speaks in a clear American accent. The Captain had said 'we have a tight schedule to be followed!' When he said the word 'schedule' he pronounced it just like we Indians or the Brits would: with the sound '*sh*'. This guy says scheduled with the sound, '*sk*'."

Gabriela could identify with that. Her boyfriend Steve Mehrotra also used the sound '*sh*' for schedule. "So who is this guy, then?"

Mark laughed loudly, "You guys are smarter than I thought. Really smart!"

"What do you mean? Who is this guy then?" Gabriela pointed out to the tall muscular blonde who had walked quite some distance ahead of them. "He is not the Captain? You are just fooling us?"

"Well, yes, he is Captain, but not '*the*' Captain!"

"What do you mean?"

Mark pointed straight ahead, "He is the Captain of the next ship we are about to board!"

Gabriela and Rajesh were in for yet another shock. It stood about a hundred metres in front of them. It was a bombardier flight, which looked like a regular short-distance passenger flight.

Chapter 50

S hahid Aziz was a worried man.

His mission was well, not a complete failure, but very near to it.

To be fair, he had saved the lives of nearly three hundred passengers on board the Eastern Airlines flight. He felt happy for the same and thanked the Almighty too.

However, he had failed on so many other accounts.

One, he lost two of his men. He might as well call them both countrymen. Officer Noor was one fine officer who had volunteered to co-pilot the flight. Mr Sanjay Sharan, although technically an Indian passport holder, had served the UAE in many ways. He had been a pilot in the Emirates airlines in the past. He was the operations' manager in the Dubai International Airport. He had bravely put up his hand to fly the Boeing in which he knew there was a bomb. Both Officer Noor and Sanjay Sharan were presumed dead. He had to break the news to their near and dear ones soon.

Second, he failed in his mission in getting the flight to Al Khair on time, although the monarchy of Dubai and Sharjah had acted in double-quick time to ensure he got a timely clearance for the same. The delays had occurred at multiple levels: the actual pilots of the flight chickening out, he sending an extra officer on board to escort Noor, everyone forgetting that the flight doors were disarmed and Sanjay having to brief Noor about the flight functions. *Oh God! How he wished that they could have been saved!*

Third, the flight had disappeared. *Apparently, it just vanished in thin air!* The Dubai or Sharjah ATC did not trace it. No crash debris was found. It was now almost eight hours since the flight disappeared and until now neither the Dubai police nor the Sharjah police was able to make any inroads. Of course, the majority of these eight hours was night-time, and maybe they would make some discovery in the morning.

Fourth, they were not yet able to trace who the Captain was. The Captain was a mysterious informant who had called only once. He called using a Matrix phone from Paris. The phone was a stolen one, and most probably it was discarded after the call. *Who was he? How did he know about the bomb? What was his interest in informing the police? If he was on the right side of the law, why was he hiding?*

Fifth, the Dubai police lost the race in following Mark, Gabriela and Rajesh. *Who were they? Why were they running away from the police? Or were they running away from Kabir? Why had they changed cars twice?* It was a highly planned escape. Hence, they must know something about the bombing. They had left the country illegally and probably made their way to Qatar, he guessed. There was no way of knowing now. Qatar, in the present diplomatic standoff, would not cooperate with the investigation. *Damn!*

Sixth, they had caught the man, who was in all probability the terrorist who had placed the bomb. They didn't still know whether Kabir Dravid was a sole mad man, or he was part of a larger terrorist organization. *Was he a member of the ISIS? Was he being supported by the Qatari government?* Whoever, but one thing was sure. He was a man of tremendous influence. The dignitary who was captured was no small person. He was a powerful man and managed to barter his freedom almost immediately after he was arrested.

So now what?

They had to find him again. If possible, they needed to get Gabriela, Rajesh and Mark as well. They had to find the Captain. They had to find any other missing link in the entire story.

The country's reputation was at stake.

His own reputation as the cool leader was taking a beating. Something had to give-in.

CHAPTER 51

Rajesh and Gabriela were too stunned to comment. They just followed Mark and the captain of the flight. They looked around. It looked like an isolated airstrip with one runway. There were no lights on the runway except for moonlight. Rajesh strained his eyes to look the farthest inland. He could see nothing but darkness. They had reached the Qatar coast alright, but it was an isolated place; nowhere near a city or town.

They entered the flight from the back end. Rajesh was used to Bombardier flights. They had a retractable door at the back end that served as a ladder for passengers to get in and off the flight. Even the pilot of the flight had to make his way through this door. After entering, there would be a 2x2 conformation of seats and cramped room.

Rajesh guessed it would be isolated inside. The entire passenger flight would be for them. *Where were they off to now?* His first guess was that they were heading further into Qatar. This could be possible as Qatar would offer them diplomatic immunity and the Captain, who was supposedly their well-wisher, could negotiate easily without them being arrested.

The second possibility was ominous. The Captain may not be a well-wisher! He might be the terrorist who was using them as bait for something that he wanted to achieve. They were being moved to a remote place in Qatar or possibly Pakistan or Afghanistan. He shuddered at the prospect.

The third possibility was the most optimistic. They probably were being moved back to the countries of origin through various routes.

Rajesh was being moved back to India, where he knew that the Home Ministry and Foreign Ministry would make sure that he was not harmed.

The last possibility was the least probable. They were being shifted to a nearby country. Except for Qatar, all countries had a neutral or friendly stance towards the UAE, and would promptly extradite them back to Dubai.

There was no use of speculating further. Mark was not going to let them know.

Rajesh looked at Gabriela, who was walking beside him, as they neared the flight. Her face shone in the moonlight and she looked beautiful, albeit tired. The breeze was making her hair fly. Rajesh couldn't help but remember romantic scenes from the Kollywood or the Bollywood movies.

Could it be possible that *she* is the terrorist; or belong to the group that is masterminding the same? Could *she* be using *him* as bait? Was the whole thing orchestrated in such a way that she was being towed away to safety and he was just an innocent bystander?

She was after all the fiancé of a billionaire in the US. Rajesh knew for sure that billionaires have clout everywhere, and it was easy for her beau to pull her out of any possible trouble. She could have called him and explained the situation to him, and he could be helping them escape! *Why didn't he think of this possibility before?*

They entered the flight. He gasped as he saw the interior of the flight. Contrary to what he was expecting to see, he saw that he had entered a private jet, not a passenger flight. It was a chartered flight. It had only six business-class style seats. It had a huge TV, a bar, a meeting table and amazing interiors. The Captain headed into the cockpit as Mark smiled and beckoned to be seated in any seat.

"Wow! A chartered flight!" Gabriela said. "We must be really special people for the Captain, I guess!"

"A *rich* Captain, a *very rich* fellow!" Rajesh muttered. The whole 'chartered flight' was in line with what he was thinking as he entered the flight.

Mark grinned. "You guessed it right. He is an important person. Note. It's not only the Chartered flight that requires money, this flight, besides being chartered, is carrying three illegal immigrants. One of them, that is me, has a genuine passport. Two are travelling with forged papers. There is no stamp of exit from the UAE. But note carefully, each of us will have a stamp of exit from Qatar."

He gave them a moment to check 'their' passports. Both of them gave an astonished look when they confirmed the same.

"Holy shit!" Gabriela said.

Mark continued, "As you may have guessed. All this costs more money than the flight itself!"

Rajesh and Gabriela sat in seats in the same row, on either side of the aisle, while Mark took the seat behind Rajesh. Rajesh peeked out of the window. It was pitch dark. *Where were they going? It was into the hands of fate!*

He put his head on the headrest and his thoughts went back to the possibility of Gabriela being the villain of the entire story.

Some things were odd though.

If her fiancé was indeed the terrorist or someone related to them, he would not choose to bomb the very airline he invested in! It didn't make sense.

Also, he didn't see Gabriela speak to her boyfriend once they had deplaned. They were together the entire distance from the flight to the hotel. It could have been possible that she spoke to him from her room, but he could have sworn that his phone already had the message from the Captain before they entered their individual rooms. It was impossible that Gabriela had time to inform her guy about the soup she was in.

The only other far-fetched possibility was that the entire story was orchestrated. Gabriela had entered his life on purpose. She had written the script of the entire story from their meeting at the airport, to their eye condition, the deplaning, the moving to the Radan hotel, and the entire escape story... *Really?* But somehow her expressions all seemed very genuine. She was equally stunned by the sequence of events. Either she was an extremely good actor, or most probably what he was thinking was just not true. Gabriela was a victim; not the villain.

He liked her. He certainly hoped so.

Chapter 52

"Enjoy your flight, folks!" the pilot announced. "We are about to take off. Ensure your seatbelts are on!"

"Where are we going, Mark?" Gabriela asked.

"To meet the Captain!"

"Where are we going?" she repeated, "Which place? At least we have the right to know that!"

"Hmmm... can't talk much about rights and responsibilities here! You are an international outlaw as of now!"

"Oh shit!" Gabriela wanted to get up and express her anger and disappointment. Just then the flight started moving and she decided not to. "Please tell us, Mark!"

"Okay, we are going to meet the Captain. Where exactly he is, even I don't know. Only the pilot knows. That's how sensitive the information is. I will know as soon as we land where further to proceed! The only thing I know is that this is not going to be a short flight. We are mostly headed to Europe..."

"What?" Rajesh said.

"Europe?" Gabriela was stunned as well.

Rajesh took a moment to see the genuineness of her reaction. *It seemed pretty genuine!*

"We are going to Europe! But, why? Oh, God! What is happening?" Gabriela cried.

"You are being flown away to safety, madam. Remember, had the Captain not intervened, you would be in the Dubai police's special custody by now, just like your pal, Mr Kabir Dravid is right now. I am sure he will not be released in the years to come!"

That was right. Gabriela could imagine what her plight would be had the Dubai police arrested her. It was a huge problem. The security of the country had been breached. There was a bomb on the flight. The flight had disappeared. Luckily the passengers were safe. Nonetheless, this was a huge problem, a terrorist activity in UAE territory. She, along with Rajesh and Kabir would be the prime suspects; they would be presumed guilty until the real terrorist and the real motive had been very clearly identified. Usually, such investigations take years. They would be in jail until then, and surely they would be subjected to all forms of torture. She shuddered.

The flight had gathered enough speed for take-off almost immediately, unlike the usual taxi period that occurred in conventional airports. Before she realised, the flight was airborne.

She looked back at her life. It seemed like an eternity since Steve had a temper tantrum and had screamed at her. Oh, God! She should have just walked away from him for a day or so. He would have anyway apologized if he wanted to. He had precisely done that. But by that time, she had been so psychologically affected that she decided it would be good for her to come on this official trip; the trip that was not meant for her anyway!

She had decided to make it up to Steve by booking onto the maiden flight of Eastern Airlines! She need not have done that! The company always paid her business class tickets in Emirates Airlines, yet she decided to travel economy in her boyfriend's airlines, just to keep him happy.

She remembered that she never managed to get in touch with Steve once this whole fiasco had begun. She had sent a message to him before boarding the flight. He was presumably fast asleep then. She could have called him after she was forced to deplane. She decided not to, for he might still be asleep. She had planned to call him after she had showered at the hotel.

But by then, Rajesh had hurried her out of the hotel. When they did that, they had locked their phones in the locker! What a fool she was! She should have called him up before she did so! Now even if Steve wanted to get in touch with her, he couldn't. By now, he should have known about the bombing, and would have also seen the WhatsApp messages! *He would be really confused and scared!*

Why did she have to develop conjunctivitis! God, I could have been just one of the passengers who were in the flight when it was called back to Dubai.

But two things struck her.

One. The flight may have never come back. She could have been dead by now. Pulverized.

Second. She realised that she never had conjunctivitis. It was a clear plan made by someone to get her out of the flight. Most probably to divert the investigations of the police after the bomb had killed so many innocent people. This 'someone' she now knew was Kabir Dravid, the maverick.

She found it hard to resign to her fate.

But what else could she do?

She had to trust Mark and the Captain. She had to trust her intuitions. She had to trust God. Mark and the Captain were her well-wishers; she had to believe that. Once she is dropped in Europe, she would be set free and Steve would somehow come and bail her out from the situation.

What would happen to Rajesh? Maybe the Indian embassy would come to his help...

She looked at him. He had dozed off as the flight was taking off, and now he was fast asleep.

She looked out. The flight had already ascended above the clouds. Mark had said that this was going to be a long flight. She had to give up. She too decided to close her eyes, hoping that sleep would overcome her.

And when she woke, she should be in New Jersey, realising that she had, in fact, dreamt the whole thing and she should laugh the whole thing off!

Hope against hope.

Chapter 53

It took him some time to realise where he was. But soon as he did, Rajesh was astonished. He looked at his watch. He had slept for five straight hours. He looked to his left. Gabriela was sipping on a coffee and staring aimlessly out the window. He looked behind to see where Mark was. He was not there.

"Where are we? Where is Mark?" he asked Gabriela.

Gabriela was startled. She looked at Rajesh and smiled, "Absolutely no idea where we are! We have been flying since last five hours!"

"Mark?"

"He is in the cockpit with the pilot!"

Rajesh laughed, "This is the third time he has left us alone! First was in the middle of the desert, the second was in the middle of the sea, now around thirty thousand feet above sea level, flying over an unknown country!"

Gabriela laughed. They were indeed at the mercy of the Captain and Mark! "Hope this Captain fellow is a nice guy! We have just trusted him blindly!"

"Where did you get the coffee from?"

"There is a dispenser. I'll make a coffee for you. I could use some activity. I am dead bored. I have slept for three hours, and then have been awake for the next two, absolutely not knowing what to do!"

"Thank you! I'll just freshen up a bit!"

Rajesh used the washroom, which was quite majestic for a washroom in a flight. After all, it was a chartered flight. Everything in here was grand, including the washroom. When he was out, Gabriela was ready with the coffee and a packet of chips.

Rajesh looked at his watch. It was still at the UAE time. It said 7:30 am. In India, it would be 9:00 am. If things had all gone right, he would be about to leave to his work after a well-deserved vacation. Instead, here he was, flying towards Europe; with a different identity. Meanwhile, the police of Dubai were on the lookout for him. He was a suspect of a terror attack. How life had completely changed in the last seventeen hours!

"Tell me more about yourself," he told Gabriela as they settled in their seats.

There was no point in resisting. Rajesh was probably the closest friend for her in the last few hours. And there was nothing more to do either.

Gabriela told him about her life; her parents moving from Argentina, her childhood; her college, her job, her frequent travels to Chennai and Bangalore, her billionaire boyfriend, his weekend parties, his investment in the fateful airlines and lastly how she wanted to surprise him by boarding the flight. She regretted not having gotten in touch with him before they set out with Mark. She presumed that life would have been much different if Steve would have known about their plight. He would have gone to any distance to help them!

Not if he himself was the terrorist! Rajesh once again thought about that possibility. But again, it seemed absurd that he would be involved in bombing his own airlines. *Absurd thought!*

"Now, it's your turn!" Gabriela seemed excited. She had given up to her fate and seemed to enjoy her little distraction.

Rajesh told her about his life, his schooling, Rakhee, Sachin aka Kabir (she already heard this part before, so he summarized it), his job, and his adventurous trip to the USA, and Manish! It seemed like an eternity since he had met Manish!

After the story was done, it was all blank again. They looked at their watches. An hour had passed since Rajesh woke up, six hours since take-off.

At that very moment, Mark came out of the door that led to the cockpit.

"Hello, guys. We have begun our descent. Pull up your seats, close the tray tables, fasten your seatbelts and keep the window shades open!" he said and laughed, although he saw that Rajesh and Gabriela both failed to sense humour here. "Also, you may want to set your watch to five thirty-five am. This is Central European Time, the time at our destination. Geneva, Switzerland.

CHAPTER 54

Rajesh and Gabriela didn't have the slightest clue as to why they were being taken to Geneva!

Rajesh asked Mark, "Why Geneva?"

"To meet the Captain. That's all I can say now."

Well, Rajesh guessed it was useless prodding Mark. He looked at Gabriela. "You have any link to Geneva or Switzerland?"

"No. Never been here in my life. I am not aware of Steve or my parents ever being here too. No connection whatsoever!"

"Me too. Never been to mainland Europe for that matter. No link whatsoever. Who must this Captain be? Considering that he may not be related to both of us, he has taken considerable pain in saving us from a false accusation and being in the UAE jail. He has also protected us from Kabir, who, in all probability was trying to harm us."

"Your guess is as good as mine!" Gabriela put up her hands in exasperation.

They both were silent for a while. Mark too was silent. He was catching a small nap.

As he looked out the window, Rajesh saw a large water body, which he guessed might be the Lake Geneva. *Wow!* He always wanted to visit Switzerland. He had always heard well about it. The Indian film industry had portrayed Switzerland in many movies. The country looked enormously beautiful in all those movies.

However, this was hardly the situation that he had envisioned when entering this beautiful country. He was not Rajesh Rajesh from India, coming here with his wife for a joy trip. He was Rajesh Rajesh from

Liverpool, holding a fake UK passport, a fugitive, and a suspected terrorist. UAE police were looking for him, and surely they would be soon in touch with the Interpol. *Hardly a time to enjoy the beauty of this country!*

The plane touched the ground at 6:15 am and then taxied to one of the hangars. This was the first time that Rajesh was getting out of a flight and into a hangar. As he got out of the flight onto the stairs, the sudden climatic change hit him. It was cold and windy.

"One degree Celsius, that's what it is now!" Mark said as he too shivered.

Although it was not more than forty-eight hours since he left New York, which also was freezing cold, it seemed like an eternity since then. Dubai had been pleasant, but Geneva was really cold; especially because he was not prepared for it and was dressed in a T-Shirt. Gabriela too was in a T-Shirt and was shivering. How he wished warm clothes were at their disposal. This was probably the only thing that Mark and the Captain had missed taking care of!

A BMW five series car was waiting for them. There was no driver in the car. As expected, it was Mark who was going to drive them! He took to the driver's seat and asked the duo to sit in the backseats. The pilot of the flight joined Mark in the front of the car. It was much warmer inside the car. Mark started driving the car towards the airport.

"When will we ever meet the Captain? We seem to be continuously travelling!" Gabriela said.

"Soon," Mark said and offered no more.

"Hmm…" Gabriela shook her head.

"Now, make a note. If at immigration, someone asks you why you have come to Switzerland, tell them that you have come here for a holiday!"

Rajesh and Gabriela had a chill up their spines. Both looked at each other and guessed that they were both thinking the same. They were to face authorities for the first time with their false identities. The slightest slip and they would be done for. They certainly hoped that things would go smoothly.

"If they ask where you will be put up, say that you will be staying at Hotel Excelsior, near Lake Geneva. Don't worry; I have a printed confirmation of the same. Just remember the name. Hotel Excelsior. I repeat, Excelsior."

So that was it. They were going to be put up at a hotel near Lake Geneva, and that's where they would meet the Captain. Rajesh certainly wanted to meet him soon and put an end to this travel. He still was not sure whether the Captain meant good for them, or he himself was a criminal who would use them as bait for something more sinister. *Whatever; he was keen to put an end to this trip!*

They approached the airport arrivals. Mark parked the car at a designated area. *(Rajesh saw for the first time a designated car park on the inside of the airport!).* They again walked a short distance in the freezing cold, before they entered the main building of the Geneva international airport.

They followed the signs to the immigration area, and the closer they got, the faster Rajesh and Gabriela's hearts beat. This was going to be dicey.

There was no line at the immigration when they got there. This was it! God bless them.

Almost as a super anti-climax, the immigration officers didn't ask a word. They just stamped the passport and let them pass. The false passport was terrific, that meant. It identified them as British citizens and no doubt was cast whatsoever. The Captain and his team had been meticulous! Also, it was reassuring to know that the Dubai police had not considered this possibility that they would be entering the European Union. There was no red flag on the way!

It was a strange feeling. After immigration, Rajesh and Gabriela were always used to going to the area to collect their checked-in baggage, but this was different. They just followed Mark and the pilot straight out of the Green Custom's channel and out of the airport.

As soon as they were out, the pilot shook hands with Mark and then did the same with Gabriela and Rajesh. They guessed it right. The pilot parted ways from the trio. They turned right and took the escalator downwards. The direction boards displayed that they were making their way to the train station. The board said that trains to the Geneva city proper started there and so did the long-distance trains.

As they reached the train station, Rajesh was surprised that Mark had not stopped to buy tickets and proceeded directly to the platforms. As they approached the platform, a train simultaneously came in. Rajesh noted that it was proceeding via the main train station of Geneva and then further to the long-distance destination called Sion.

Gabriela and Rajesh simply followed Mark. He entered a second-class cabin and the three were seated there. The second-class cabin looked awesome and really clean.

Rajesh allowed Gabriela to take the empty seat while he seated himself next to Mark. He stretched a bit.

"Which station do we need to get down for Excelsior?"

Mark replied, "For Excelsior, we need to get off in eight minutes at the main Geneva railway station..."

"Oh! Okay," Rajesh presumed that there would be a room in the hotel arranged for them and he could take a much-needed hot bath.

"... but we are not going there. We are going to another town from here, which will take an hour at least. So sit back, relax and enjoy the world-famous Swiss rail!"

Chapter 55

"Now, where?" Gabriela sounded tired, frustrated and irritated. "To meet the Captain!"

"Of course, I know we are going to meet him, but I am asking you, Mark: when and where are we going to meet him?"

"I am not supposed to reveal that, Miss. We are on a secret mission and even the walls here have ears."

As he said that, the train started moving.

"Do you realise that I can run away from here? I need not follow you anymore!"

"Why will you want to do that after everything the Captain has done for you? He has saved you from a certain hell; well, almost!"

"Almost means?"

"Well, the chance remains that the Dubai police may trace us here! So we must follow the Captain's orders to remain safe!"

"I can just get down on the next station and ring up my fiancé in New Jersey! I am sure he can help! Rajesh, listen to me! We should do that!"

Rajesh considered the possibility and he could see Mark was allowing him to do so. Mark was smiling. There would be a glitch surely. The train moved out from the station into the bustling Geneva metropolis.

"Well!" Rajesh said, "I guess that might be foolish to do. The Dubai police, by now, would have surely tapped all the phones of your fiancé. They would be expecting you to contact him!"

"Okay, I won't call him, but we can call someone! The US embassy, perhaps! Someone!"

Mark intervened, "As far as the US embassies are concerned, you are no longer their citizen. Are you? You hold a British passport!"

Gabriela fell silent. Her brain refused to give up as she explored some more possibilities in her mind. She looked out the window. The sunrays had just begun to light up the winter morning. This day she should have got up and looked out of her hotel room in Chennai, but here she was, thousands of miles away, in Geneva. She was a fugitive with a false passport who couldn't reach out to her near and dear ones. She wondered which of the possible fates would have been bad... being blown up in the flight versus being tormented by the Dubai police versus where she was now. She was, in fact, taking a leap of faith here. All three situations at this moment seemed like torture.

The train stopped at the central station of Geneva where they were supposed to get down according to the information provided to the immigration officer. The Station appeared busy at even at this early hour, at 7.30 am.

Gabriela decided not to get further excited again. She had to save up some energy as much more was yet to come, she presumed.

The train trip went on and on. Rajesh identified some landmarks on the way. First was Nyon, where the football association of Europe was located. He had started following football since long, almost twenty years now, and was aware of this place. The train then passed a large station called Loussane, which appeared to be a large junction. He realised that the track they were following was the one that went around Lake Geneva in a clockwise manner, as he was able to distinctly outline the lake on the right-hand side throughout the trip.

The countryside and lakeside looked amazingly beautiful. How he had wished that he had come here first for a leisure trip! There were so many photo-taking opportunities. He looked at Gabriela. She was silent but also appeared to be immersed in the beauty that lay outside the window. *There was nothing else to do!*

Mark appeared less impressed with the scenery. Possibly he had been here at least a couple of times before, if not more. He had picked up a magazine and a newspaper at Loussane and just finished flipping through the newspaper.

Mark looked at Rajesh and Gabriela and smiled. "Guess what, guys? We are famous already!"

Rajesh shuddered. Their names must have been in the newspaper. He picked it up in a hurry. There it was! There was a small column on the front page of Swiss times.

Hundreds of deaths prevented in an aborted terrorist attack with a powerful bomb that has managed to pulverize the flight after the passengers had been deplaned. The Dubai police reacted well in time to an 'intel' and prevented a major bomb ripping through a full flight. The passengers had been deplaned and the flight was to be wheeled away to safety. The flight had two officers on it when it mysteriously lost contact with the Dubai airport. Four suspects are being tailed and no international group has yet claimed responsibility. More details would follow on page 5...

He hastily turned to page 5. His eyes first searched for their names, and surprisingly, the names were not yet revealed.

However, for sure now, they would be hunted down.

CHAPTER 56

*A*borted *terrorist attack, Passengers safe, Flight missing, two presumed dead.*

As per the statement by the Chief of the special investigation team of the Dubai police, Officer Shahid Aziz, the flight EA001 had its maiden flight from Dubai to Chennai. It was indeed supposed to be a joyous occasion for the airlines. It had taken off at 1500 hours. However, the Airport security team had got an Intel alert that the flight had a powerful bomb on it. When asked specifically, Officer Shahid refused to comment on how the bomb had passed the Dubai airport security, saying that investigations were being carried out. The flight was recalled and all passengers were successfully deplaned at 1700 hours. The flight was then supposed to be flown away to safety to an isolated airstrip in Sharjah, with appropriate precautions taken. Two brave pilots, Sanjay Sharan and Noor Aziz were in-charge of flying the flight.

Mysteriously, the flight lost contact with the ATC at Dubai and Sharjah at around 17:40, the time when it would have been flying over the deserts of Sharjah. No information on the flight has since been received. Civilians reported no crash and no debris has been found.

The location and the circumstances in which the flight disappeared have led to many speculations. Sources say that the flight was closely being followed by the ATC, hence, it would be unlikely that the flight had veered off its flying path without being noticed, similar to the ill-fated Malaysia Airlines flight. The absence of debris made the possibility of a conventional bomb unlikely. Sources believe that the bomb was very advanced and the most devastating known to humankind yet. It had *escaped the Dubai Security and also had successfully managed to blast the flight into smithereens. Further update on this regard is awaited.*

No international group has claimed responsibility for this attack, probably because it was a failed attempt. Officer Shahid Aziz mentioned in a late-night update that they had zeroed down to four suspects, who were being followed. Their identities could not be revealed for security reasons. He would leave no stone unturned to find out who the real culprits were and bring them to justice real quickly.

What is worrisome in the whole incident is the conventional security measures at the Dubai airport, believed by many to be the most robust in the world, failed to detect the 'bomb'. If this is the case, what is the world coming to? Experts in the field said that they would submit their opinion later in the day as to what the explosive could be. However, there is a growing suspicion that some human manipulation may have been possible to bypass the security measures. Time will tell.

So that was it. The Dubai police had narrowed down to four suspects: which Rajesh guessed aloud were Kabir, Mark, Gabriela and he. Kabir was caught, but he seemed to have not revealed anything yet. The three of them present on the train were still the suspects.

Gabriela had picked up the paper and was reading it in her mind. With every line she read, the grimace on her face seemed to grow.

Rajesh studied Mark. He was looking unaffected by the news piece. There were only two inferences. Mark was a cold-blooded criminal. Either that or Mark was on the right side of the law and was protected by the Captain, who in turn was a man with immense influence on anything that might happen to the trio. If Mark were anyone else but the two, he would have been affected by the fact he was an internationally hunted fugitive himself! *Oh God! What if he is a criminal!*

Rajesh decided to give in to his fate and looked out the window as the train approached Montreaux. *Oh, he remembered this place!* It was mentioned in one of his favourite songs, Smoke on the Water, by Deep Purple; as Montreaux on Lake Geneva shoreline. He felt good that he was here, but how he wished it were a holiday!

"We get off at the next station!" Mark said.

It had been an hour and fifteen minutes on the train.

"Okay!" Gabriela said. "The situation that we ran off from has become world-famous. Soon, we too will become world-famous!" She gave a wry smile. "And here we are, blindly taking the leap of faith; with a man who apparently is unfazed by the events in the world!" She gave a strong look to Mark.

Gabriela had just read out what Rajesh was thinking.

"We will be getting down at the next station!" Gabriela continued, "But that doesn't mean anything. As we will be getting on to some other mode of transport to somewhere else; another train, or flight, or bus, or car, or helicopter, or who knows; maybe a spaceship?" She was quite clearly perturbed. Her sarcasm had hints of fear of the unknown.

"The Captain will take care of us all!" That was all Mark had to say. He too apparently read the minds of Gabriela and Mark.

After five minutes, Mark got up and headed towards the door. "Come on!" he told the others, as the train pulled into another station.

Rajesh and Gabriela followed him to the door. The train stopped and the three got down. The sun was shining bright, yet it was very cold, to say the least.

They looked at the name of the station. It read 'Aigle'.

Aigle? The place had no significance at all! However, the Captain was indeed a mysterious man. He chose mysterious places.

But as the two had guessed already, Mark pointed out "That, my friends, is our next vehicle!" He pointed out to another train, which stood at the station, possibly on a narrower gauge rail than what they had come by. It was going to be another train ride. *To where?* It was futile to ponder or ask!

CHAPTER 57

The smaller train left in ten minutes.

The scenery was becoming more beautiful. Farmlands and mountains further away dotted the scenery. The stations that passed were of unheard places as far as Gabriela and Rajesh were concerned; Ollon, Collombay and finally they were at a terminus called Monthey. Rajesh could see quite clearly it was a terminus; the train could not go any further. Yet, Mark didn't get up from his seat. There was no one else in their compartment; they were in with the sole other passenger having got down at Collombay.

What was this now? Rajesh wondered why they were in a train that had started back in the opposite direction! It was surely some part of a larger plan to throw off the possible policemen who may be tracking their moves.

The reason was clear soon. The train that had moved in the opposite direction had changed tracks and was moving towards another destination; not back to Aigle.

The train suddenly started ascending. It was clearly going up the mountains. It passed a station quite simply called 'Hospital'. Slowly, snow started appearing as part of the scenery outside. It looked beautiful. The train passed another few stations as it ascended. Again, Rajesh had never heard of these places. The snow was now thicker as they ascended further.

"We need to get off next," Mark said. The time was nearing 9:30 am.

"Will this journey ever end?" Gabriela said. "Oh, how I need to rest!"

"Me too!" Rajesh said. "My trip started more than forty-eight hours ago. At Boston! I travelled Boston to New York, New York to Dubai airport, airport to inside the Eastern Airlines flight, from the flight to Radan hotel, from there to Sharjah, via Abu Dhabi to a port in UAE, to Qatar, to Geneva and then a huge train trip to here... amidst the snow-capped mountains of Switzerland."

"Knowing these guys, there must be a helicopter here that may fly us to Siberia or somewhere else!" Gabriela smiled sarcastically.

Rajesh sure hoped what she said was not true!

Mark got up and walked up towards the door, Rajesh and Gabriela followed suit.

They got down at the next 'station'. *Well, it was as big as a pavement only!* The station was called 'Val de Ileaz'.

Val de Ileaz was visibly a very small town. It looked dainty. The weather was chilling cold. Rajesh and Gabriela immediately shivered and put their hands in their pant pockets.

They followed Mark who had made his way out of the station to a small parking spot nearby. The snow had been neatly shovelled and piled up by the sides of the parking space.

A Land Rover stood there. Again, no surprises. Mark had the keys to the car. He got into the driving seat and asked them both to be seated.

They both sat in the backseats, as usual.

"Oh God, yet another drive!" Gabriela said.

Mark started the car and they moved onto the small streets. Mark seemed to be driving the car further uphill. The town looked beautiful, but as soon as the beauty had sunk in, the car was already out of the town, up the snowy Alps. The road had many hairpin curves as they moved on. They were travelling through a forest with trees covered by snow. *Breathtaking views!*

After twenty minutes on the road, they approached another settlement. It looked like a ski place, as many tourists seemed to be there. The car traversed the streets of this place and finally pulled into a gated compound.

"This, folks, is the end of our journey. We have reached our destination. Hotel 'the Place' in Champoussin village, Western Switzerland!"

Wow! Had the journey really ended? Rajesh and Gabriela heaved huge sighs of relief!

"The Captain is here, I presume?" Gabriela asked.

"Well, he won't be here anytime soon. He is driving from Paris and will be here later tonight. Until then, you can check into your rooms and have some good rest! As long as you are here, you will not be hunted down for sure and no police in the world will reach here soon. So, have a good day's rest fellows!"

"Really?" Gabriela wondered aloud. Yes, she thought of escaping, but Mark had made it clear, mincing no words. As long as they were here, they were safe. It was indeed a foolish idea to venture out alone.

Rajesh and Gabriela followed Mark quickly into the resort. It was biting cold. The temperature indicator at the reception read minus five degrees Celsius. It was barbaric to be here without warm clothes.

Mark quickly completed the check-in formalities. For some reason, none of them was asked for photo identities or credit cards. Three sets of key cards were handed over.

They set out of the reception area, again into the biting cold.

"Don't worry folks!" Mark said, "The Captain has arranged new sets of clothes, which also include warm clothes in all our rooms!"

Rajesh was indeed amazed by the details that the Captain had taken care of. He wondered why they were being treated with such VIP status and that too high up in a skiing resort in Switzerland. He wanted to enjoy this place. However, it was not easy to forget that the Captain's true intentions were still unknown, and probably the Interpol had already been alerted.

They were shuddering in the cold as they finally reached the building in which their rooms were. Luckily, once inside the building, it was much warmer.

The rooms were next to each other. Mark entered his room and told them both to rest. *He was almost arrogant in his confidence that the two of them would not escape!*

Mark and Gabriela entered adjacent rooms. It was the second time in twenty-four hours that they had done so.

They only hoped that this time there was no Kabir Dravid checking into the room next to theirs. A terrorist. An outlaw.

As a matter of fact, they hoped that no man on the right side of the law would also be anywhere near them!

What a strange situation to be in.

Chapter 58

Rajesh's room was a small studio room, with an attached kitchen and bathroom. He opened the wardrobe, and as promised there were neatly folded clothes, a sweater, a jacket, gloves, socks and shoes. He walked up to the kitchen where there were some chips and fruits. He picked up an apple and started munching on it. He went to the balcony.

Oh! The scenery was so beautiful. Nearest were houses. Their roofs were covered with snow, with smoke billowing out of some chimneys. The snow on the roads in between the houses was shovelled, and mainly tourists walked on them. Beyond that were skiing areas, where he could see many people making the most of it. Further beyond were the forest and more snow-covered mountains.

He soon re-entered the room as it was too cold outside. He shut the balcony door and turned on the heater of the room. He decided he should first have a shower and change.

As he was showering, he tried to guess who the Captain could be. Whoever he was, he surely was someone of prime importance. His mind raced from one weird thought to another; the President of the US? Was it the President of Russia? Or maybe the Prime Minister of India? Maybe he was Osama Bin Laden's son? Maybe he was someone from Dubai Sheikh's family? Or perhaps the Pope? Or wait a minute... could it be the Great Guru Amar? Why not? Maybe he wanted to prove to the world that he had worldly powers! How could that be?

He dried himself and put on another T-shirt and jeans. He decided to rest his back on the bed for a while before he made his way for lunch in a while.

He rested on the bed and decided to catch a nap. It was 11:00 am; he slept.

The next thing he realised was that it was 5:00 pm.

He made himself a cup of tea, wore his jacket and went to the balcony. He saw Gabriela sitting on a ledge there. She wore a jacket and a tight cap. She was just staring at the natural beauty.

It was amazing how she always needed much lesser sleep than him. She had slept lesser than him on the plane and also now. She looked at him and smiled.

"Hi! Can I join you?" Rajesh asked.

"Yes, do that!" she said.

Rajesh went back to his room, wore his socks, shoes and gloves and left the room. Mark was seated in the lobby, reading a magazine.

"Hi, mate? Had a good sleep?"

"Yes! I wonder how you are going on and on without any sleep!"

"To be fair, I did sleep for three hours. I will sleep peacefully after I hand over you guys to the Captain!"

"Hand over? That sounds ominous!"

"Not at all! He is your well-wisher. Last I heard he would be in his cabin by 8:00 pm. However, dinner here is served early. So wherever you are heading to, come back by six-thirty. After dinner, we will achieve what we set out to achieve; that is – meet the man himself!"

"Too much suspense! Too much!" Rajesh shook his head. After that, he headed out of the building into the cold. He caught up with Gabriela. They decided to go for a walk.

"Should we run away?" Gabriela asked the futile question again.

"I don't know really, Gabriela. We have possibly the Interpol looking for us. We have possibly a terrorist group that Kabir represents looking for us. Worse, if we run away, we could have the Captain, whose intentions are not yet clear, trace us within a jiffy."

They decided to chuck the idea again. They walked on the roads of Champoussin village. Many tourists were filling up the two bars in the village. It was cold and it was slowly becoming dark.

They reached the end of the village and turned back, having decided that it was not a good idea to walk into the forest area. They reached the resort in time for the dinner. Mark waited for them at the main reception and then led them to the restaurant. It was amazingly tiny for a resort as big as this.

The dinner tasted really good, considering that this was the first whole meal Gabriela and Rajesh had since the last one at Dubai airport before boarding the fateful flight. It consisted of grilled chicken, mashed potatoes, cauliflower, carrots and tomato sauce. Red wine was on the house.

This was it! The time was 19:45. Mark returned from the restroom, "Okay guys! The Captain is here! Let's make a move to his cabin."

Rajesh and Gabriela felt the same way. It was a unique mixture of happiness, anxiety, fear and relief. Neither knew how to express the same in words. They simply followed Mark out of the restaurant.

Mark pointed to a Rolls Royce Phantom parked outside one of the cabins. "That is the Captain's car!"

He walked swiftly towards the cabin. "You guys wait here," he said as they reached the opposite side of the road. "I'll see if the man is ready to meet you."

Rajesh and Gabriela shuddered. They were to meet the Captain after all that had happened.

The next few events happened all in a matter of a few seconds.

A man, dressed in all black, carrying a rifle also reached the door at the same time as Mark. Rajesh had seen him before, but Mark did not recognize him. Mark proceeded to greet him, "Hello, sir! Have I seen you before?"

"Nope. I don't intend to see you again too." Kabir Dravid pumped two bullets point-blank at Mark's chest, who collapsed without emitting a sound, as blood spurted out of the gunshot wound like a large coloured fountain.

CHAPTER 59

Gabriela and Rajesh froze. They knew what was going to come next. There was no closed space where they could run to. They were sitting ducks, basically.

This was it: the moment where your entire life flashes before your eyes; the time right before your death.

Kabir aimed the gun at them, ready to shoot.

But just as he was about to do so, he was distracted. A bright light shone from the uphill side of the road, from within the resort. In fact, it was not one, but two blinding headlights of a Jeep. It came hurtling down the road.

Before Kabir could regain his composure and be ready to shoot, the Jeep had made its way and stopped right in between the gunman and the terrified duo of Gabriela and Rajesh. The driver of the Jeep flung open the rear door and screamed at the two of them to get in.

They had no choice. Gabriela, followed by Rajesh, got into the rear seat and Rajesh instinctively shut the door behind him tight. The movement was very quick. It was strange indeed as to how quickly they both had got into the vehicle, almost at superhuman speed. However, this was a pure survival instinct. They had to protect themselves from the madman.

Neither of them could see the driver's face clearly, and he too offered no introduction. He just slammed on the accelerator and the SUV set into an immensely quick speed in a matter of seconds.

They could hear clear gunshots, even though all the windows of the Jeep were shut and its engine was revving up loudly.

"He is shooting at us! The maverick!" Rajesh shouted.

Gabriela prayed.

However, with the speed they had gathered, they had already made their way up to the gate of the resort. The driver braked suddenly, sending Rajesh and Gabriela hurtling forwards. He then took a sharp left turn and again accelerated, this time down the main road, heading surely out of Champoussin village.

Rajesh could feel the potato and chicken come up his food pipe and into his throat. He last felt this way on a roller coaster ride in Mumbai. He wanted to throw up badly. In the last few seconds, he had experienced near death.

Gabriela was in tears. He could imagine how she would be feeling now, as he himself wanted to cry.

Who was this guy who was driving them away? He was a Godsend. Was he the Captain himself? Possibly. But this was not the time to hold an enquiry. He was driving the Jeep at immense speed downhill. It was survival time.

The Jeep had left Champoussin village and had entered the forest. Now the driver eased the speed just a little bit but was still quite swift. Anything could happen next. Kabir must have gotten into his car and for the hot pursuit.

"You guys okay?" the driver finally spoke up.

"Yes, alive!" Gabriela answered. "What just happened now? Who are you? And who was the madman who shot at us just now?"

The driver was about to answer, but they had come to an area that had sharp hairpin bends, so he had to concentrate.

Rajesh was surprised that Gabriela had not recognized the shooter.

"You didn't see him? He was Kabir! How the hell did he get here? I thought Dubai police had him arrested!"

It was Gabriela's turn to get astonished, "He is Kabir Dravid? I have never seen him before! I have only heard about him from Mark and you until now. This is the first time I am seeing him!"

As she said that the Jeep took yet another stomach-churning turn at high speed. It was clear that the driver was not bothered about traffic coming from the other direction. It was a time when no one travelled these roads, high up in the Swiss mountains.

Rajesh nodded. *How true!* She had only heard about Kabir! She had indeed never seen him. It was Rajesh who sighted him getting onto the flight, at the airport when they were deplaned and at the hotel when Kabir was being questioned.

It was clear that the driver had to negotiate another few turns and was not in a position to offer any answers. It was only they both and speculations.

"Yes, he is Kabir! For sure it's him!" Rajesh blurted. "That ass really wants us dead. That is for sure!"

"How did he escape the police? How did he follow us to this remote place? We have changed so many cars, ships, flights and trains to get here. Yet, he has managed to trace us here. He is surely mad. And what frightens me the most is he will surely follow us again, wherever we are. He will ultimately kill us! Oh Jesus! What have I done to deserve this? What does this guy want?"

"I have no idea, whatsoever."

"Oh! Why did you have to break his leg? He is behind us for that only!"

"I don't believe he is so freaking out of his mind. I have given it a thought! He may be a terrorist; he may want to kill people. But why is he behind me? Is it only because I had broken his leg? Is that why he is chasing me around the world? I really doubt! If he is so well connected, he could have finished me off years ago, assuming that's what he wants! Why will he be behind my life especially now? He has just spearheaded one of the most brutal attacks in the history of humankind. Why will he want to take revenge on a relatively unimportant agenda now?"

"Unimportant? You broke his leg and maimed him forever?"

"The word is 'relatively' unimportant!"

"Okay, okay I get it!"

The road was straight now.

"Okay guys, it's gonna be a long drive now," the driver said. It was an Australian accent that he spoke with.

Rajesh had heard this voice before.

Everything seemed to be connected to his life! Gabriela was indeed a poor victim, he guessed.

He had heard the voice before. The car reached Val de Ileaz and finally, a streetlight fell on the driver's face. Rajesh was stunned, having least expected this person to be driving the car: not in his wildest dreams.

The driver was the 'Regatta yachtsman', the person who sat with him in the New York to Dubai flight. The person who was apparently also tailing him all this time. Ken.

Chapter 60

Before Rajesh could react, a phone rang loudly. It took him a moment to realise that the phone was on hands-free and the phone ring was coming out of the car's audio system.

Ken pressed the answer button on the phone wheel.

"Ken here."

"The guy is captured alive and bound. You can now slow down. Proceed to base."

"Cool."

The guy? Did they mean Kabir? A lot of questions needed to be answered. What had happened in the last few minutes was complete mayhem.

Ken cut the call.

Rajesh looked at Gabriela, who appeared too stunned to speak a word. He then looked at Ken. "So, Mr Ken. You are the Captain!"

Gabriela woke up suddenly. "Wait a minute? You know the Captain?"

Ken chuckled, "Yeah, you can answer her, mate!"

Rajesh shook his head in disbelief, "Well, yes and no. I only apparently know this guy. He travelled with me from New York to Dubai in the same flight. He was seated right next to me! But I know him as an Australian yachtsman, travelling to Singapore from New York via Dubai. He was supposed to be sailing at the Singapore regatta. And guess what? I was supposed to be seeing his regatta video on YouTube tonight!"

"What? I don't get it!" Gabriela asked.

"Yes, I don't get it myself! I only told you what I know of him. It's obvious that he is no yachtsman! He is the Captain himself! He has been following me from New York. He is responsible for our escape from Dubai to here! I am yet to put all the pieces together! I am just not able to understand anything myself!"

The Jeep had slowed down to a more comfortable pace and was heading down the mountain. It crossed the town of Troisstorents and headed towards Monthey.

"You are the Captain?" Gabriela asked.

"No," Ken replied simply.

"What is happening? Care to explain?"

Ken smiled, "First of all lady, I think both of you must at least thank me for saving your life!"

Rajesh and Gabriela looked at each other. *How true!*

Rajesh's mind wandered back to the incident. Mark, the person who had been with them for almost two days was dead. The madman Kabir had shot him point-blank. And yes, it was true, had Ken not come with his car right in between Kabir and them, they too would be dead now.

"Right, buddy. I guess I have been selfish. You are absolutely right. Thanks for being there when it mattered the most!"

Gabriela had also gone through a 'flashback' in her mind, and she too realised that she had been wrong in not thanking Ken. "Thanks, Ken. I really mean it!"

"Welcome guys!"

"But come on, Ken. It's really strange; you know. We really don't know what is happening!"

"Okay. I am Ken Anderson. I work for the Captain."

"Oh! The wait for the Captain continues! Who is this mysterious person?" Gabriela asked.

"Yeah, the wait continues. We were tipped off of this possibility at the resort. Unfortunately, we couldn't do much to save Mark on time! But at least we managed to get you both out in time!"

This was strange, Rajesh thought. Mark was a colleague of Ken (of course, he still didn't clearly know who Ken was), both worked for this strange powerful person called the Captain. The strange thing is he didn't seem to show much remorse in the fact that his colleague had just been shot dead in a gruesome way. He only stated it as a matter of fact.

He was more interested in getting Rajesh and Gabriela out of the scene quickly.

This degree of apathy when a comrade died could happen only in two circumstances; one: both Mark and he were hard-core criminals and were used to colleagues dying around them. Or they were soldiers; soldiers in a war, where some were expected to die, and the colleagues around them were expected to carry on with the ultimate objective of the battle at hand. In this case, both Mark and Ken had only one objective; to get Gabriela and him to the Captain.

They must be really important people; both Gabriela and he. Or maybe she was the important person and he was just being dragged along.

That was unlikely. Kabir and Ken were more directly related to him than to Gabriela. Something was strange.

The Jeep had now reached Monthey, and was proceeding in a direction that was away from the railway line that had brought them to Monthey from Aigle. Rajesh realised that they were headed somewhere else, not back to Geneva.

He asked, "Were you tailing me all the way from New York? Why am I so important to you?"

"Only the Captain has the right answers to these questions!"

"Enough!" Gabriela said. "What is going on here, Rajesh?"

Rajesh was taken aback. Gabriela had quite literally said it in a tone that was pointing an accusing finger at him. To be frank, he had seen it coming soon, but he was surprised, nevertheless. "What?"

"It's clear that this whole operation is centred around you. Ken has tailed you from New York to Dubai. Kabir is a terrorist who had been grievously injured by you in the past! It's clear that both the good guys and the bad guys in the story are linked to you. I am just an innocent bystander and my life is screwed because of you! Why did you do this to me?" She wept for the first time.

Chapter 61

This was quite contrary to what Rajesh had thought when they had boarded the chartered flight at Qatar; he had thought that the entire plot centred around Gabriela and he was the bystander. Here the accusation was reverse.

Come to think of it; she was justified to feel the way she felt, but he had to defend himself, nevertheless. "Look, Gabriela. I promise. I don't have the slightest clue what is going on. There is no reason why Kabir, who is now a world-renowned terrorist, would want to extract revenge at the time he was carrying out such an event of grand scale. Also, I have no idea who this Ken is. All I know is that he sat next to me on a flight, that's all!"

The Jeep had reached a place called Saint Maurice and the road signs said the next big place on the road was Martigny. Rajesh had never heard of these places before.

"Yeah, yeah. That's true. I know!" Gabriela said. "But, just imagine my plight! I am a software business consultant, who was on my way to Chennai. But now I am being dragged against my wishes to somewhere in Switzerland!"

Ken spoke. It was déjà vu. He spoke just like his friend, Mark, "At least you are a software consultant who is alive. Had you been on the flight, there was a good chance of death. And had the Captain not smuggled you out of Dubai, you would have been in the Dubai police's torture chamber!"

"But…"

"Now listen, guys. No point in this chitter-chatter. Right now, both of you should be lucky that you were not on that flight and possibly bombed down. Nor are you in Dubai, where the police would wind you up. Most importantly, both of you were not split wide open by the Kabir chappie, whose real intentions in following you halfway around the world are not known even now!"

Gabriela took a deep breath. After all, it was not even an hour since they had a near-death experience "Yes, I suppose you are right. But I am sure your guys have got him already. And you will extract the required information."

Rajesh interrupted, "Now, remember one thing. The Dubai police caught him. Yet he managed to escape. He must be a highly connected individual. He might give you the slip as well!"

"Yeah, we came to know about that just a little while ago. The Dubai police are quite hush-hush about the fact that he was caught in the first place. However, our sources in the police say that he was let out on barter with some famous personality. We are not sure, but you are right. He is a well-connected and dangerous person. However, I am not sure how much clout he holds here; deep amidst the Alps in western Switzerland! We will be careful nevertheless."

"Hmmm…"

"Now sit back and take some rest. We will be reaching our destination I guess by ten pm only. After that, you can either take rest and then meet the Captain tomorrow, or meet him tonight. What do you guys want?"

"Obviously…" Rajesh started.

Gabriela interrupted and spoke the same thing that was on his mind. "We have rested enough in the day. I want to meet the Captain!"

"Then, I guess you guys might as well take a snooze in the car now. It will be a long night!"

"Really, what does the Captain want us to do in the night? Dance for him?" Rajesh smirked.

"You shall see. You shall see."

What other answer did Rajesh expect? These guys were maintaining suspense until the end.

The three fell silent. Gabriela was trying to sleep but was failing. Rajesh didn't even try. He had slept enough. Besides, his mind was super excited. He was not going to fall asleep for sure!

They passed the exits to the towns of Martigny, Saillon and Sion. Again, Rajesh had never heard of these places before. The car was maintaining good speed. *Where were they headed?*

After an hour and a half on the road, much earlier than what Ken had expected, they pulled out from the highway and started moving into a town.

"This town is called St. Leonard, and this is where the Captain is."

"Really? I don't believe it!" Gabriela said. "I won't believe that we are anywhere near the Captain until I have actually seen him."

"Justified!" Ken said as he took the car into one of the smaller lanes, lined by neat houses. Almost all houses had their lights off. The citizens were almost surely asleep.

They reached the end of the street and the car entered the gate of the last house on the street on the left-hand side. It seemed exactly similar to all the other houses on the street. There was a small garden on the left side of the porch. The façade of the house gave the look that it was made up of stone. The windows looked majestic. The roof was tiled and there was a chimney.

Ken stopped the car and the three of them got out. Had the moment finally come?

It had.

This moment was to be the moment of glory; an enormous sense of achievement. Rajesh and Gabriela had travelled halfway around the world in almost all possible forms of transport for *this* very moment.

The man stood at the door: an Indian, surely. He greeted them. "Hi, Ken." He waved at Ken who acknowledged him with a wave. "Hello, Mr Rajesh and Miss Gabriela. I am Captain Naveen Sharma. Pleased to meet you."

Chapter 62

It was freezing cold, but that did not seem to bother either Gabriela or Rajesh.

Rajesh gauged the person. The Captain was as tall as him, six feet two inches for sure. He was very well toned and had a slim body. He was wearing a sweater, but Rajesh could make out that his arms were muscular. He had black hair and quite a handsome face. He looked his age, if not younger.

Rajesh was sure that he didn't know who this person was, for sure. His face was not even a *bit* familiar. He was a stranger, as far as he was concerned; a stranger who had spent enormous money and resources for smuggling him out of Dubai. He looked at Gabriela.

Gabriela also showed no signs of recognizing who Captain Naveen was. *Was she acting?* No. The expression on her face seemed genuine. She, in turn, was now checking Rajesh out for the same.

"Come in guys. It's really cold out there!" The Captain said. He signalled them to follow him and led his way through a small veranda, into the house.

His voice and his physical appearance reminded Rajesh of the popular Bollywood actor Akshay Kumar. Gabriela, Ken and he followed the Captain into the house.

The house was much warmer. They removed their coats and hung them at the coat hanger that was right next to the door. The interiors of the house were chic. They entered first into a drawing room that had some sofas and a centre table, among many other showpieces that added beauty to the room. They were led into another room, which was a hall and a dining room. There were a large sofa and many chairs on the right side of the room. There was a showcase that had many utensils made of bone China. The walls had some medals hung. There was a large replica of the Mona Lisa on one of the walls. The yellow lighting and the cosy temperature gave an amazing feel to any guest, Rajesh guessed.

"I had some tea made for you guys as soon as I knew you were close by. My butler, Raj will be here soon. Meanwhile, please make yourself comfortable at the sofa." He pointed further, "There is the restroom if you need to use it."

Gabriela did so. Rajesh suddenly felt a bit scared. He was in a house in a place called St. Leonard in Switzerland. He was with unknown people. *Was Gabriela part of this team? Was he being lured into a trap? What the hell was happening?*

"It's strange. I just have not understood what is happening!" Rajesh told the Captain as he sat.

"You will surely!" the Captain said as he disappeared into the kitchen at the far side of the room. He came back with his 'butler', who looked like an average Indian help from North India. As he served tea, Gabriela was back. Rajesh strangely felt less apprehensive once she was back.

"Please don't keep us in any more suspense. Why are we here?" Gabriela asked.

"You are here for a specific purpose. As per the Interpol, both of you are fugitives, possibly terrorists. If you serve the purpose for which you have been brought here, you guys will have automatically proved your innocence to the world!"

That sounded nice. However, it still failed to reduce the suspense in the air.

"Okay..." Gabriela said. "But do we know you? You have taken extra care to bring us here so safely? Who are you? Why are you interested in us proving our innocence to the world?"

"Because, as you do so, you would have achieved for me, what I have set out to achieve in the last ten years!"

Chapter 63

They had already made their mind up that they were not going to sleep immediately. Gabriela and Rajesh were desperate to know why they were made to travel all this way. The Captain had left an interesting proposition. They had to follow his instructions, and they will be proved innocent. In doing so, the Captain would have some ulterior motive succeed. So be it.

Captain Naveen asked Ken, "Shall we go in your Jeep?"

"Sure, sir." Ken was cool in demeanour but addressed the Captain with respect. It was evident that both Mark and Ken really respected the Captain. *How did the Indian command so much respect over these two guys; one from the US and the other from Australia?*

Ken headed to the car. The Captain changed, and Rajesh used the washroom. The four of them were out soon, back with their jackets on in the freezing cold.

The Captain sat in the front seat next to Ken, with the 'visitors' seated behind. They went back the same road that was lined by the houses. Once on the main road, they took the road that led further away from the expressway that they used to get here.

After a brief five-minute ride, they reached a small building. Ken parked and the four of them got down. The building looked like a ticket counter of a tourist spot. Of course, it was absolutely isolated at this time. It was nearing midnight now.

The Captain walked past the building and reached a gate. The gate was locked from the outside, but the Captain had the key. He allowed the three to pass before bolting the gate from the inside. They entered what seemed to be a department store; *or was it some souvenir shop?*

Rajesh managed to read a board on the wall. A dim light lit it. It said, "Welcome to the Saint Leonard underground lake."

Underground lake? What could that possibly mean? Whatever it was, it sure was a place for tourists. It was evident that people visited here always. Why were they brought here?

There was not much time to speculate. They had again left the building from the other side and were out in the open. He noticed that Ken and the Captain shone powerful torches as they descended downstairs. They were entering 'underground'.

The steps were steep. They had descended almost the depth of three standard storeys below the ground. They had now reached deep enough to be cut off from the streetlights above them. The only light was that of the torches. They followed the leaders gingerly.

Then they saw it. It was beautiful. It was indeed a lake in the underground. Numerous rowboats were at the jetty. The Captain stood next to one of them. "Ladies and gentlemen, please be careful as you step on the boats. It can be slippery!"

Ken first got onto the boat and held a hand out for Gabriela and then for Rajesh. Ken went to the front end of the boat and steadied himself at the seat with the oars. Rajesh and Gabriela sat on their seats as the Captain joined them.

What on earth was this? A lake under the ground! And they were going boating in it!

As soon as the Captain released the rope and was seated, Ken started rowing. The boat started moving away from the shore, into pitch darkness.

"You guys must be wondering where on Earth we are!" the Captain said.

"We sure are! This looks so scary!" Gabriela said.

"We are at the Saint Leonard's underground lake."

"And so we read..." Gabriela said.

The Captain ignored her and continued. "It is formed where a bed of gypsum, which had been trapped between layers of impervious Carboniferous strata, has been dissolved by groundwater. It has a length of around three hundred metres and a width of twenty metres. It is in fact, the largest underground lake in Europe."

What? That means there are more underground lakes in the world! Rajesh had never heard of them before!

"It was discovered in nineteen forty-three by Jean-Jacques Pittard. Prior to nineteen forty-six, the water-level was much higher, but an earthquake with a magnitude of five-point-six on the Richter-scale opened additional fissures in the cave. This was on January twenty-fifth, nineteen forty-six and this made it more readily navigable. Its water is constantly at eleven degrees Celsius. Always! You can touch the water. No crocodiles here for sure!"

The fugitive duo did so. It was pleasantly warm, considering that the ambient temperature might have been not more than three or four degrees.

The rocks on either side were now lit with some electric bulbs, which gave an awesome feeling. The lights intermittently lit the underground tunnel and the reflection shone off the water.

After a brief period of awe, Gabriela got to the point. "What are we doing here? This looks like a tourist spot and nothing else."

"What we are now seeing is the tourist spot. There remains a small detour in a cave within this lake that not many people are even aware of. Rest assured, no tourists would ever wander down there even by mistake. But remember, we are no tourists. We are here for a mission!"

CHAPTER 64

The boat moved towards the edge of the tunnel. The Captain had said that the length of the lake was three hundred metres, but they had hardly travelled half of that. The lights on the edges of the tunnel lit the rocks.

Rajesh wondered. *Why were they headed towards the edge when there was no shore there? Did the Captain expect them to climb onto the rocks and get into a secret tunnel?*

The boat was being rowed parallel to the rocks very near to the edge. The lights on the wall were ten metres away from each other. They reached a place where neither the light before them or behind was able to reach. It was dark here.

Then, Rajesh saw it. The boat now entered a smaller cave going off at a forty-five-degree angle into the sidewall. The tunnel was totally dark. The Captain shone his torch and it lit it brightly. This tunnel had a lower ceiling and there were points where the Captain asked Rajesh to crouch low. The Captain and he were tall enough to have their heads hit the ceiling. *Where on earth were they headed?*

The tunnel ended and the boat was rowed into a small atrium of sorts. It was a large cave. The ceiling was higher. The edge of the lake was in sight at the far end of the cave, and Ken rowed the boat to the edge. There was a pier to which he tied the rope of the boat. He got up first and stepped onto the rock, which formed the shore of the lake, which was just visible in the torchlight.

Rajesh expected him to now give a helping hand to Gabriela.

Ken did not do that. He walked away from the three on the boat, almost into total darkness. It was evident that he had been here multiple times before, as he didn't care to use the torchlight. Rajesh could see his silhouette in the dark. He had stopped and was doing something...

Suddenly, a bright light lit up the entire cave. Ken had switched on the powerful LED lights that were arranged in a neat line all around the cave's wall. Although they were LED lights, they still hurt their eyes, mainly because of the fact that they had been in the dark for so long.

Rajesh could not keep his eyes open for a while. After almost fifteen seconds, the surroundings started becoming more evident.

The 'cave' was indeed a dome. It was a natural dome and it served as an atrium to some structure that lay beyond the edge of the lake. In modern buildings, cars could drive up to the Atrium of the buildings. Here, the boat reached. He looked at the place where Ken was standing. Ken stood near a huge iron door. Rajesh, at once, knew that they were going to enter the door and go into yet another secret chamber.

Ken got back to the boat now. This time, he did give a helping hand, one after the other to Gabriela, Rajesh and then the Captain. Once all of them were on the shore, the Captain led them to the door.

As they reached the door, Rajesh was surprised to see that there was no latch on it. *Was it a door? If so how were they going to open it?* He just decided to observe.

The Captain headed to a small structure near the door. It seemed like a small 'letterbox' that the apartments in the eighties and nineties used to have. He opened the box. It was a biometrics machine.

The Captain first placed both his thumbs, then four fingers of both hands. He then placed his eyes close to the machine. *Well, well, this was some heavily guarded place!* It could only be opened with such stringent biometrics. It must be something really important.

The door suddenly opened inwards. Basically, Rajesh realised that there was no way of opening the door from the outside besides the biometric coding. The Captain headed inside and as he did so, lights automatically lit up.

Rajesh and Gabriela followed. The hitherto rocky surface had suddenly turned into white polished marble. They had entered a small well-constructed room. The room seemed empty except for a cupboard; an old fashioned wooden cupboard. *What now?*

As soon as Ken entered the room, he shut the door behind him.

Where were they? They were locked up in a small concrete room. Why?

He soon realised that this was yet another entrance room to something that was further guarded.

Ken said, "This, ladies and gentlemen is the place where we need to change our footwear." He pointed to a small shelf where there were neatly stacked rubber flip-flops. He himself started removing his shoes.

The three others followed suit. It was as if they were entering a laboratory or perhaps an ICU of a hospital.

Again, the Captain repeated the biometric steps at yet another 'letterbox' type of contraption. This time the distal wall started moving upwards... it was not a wall, it was a shutter door!

Rajesh wondered what lay beyond that.

They were in some secret laboratory constructed deep underground... near an underground lake in Western Switzerland. The time was past midnight. Rajesh had no idea how and why he was in such an eerie location at such an unearthly time.

He surely must be dreaming.

CHAPTER 65

They entered through the door. Rajesh and Gabriela were absolutely amazed at what they saw next.

The room was as big as a football field. The ceiling was at least three storeys high. It was a huge factory-sized complex constructed deep underground. It was totally unexpected. The sheer enormity of this 'hall' stunned Gabriela and Rajesh into awestruck silence.

There were no 'rooms' as such, but there were many cubicles separated by glass sheets; some were small, some were large enough to hold a small plane. These glass partitions enclosed many machines, tubes, wires and computers.

Even at this time of the night, they were not the only people here. At least twenty other people were visible from where they stood, all working with immense concentration at different places.

The Captain finally spoke. "So, Miss Gabriela Fabregas and Mr Rajesh; you are the privileged first two 'common citizens' of the world to enter this enclosure. No one else can enter this complex unless authorized by a security team called 'Montag'. The 'Montag', a word that means Monday in German, is a security team picked by the governments of twenty-three countries. They have allowed you two to be the first non-member people to enter.

Oh God! What was this? Rajesh could only smile. In a matter of a few hours, Gabriela and he had changed from ordinary citizens to international fugitives travelling with false passports, to a privileged couple authorized by the governments of a few countries to view a top-secret place. "Where are we, Captain Naveen?"

"We are at the offshoot lab of the CERN."

"The CERN? What is that?" Gabriela asked.

"The European Organization for Nuclear Research, known as CERN, is a European research organization that operates the largest particle physics laboratory in the world. It was established in nineteen fifty-four, right, Ken?"

Ken nodded, "Yes, nineteen fifty-four it was."

"Well, yeah, the organization is based in a northwest suburb of Geneva on the Franco-Swiss border and has twenty-three member states. CERN is an official United Nations Observer.

"The CERN's main function is to provide the particle accelerators and other infrastructure needed for high-energy physics research – as a result, numerous experiments have been constructed at CERN through international collaborations."

"Jesus Christ! Why are we here?" Gabriela asked. "I am a software consultant for IT companies. What have I done to earn this privilege?"

The Captain ignored her. "Well, we are not exactly at the main site of the CERN, but an offshoot site. Ninety-nine per cent of the people in the world don't even know the existence of this place!"

It was Rajesh's turn to speak up. "Wow. Now Gabriela and I are in that one per cent! I am a reporter for a small TV channel based in India. I am sure I too am extremely underqualified for this privilege! If you had to bring some reporter in, it should have been someone from CNN or BBC!"

The Captain sounded a little impatient. "Of course, you will know soon why you two were the chosen ones! Do you want to sit here and ponder about it for a while…or maybe we should just move on?"

Rajesh and Gabriela looked at each other. *Well, they had to move on!*

"We will follow you, sir!" Rajesh said. He made sure he didn't sound sarcastic, although he wanted to be.

The Captain moved ahead, followed by the three. He first moved to a relatively smaller room. It seemed to be filled with multiple small similar-looking machines. That did look rather strange.

They all had a similar-looking front. There was a pillar-like structure, which was sliced horizontally right in between, the upper part of the 'pillar' was supported by a powerful fulcrum. The lower part of the 'pillar' was firmly fixed to the base.

They were of numerous sizes. The Captain picked one of the smaller ones. This was as small as a routine microscope.

"This is what we have got you to witness. This is ten years of my research gone in here. To develop this chap... this is called the 'Compressor'."

"Compressor?" Rajesh repeated.

"Yes. Can you see the space between the upper and lower portion of this rod called the Compression arm rod?" He pointed to the space between the upper and lower parts of the 'pillar-like' structure of the machine.

"Yes," Rajesh said. *Where was this getting? Why had they come so far to witness something to do with Civil engineering?*

"This, my friends, is the most powerful compressor in the world. It can compress anything to the smallest imaginable dimensions!"

Rajesh and Gabriela could still not understand why they were here to witness such an anti-climax: something as futile as this.

Rajesh remembered the '*girni*' that he used to visit with his mother when he was young. '*Girnis*' were neighbourhood places in India where people used to take purchased wheat grains to. The *Girnis* used to pulverize the grains into a fine powder that could be used as flour for cooking.

Gabriela remembered the stone crusher that was used to compress rocks into small stones next to her house in New Jersey.

Neither of them found this machine unique.

However, they were sure that there was something indeed crazily unique about this. Twenty-three countries had probably spent billions of dollars to develop this contraption and had kept this a secret. They were to find out why.

The Captain had said that their freedom depended on it.

CHAPTER 66

"*Girni?*" Rajesh couldn't help but say it out loud.

The Captain immediately recognized what he meant, although Ken and Gabriela were clueless. He laughed loudly. "*Girni? Girni!*"

Rajesh also chuckled.

The Captain said, "Let me explain to the others what '*girni*' means. It is the machine used to… you know… crush wheat grains into flour."

"It does seem like that," Gabriela said. "I had a stone crusher in mind."

"Stone crusher!" Again the Captain laughed loudly, but this time Gabriela and Rajesh didn't laugh.

Ken did laugh though, "A few billion dollars spent for developing a stone crusher! Sure!"

"That's what we see thus far, Captain!" Gabriela said. "I'm sure you are going to explain what it really is!"

"Yes, I will. You will witness what this machine does in a few minutes itself." The Captain went to the far end of the room. There was a jar. It seemed full of small metal balls, each probably around half a centimetre in size. "These are ball bearings."

"Hmmm…" Gabriela said. Rajesh had said that he too had studied engineering in his graduation. *Sure both of them knew that!*

The Captain pressed a button on the Compressor. It made the two arms of the compressor move a little apart. He placed one ball bearing in between them. He pressed the button again. This time the two arms moved towards each other just enough to immobilize the ball bearing between them.

"Now, people, we will begin the compression. But we must not do it here by strict rules."

"Then where?" Rajesh asked.

"Follow me."

They came out of the cubicle. The Captain led them past some other cubicles. Few of the people who worked there acknowledged them and waved. Rajesh guessed that they might all be highly paid scientists. No one seemed to be bothered as to who Rajesh and Gabriela were. Rajesh imagined the Captain commanded enough respect not to be questioned.

They reached the opposite end of the 'hall'; the side opposite to where they had entered. There was yet another metal door and yet another biometric box. The Captain followed the rituals and the metal door opened.

Again astonishment followed.

Here was yet another hall. This time it was as big as a basketball court. The lights lit up as they entered. Rajesh looked around.

This hall was absolutely empty. The floor was made up of probably carbon fibre. The walls and ceiling were made of some strong metal, not concrete. High up the walls, there were some glass windows. *Eerie!*

The Captain made his way to the centre of the hall and placed the compressor right there on the floor. He then pressed yet another button on the machine. "Ladies and gentlemen, the Compression has begun. It will be completed in fifteen minutes; enough time for us to make our way to the observation desk."

He started to walk back towards the door. The trio followed suit. Rajesh wondered as to why they were not allowed to witness the crushing of a ball bearing from a close distance. *Did it contain explosives? Was this ball bearing heavily filled with a highly compressed explosive? Was this the bomb on the flight?*

He could only guess...

They reached the door and were back into the main hall. The Captain shut the door behind him. It could now only be opened by biometrics.

They entered an elevator that was right next to the door. Rajesh hadn't noticed it when they had got here initially. The elevator took them up, two floors. They then entered a room: 'the observation' room. The room had large windows made of glass. Rajesh and Gabriela realised that they were now staring at the second hall through its windows.

They had reached the observation room in three minutes flat. The Captain had said that the ball bearing would be compressed in another twelve minutes. So, what was the big deal? Rajesh was dying to find out.

"So, now," the Captain said, "tell me, what can be the smallest size this ball bearing can be crushed to?"

"Powder," Gabriela said almost immediately, jolly well knowing that the answer was not going to be that simple. She just wanted the Captain to go on.

"Use your imagination a bit more…"

"Microscopic granules," Gabriela said immediately again.

"Better…"

"Come on! I am sure that the two surfaces of the compressor cannot get closer than that. It cannot reach a point where there is lesser space between the upper and lower surfaces!"

"That's where the billion dollars comes in!" Ken said. "Shall I explain, Captain?"

"Yes, go ahead."

Ken continued. "Yes. One would be sure to imagine the same. The two surfaces can't get closer than what you said. However, this material is special. It contains a miniature nuclear reactor within both surfaces, the circuits of which set off when the two surfaces come close together. Once the nuclear reactor activates, it pulverizes the material between them even further; and guess what? It compresses them from all directions of the sphere…can you guess what happens next?"

Rajesh spoke, "It means it breaks it up to individual atoms?"

"Well, yes and no."

"Means?"

"*Yes* is for the fact that it breaks it into atoms, but the *no* is for the fact that they don't break 'up'. Did you get what I mean?"

"No," Rajesh and Gabriela said simultaneously.

"The compressor in actuality breaks the material into subatomic particles also…into electrons, protons and neutrons, and finally into quarks, but the particles don't dissipate. They are compressed further and further…"

Rajesh was getting it. "A black hole!"

CHAPTER 67

Gabriela looked at the Captain and Ken to see what their reaction was. They nodded in affirmation, almost proud that Rajesh had said that. "Come again? A black hole? I still don't get it! Sorry, I seem to have forgotten physics all together!"

"Can you explain, Rajesh? It is better if a relatively lay-person explains it rather than two nuclear physicists," Ken said.

Wow! For the first time, it struck to him that Ken and Captain Naveen were, in fact, nuclear physicists. All this time, Rajesh viewed Ken as a yachtsman! He viewed the Captain as a rich billionaire with immense political influence. None were what he thought they were!

He didn't waste time though. He realised that time was running down for the compressor to do its work. "This is a theory in astrophysics."

"No longer a theory," the Captain quipped. "Sorry. Go on."

"Well… in astrophysics, they say that if a large particle gets compressed into a smaller and smaller size, it eventually reaches a point. That point is called 'some' radius…"

"Schwarzschild radius," the Captain said.

"Yes. Beyond this point, the entire mass of the object will have such high gravitational pull that it will collapse into itself and create an area of such high gravity that it will pull anything that is within a certain distance from it."

"The black hole!" Gabriela said, "Even light cannot escape from it."

The Captain took over, "But it's not so easy in practicality to 'create' a black hole. It happens naturally in the Universe because of the immense energy individual stars have at their core. Remember, the Schwarzschild radius for individual masses is extremely small. Can you guess this…if the entire Earth had to be compressed into its Schwarzschild radius, how small would be the mass of the Earth before it becomes a black hole?"

"No idea," Rajesh said.

The Captain teased them. "Remember, the earth weighs approximately six trillion kilograms; that is six followed by twenty-four zeroes. It has a circumference of approximately forty thousand kilometres. Your options are; as small as India, as small as Switzerland or as small as London."

"London," Gabriela guessed quickly. She was clearly impatient.

"Mr Rajesh?" the captain asked.

His reply was the same. "London."

"No, none of the answers is correct. Believe it or not, the earth in its entirety must be compressed to the size of a coin!"

"What!" Gabriela was genuinely surprised.

"Yes imagine this, if the earth had to be compressed so much… how much will this ball bearing need to be compressed to? I don't want an answer. I want you to just guess!"

Rajesh and Gabriela were indeed guessing. It would have to be in less than nanometres…maybe even lesser.

"What happens to all the mass that gets swallowed up?" Rajesh asked.

"That, my friend, is what we have brought you here to Switzerland for! Right now, I want you to observe the Compressor. You are about time…" the Captain looked at his watch, "a minute to be exact to witness one of the conclusions of my years of research.

Rajesh and Gabriela had guessed somewhat what they were about to witness. They both imagined the sound and sight of an explosion.

However, what they witnessed just astonished them.

The Compressor was right in the centre of the hall now. The next second it disappeared. Disappeared in thin air. There was no sound preceding its disappearance. It was just, to put in simple words, gone.

Chapter 68

Rajesh and Gabriela followed the Captain and Ken back to the house at St Leonard. They followed the same circuitous route that they had come by. They went back through the gate, the footwear room, the atrium in the cave, back onto the rowboat, through the tunnel, onto the underground lake, back up the stairs and through the souvenir shop. They were back onto the SUV and were headed back.

The Captain had told them that any further information would be provided at home only, which left time for Gabriela and Rajesh to introspect.

Rajesh could see the possible connection, but he didn't understand the significance. This Compressor was the bomb used on the ill-fated Eastern Airlines flight. It obviously was compressing something larger. It had compressed an object that was really large, which was enough to cause a black hole that swallowed the entire flight.

Of course, there were no explosives involved. There were no wires or batteries. It looked like a simple microscope, to say the least. That explained how it had escaped detection completely at the Dubai airport.

But some things troubled him.

How was the Captain involved in all this?

Was he a nuclear physicist or a terrorist or both?

Why did he use his invention for such a dastardly act that could have killed hundreds? It would have started a war-like situation and would have been disastrous.

Why were Gabriela and he deplaned from the flight? Why were they hauled all over the way from Dubai to Switzerland? Had things gone according to plan, the two of them would have been saved while the plane would have been sucked away with all its passengers on board?

Wait a minute! Who was Kabir Dravid? Wasn't he the terrorist? Then probably he had done some business with the Captain. It was becoming increasingly clear that Kabir was the terrorist while the Captain had invented the bomb used for the terror act.

Then why were Mark and Ken so keen to save Gabriela and Rajesh from Kabir and bring them to the Captain; especially if Kabir and Captain were business associates?

Rajesh's mind was going crazy… His life was a complete mystery and he was yet to find out answers. He hoped he did so soon.

The SUV now pulled into the corner house of the Captain. The time was 2:30 am and the air outside was now freezing cold. The Captain quickly opened the main door and ushered the three inside.

"So guys, would you want to get some sleep before I tell you anything further?" the Captain asked.

Gabriela looked at Rajesh, who shook his head to say no. "No. We can't sleep unless some suspense is solved!" she said.

"Okay, let me get some coffee, then. I need that. I am sure Ken and you two wouldn't mind it either!"

"Yeah, okay. Appreciate," Gabriela said.

There was an enforced break. This was indeed going to be a long night. All members used the restrooms before they got together in the hall with the coffees.

The Captain started, "So, let me begin by asking… what do you guys make of it so far?"

Rajesh took that question. "Captain Naveen, it's clear you have invented the Compressor. And this was the weapon smuggled in by Kabir onto the flight. So, obviously, your invention is now being used to strike terror attacks! Why Captain? Why?"

"Yes, you are absolutely right. I have invented the Compressor. And for sure it was the 'weapon' used to blow up the Eastern Airlines flight."

This was it then. The Captain was the mastermind behind inventing the most powerful bomb on the planet, and he had sold his invention to the radical group, of which Kabir was a member.

Rajesh and Gabriela had escaped from the clutches of a cruel man. Now they were with an even more dangerous one. It was clear that '*Captain dangerous*' had some sort of fallout with '*Kabir the cruel*'. Kabir wanted to kill them, but the more dangerous Captain wanted to save them.

In the eyes of the world, they themselves were bloodthirsty criminals. They were done for.

CHAPTER 69

"Let me start from the year two thousand eleven. I had just finished my short service commission in the Indian army. Hence, the 'Captain' name has stuck on. I applied for an interview here in Geneva. I got here on my merit."

"An Indian army officer is now inventing bombs to crush the world!" Rajesh exclaimed.

"I am no longer an Indian army officer remember! I am free to do whatever I want. I am a civilian now!"

"Whatever…" Rajesh said in disgust.

"Okay. Let me make things clear. I am a trained physicist. I have qualified with honours in the National Defence Academy and have been sponsored by the army to study physics at the Hyderabad University. I served the army for five years after that. I have come here to Switzerland to be part of a group of responsible nuclear physicists. So cut the crap about *me* being a bad guy!"

Rajesh sure hoped what he said was true. Yet, there was a connection between him and the flight that was blown up. He had to hear it all before commenting.

Gabriela felt the same. She decided not to comment.

The Captain continued as if he had expected the non-response by the duo. "As soon as I was inducted, I was assigned to be a part of the team that was to research and present a hypothesis as to how it was possible to do what we just witnessed; that is to crush routine objects to points of singularity. Remember, generating quarks and atoms has been the long-time work of the CERN. However, these particles had to be generated with huge energies being involved… by nuclear fission methods. We were to find out how this is possible in simpler ways."

"Why would people want to do that?"

"Good question. It was mainly to solve the problem of non-biodegradable waste. As the Earth is getting loaded, more and more non-biodegradable waste is being generated. Our ocean floors are loaded with plastic. Fish are dying because of the same. It won't be long before the entire ocean ecosystem disappears and this would have devastating consequences on the entire human race!"

The Captain paused. He was expecting some biology-related questions as to how that was possible.

Rajesh and Gabriela just looked at each other. They were awestruck. *Really, could this be possible?*

Gabriela said, "Wow! That would be great if that really happened. Instead of blowing planes up!"

"My research hypothesis was the one that was accepted. Remember, it took me five winter months of burning the midnight oil just to come up with the hypothesis. It was a dream come true!"

Rajesh felt proud of his fellow Indian, but still, there were things that were uncomfortable and not clear. He waited.

"I was now assigned a team and a budget to develop what I had proposed. In my team was Kenneth Anderson – a brilliant physicist, a gold medallist from Gold Coast Australia…"

Ken bowed.

Rajesh looked at the 'yachtsman' Ken. *How his perception of Ken had changed!*

"… and Suleiman Schmidt; a gold medallist from Munich."

Who was he now? Was this the real name of Mark Andrews; the concierge from the Radan hotel, who had got them from Dubai to Champoussin village?

"This was an amazing team, I tell you. It took us years of research, planning and failures, I'll spare you the details, to get this baby ready; the Compressor.

"The Compressor is one of the most advanced inventions by mankind. It owes its development to scientists, right from Galileo, Copernicus, Newton, Einstein and Hawking to the thousands of unnamed scientists who have studied astrophysics and quantum mechanics. Rest assured, it would have made all the mentioned scientists really proud! But there was a catch here… in fact, there were quite a number of issues here."

"What?" Gabriela and Rajesh said simultaneously.

"Two main issues. There were two groups of people who had eyed this entire invention wrongly. One was the ISIS, the radical terrorist group. Suleiman Schmidt was an excellent scientist. He was a dedicated and brilliant worker. He was a mildly religious Muslim, but he was the target of a dedicated radicalizing team of the ISIS. It is now evident that they had identified him as a highly potential target and had got onto their work diligently. We knew Suleiman well until the end of two thousand and twelve. After that, the team had done its job so discretely that Suleiman was a total wreck by the year two thousand and thirteen, and we knew nothing. They made sure he didn't leave a damn clue of what was happening. Suleiman was successfully transformed into an ISIS member. The radical group had reached CERN! You can see where all this is getting to…"

"Suleiman sold out this invention to ISIS! Oh my God! Oh my God!" Gabriela said.

"Kabir Dravid is an ISIS member! He is not even a Muslim!" Rajesh's thoughts had progressed further.

"Oh, we don't know his real name! He might be one!" Ken said.

"His real name is Sachin! He named himself Kabir! I know this chap for years now. It's evident he is working under an alibi, but it still doesn't explain shit!" Rajesh said.

"Suleiman had just given this work for free? You must be kidding!" Gabriela asked.

The Captain replied, "He had given his work for free. Yes, he did… that asshole. But as you would have guessed, it is not easy to walk out with this machine so easily. What you have seen was a smaller version of the machine. Now, if he had to create a machine that could create an explosive that was large enough to blow up a Boeing aircraft, he had to use machines of variable sizes, large and small. They would have progressively compressed a large matter into smaller sizes."

Ken interrupted, "Yes, there is a pickup device. It transports compressed material from one compressor to the other. That itself is as large as a fridge. He had to smuggle one pickup device too."

"Yes," the Captain continued. "You should by now have guessed that this would have involved breaking out of one of the most complex twenty-four by seven monitored places. Its transfer would involve at least a billion dollars, I can tell you! And surely he is an international fugitive now. He himself would have been paid off handsomely!"

Ken interrupted again, "At this moment, only a very few people besides the authorities know of his disappearance. It has not been made public yet, as it would wreak havoc. Therefore, you saw the other scientists were not bothered much when we saw them today! And you two guys are the chosen ones from the outside world to know this."

"The chosen ones!" Rajesh repeated. It sounded ominous.

Chapter 70

"Why are we the chosen ones?" Gabriela asked.

"You will know soon. Soon," the Captain said, building up the suspense.

"Aye, aye, Captain!" Gabriela said sarcastically.

Rajesh said, "You said there were two issues with the invention. One was the fact that Suleiman Schmidt smuggled out the Compressor and the fridge-sized pick-up device from the CERN. He had smuggled it out to the ISIS who used it for the bombing. What is the other issue?"

"The other issue is with another group of people who have a strong sentiment *against* this invention!"

"Who are they?" Rajesh asked.

"Why would anyone have a problem with anything that helps in removing plastics from the ocean?" Gabriela wondered aloud. "It seems to be a problem that everyone should be equally concerned about."

"For that query..." the Captain began and then paused a bit, "we need to answer the previous question that you had asked me. Do you remember what it is?"

"No..." Gabriela said.

"I remember," Rajesh interrupted. "I asked you what happens to all the mass that has been sucked into the black hole. You said that the answer to the question was the reason why we both are here for!"

"Yes. Exactly. Then, what do you think happens to all that mass?"

"Dunno." Rajesh shrugged.

The Captain looked at Gabriela.

"No clue." Gabriela had actually given it a brief thought. "I always knew that black holes suck in everything in them, including light. But yes, come to think of it, what happens to all of the stuff?"

The Captain answered, "For centuries it was believed that black holes were the deathbed for anything that was sucked in. However, it doesn't make sense, does it? All matter can't just disappear. It was believed that in the centre of the black hole there is a point of infinite mass and infinite density. But what happens to it?"

Both Rajesh and Gabriela were just silent. This was getting too much for them.

"Hawking came up with the explanation. He believed that the matter actually escapes as radiation from the centre, and he called it 'Hawking radiation'."

"Okay?" Rajesh retorted simply.

"He himself changed it into another hypothesis... I won't go into detail – he said that radiation is converted into useless particles of information that escape from the event horizon; that is the edge of the black hole..."

Gabriela and Rajesh understood that lesser.

"Now scientists are believing that the centre of the black hole can serve as the beginning of a new Universe, where all the mass escapes into another yet unknown dimension; the fifth dimension..."

"What! Wait a minute! I can't understand a thing now!" Gabriela said.

"We, as human beings can see things in four dimensions, how far it is lengthwise, breadthwise, depth-wise, and where it is as far as time is concerned. Four dimensions. But this point of extreme gravity can serve as the gateway for the fifth dimension, which we cannot see. It is the start of an alternate universe."

"Well, whatever!"

"Okay, let's put it this way. Do you know what the Big Bang is?"

"Yes," Gabriela said. "It said that the entire universe was created by a huge explosion!"

"Explosion of what?" the Captain prodded.

"Something made up of all the matter of the universe!" Gabriela said.

Rajesh was beginning to see sense. "The entire matter of the universe was a point of singularity... a point of infinite mass and infinite density.

It exploded and we, the entire universe that we know of came into existence!"

"And this point of singularity, where did that come from?" The Captain prodded further.

"Shit! I know where you're getting Captain!" Rajesh said. "You are saying that the entire universe was a point of singularity, which in turn had been created by a black hole existing elsewhere? Really? Can that even be true?"

Gabriela "Good Lord holy Jesus Christ!"

The Captain laughed loudly. "Gabriela says, 'Good Lord!'. That is the catch here!"

"What?"

"Can you see this coming? Religion clearly teaches us that God created the universe as it stands now! He said 'Let there be light!' and the universe began!"

"Hmmm…" Gabriela said.

"You take any religion, it says God created the universe. In Hinduism, we believe that Lord Brahma was the God of creation!

"But this, my friends, is the ultimate proof that no God was needed for creation! The Compressor proves without any doubt that a point of singularity can be reached and the entire matter could just disappear without leaving any traces in the present universe! This is an absolute contradiction to the theory of 'Creation'."

"Oh, man!" Rajesh stood bewildered.

"So you now understand, the group of people who don't want this invention to be made public, will understandably be the world leaders of religion in the present date. The Muslims and the Jews presently have no particular present-day leader. However, Christianity is represented by the Pope, the followers of whom might want this information to be gone forever! And in Hinduism, there is one particular gentleman, who seems to have taken the agenda seriously, the Great Guru Amar…"

Chapter 71

The Captain got up and went to the kitchen. As if by cue, Ken moved to the drawing room at the same time. It was clear that the duo wanted Rajesh and Gabriela to introspect.

Rajesh sat silently while Gabriela connected the dots.

"Hey!" she said. "This was the guy who you were doing an article on! That was it then! You and I have been tugged all around the world so that you can do a ground-breaking article on the religious man whom you so despise!"

"Hmmm…" That was all that Rajesh could muster. *Was that it then?* Rajesh built the story in his mind and then spoke it aloud.

"Really, Gabriela? Let's build the story.

"Suleiman Schmidt, the transformed nuclear physicist to ISIS member, smuggled out Compressors of various sizes to the terrorist group. How did the terrorist organization finance such a great heist? We still need to know. But, okay, they got the weapon.

"The terrorist group sends Kabir to check in the smallest size compressor onto the flight. The smallest size compressor is compressing a very large object, which has been compressed into a relatively smaller object by larger compressors. A pickup device has now transferred it onto the smallest compressor. The smallest compressor will compress the object to its singularity point after a while on the carriage compartment of the flight…"

"It could be in the hand baggage as well!" said Gabriela.

"Yeah! But I am sure the passengers who had been deplaned would have noticed a suspicious piece of baggage left behind by Kabir on the flight!"

"Yup. That's true."

"Our Captain meanwhile knows that the bomb is on the flight. Again, we don't know - how. So he decides to deplane me first so that he is sure that I could be alive to tell the story. We still don't know why he deplanes you, but he does."

"Okay!"

"He makes sure that the people on the flight are safe next by raising the alarm. Still, why he did that after the flight took off, no one knows!"

It was Gabriela's turn to say, "Hmmm..."

He then makes sure we travel all the way to Switzerland to meet him to achieve what he wanted to achieve. Kabir, meanwhile, knows about the agenda and has been sent by ISIS to make sure that we don't!"

"Or maybe he is sent behind us so that we lead him to the Captain and the terrorist group could blow the shit out of him!"

"Yes, that is more probable, I guess!"

"But the Captain managed to outsmart him! And here we are! We are here to help the Captain to denounce religion as well as give him a clean chit. After all, it was he who invented this Compressor!"

"Two strikes in one!" Gabriela said.

They both looked at each other for a while.

"Our story makes very little sense! There has to be some other angle!" Rajesh said.

"I agree. Our theory is bullshit!"

The Captain and Ken returned right at that moment. It was as if they had been overhearing Gabriela and Rajesh while having some fun at their expense!

"So Captain!" Rajesh said, "I am sure you left us both to have a small chit chat. And yes, as you must have guessed, we have come up with our own story. But still, it doesn't make sense whatsoever!"

The Captain laughed loudly, and Ken chuckled.

"It still doesn't make sense why you would save me!" Rajesh said. "I am a small-time journalist at a rather insignificant news channel. Yes, I did some scripts on the Great Guru Amar... but that is the reason you saved me? And then why did you save Gabriela?"

Again the Captain laughed. "I saved each and every passenger on that plane, my dear!"

"Then again, what was special about us that we were deplaned earlier than the others? It was clear that neither of us had conjunctivitis! It was some chemical sprayed in our eyes!"

"Well, let me put it this way. The terrorist organization had made a huge blunder in their planning. They had chosen a flight to be bombed. But they did not know that the flight had you two, Gabriela Fabregas and Rajesh Rajesh, on it!"

CHAPTER 72

"What!" Gabriela said. "The ISIS is a merciless group of people! But you say they made a blunder because they had a reporter and a software consultant on board! I can't speak for Rajesh, but I can't imagine being a person of any importance!"

"Well?" Rajesh said.

"Well guys, let me tell you. Gabriela is a person of prime importance for one single reason. Rajesh is of importance for three different reasons!"

"Really? Am I to feel privileged by that?" Rajesh said.

"I am of prime importance!" Gabriela said. "How on earth? I repeat – I am a software consultant! What do *I* have to do with CERN, nuclear physics, the Compressor, or the ISIS? What do *I* have to do with the Pope or the Hindu Guru? What enmity or friendship do *I* have with Kabir Dravid?"

She was clearly making references to the possible ways he could be involved, Rajesh thought. He had something to do with Great Guru Amar, as well as he had an enmity with Kabir, but he could still not make any sense.

"To answer your questions, I must continue with my story," the Captain said curtly.

"Please do, Captain!" Rajesh said.

"I'm all ears!" Gabriela said.

"It was April two thousand and eighteen. Ken and I had decided to take a vacation, leaving Suleiman to carry on with the work. Ken and I decided to go to Interlaken and Jungfrau. We booked a cottage at Grindewald for a week. These three are famous tourist destinations in

Switzerland. They are amazingly beautiful. That one week was enough for Suleiman to carry out his plan.

"When we got back to St. Leonard, we saw that Suleiman had not turned up for work. However, we got into our offices and started working. We didn't notice anything abnormal. All the scientists were at work as usual. Late that evening, we decided to unlock the storeroom where the pickup device was kept. That was when we realised; the pickup device was no longer there. In another fifteen minutes or so, we could realise that four compressors of different sizes were missing!"

"We panicked. We tried to call Suleiman, but his phone was switched off. We headed to his house. It was locked. It was then we realised that something was horribly wrong. Suleiman had been kidnapped or killed, was our first thought. He had been forced to remove the stuff.

"We had to report to our director. An investigation was ordered and the search of the CCTV cameras began. Amazingly, the CCTV cameras in and around our lab were all shut for an hour on one of those days. I can tell you, it was not an easy thing to accomplish. It was either a high-level payoff or it was a really complex hacking device that did it! We never knew how Suleiman had been kidnapped or killed, and how the devices were smuggled out.

"However, there was one major issue with Suleiman's plan. He was spotted in the back seat of a Mercedes with tinted glass. How; you may ask. The driver of the car had pulled down the windows to swipe his card at a toll near Sailon village. His picture was captured on CCTV. He was quite comfortable and relaxed. It was then we realised that Suleiman was not kidnapped, he had escaped. He was the mastermind behind the disappearance of the compressors and the pickup device!"

"The Interpol were now involved and the top-secret team was assembled for this mission. There was a dangerous man on the loose somewhere with a machine that potentially could lead to a lot of destruction.

"And kudos to our security team to come up with a security idea that was ingenious. Only I, among the entire team, knew one thing. They had embedded the pickup device with a GPS transmitter, which transmitted the device location. The hitch was that the machine had to be connected to power for it to transmit. We were frustrated that it hadn't picked up any signal from the time it disappeared.

"The investigations were reaching a standstill. Our assignment was frozen for a while by the institution until any further advancement of the investigation was reached. We were headed to an impasse.

"Suddenly, things changed in a week. In July two thousand eighteen, the machine was switched on. The GPS had traced the machine to Iraq, to an area under control by the ISIS. Our worst fears had come true. My dearest invention, the invention that was made to serve humankind, had landed in the hands of an extremist group. They could now go on and create havoc! But at least the investigating team knew where it was now. They could use drones to destroy it, hoping that Suleiman had not already cloned it elsewhere.

"In the same week, Suleiman was traced in Santa Monica, in Los Angeles, California. The Interpol had used the single clue from the black Merc that he was travelling in, and their investigations had successfully traced him, living in LA as Karl Werner, just as another tourist with a B1 B2 visa."

"Holy shit. He entered the US with a false ID. How is that even possible?" Gabriela asked.

"Anything is possible. Money talks. He had a fake Hungarian passport with him."

"Shit!"

"But the instructions to this special team of the Interpol were clear. They were not to make high profile arrests unless the entire matter was solved. They trapped him in his own rented house and used every possible way to extract information from him."

"But he has his civilian rights!" Gabriela said.

"Not when he is a maniac radical scientist, who travelled to the US and provided the ISIS with potentially the most devastating weapon known to mankind!"

Chapter 73

"They must have used third-degree torture!" Gabriela said.

"I don't know!" The Captain's emotions were rising. "But he certainly deserved one. He stole my baby. I had conceptualized the Compressor after so many months of research. Ken and I, and for that matter, Suleiman too had put in so many years of hard work to achieve this, for the betterment of mankind. The taxpayers of so many peace-loving countries funded it. This prick sold it out to achieve the destruction of these very same countries! He deserves to be shot in public!"

Gabriela was silenced. "Yes, he deserves it, I suppose!"

"The questioning of Suleiman led to an important pieces of information. We now knew two pieces of information.

"One. The first target of this bomb would be a flight. That's all he knew. Where and when? He had no idea.

"Second. The entire operation was funded by one of the billionaires in the United States. We have to call him Mr A at the moment."

"Who is this Mr A?" Gabriela pounced. "If I have to guess, he has to be one of the business rivals of my fiancé, Steve Mehrotra! He had chosen to bomb his first flight!"

The Captain waited as if he knew that Rajesh would wait a minute and then retort.

As expected, Rajesh did the same. "This is the connection between Gabriela and the whole story!"

"Yes, but it still doesn't make sense! Why would Mr A want to deplane me then? He should have let me blow away to smithereens!"

"The Captain deplaned you, not Mr A!" Rajesh said. He himself was not convinced of what he had just said and the three around him could feel just that.

"Captain, please continue!" Gabriela sounded as if she was ordering, not pleading.

The Captain smiled. "Mr A is probably one of the members of the World Elite group. The Elite group benefits by doing business with members of both sides of all wars. They are supposed to have invested and then gained huge returns by funding wars since time immemorial. They have instigated governments, played huge roles in the outcomes of elections, probably fund half the banks of the world, and dictate policies of almost every country.

"Mr A is surely investing some billion dollars to fund the ISIS now, but surely he will gain his returns by doing business with the rest of the world to hunt them down. A very shrewd person indeed, isn't he? At least hundreds of millions of people would die, but he would have made his cash."

"People could stoop to any levels for money. This is a mass scale murder!" Gabriela said.

"Money!" Ken spoke after a long time. He spoke only one word, but it had a deep meaning.

The Captain continued. "The intelligence agencies of many countries already suspected the hand of Mr A in funding the ISIS, but no one had any conclusive proof. There was no way we could walk into this billionaire's home and just pick him up. Conclusive proof was required.

"Meanwhile, we didn't know which flight was going to be involved, remember? It could be anywhere in the world! We narrowed down to Dubai when we picked up the GPS signal of the pickup device in Dubai in December two thousand eighteen. The UAE intelligence narrowed down on the area and intercepted all calls from there. It was clear that the bombing was going to occur on the fateful Tuesday afternoon, around 5:45 pm. But still, only code words were being used. We didn't know how the bomb would get in and which flight would be involved.

"But the intelligence agencies were clear that the terrorists were making some last-minute changes to their plans. The date remained the same, but some late change in plans was going on. Possibly the route of entry was being changed."

"Kabir had made his entry now!" Rajesh guessed aloud.

However, the Captain just continued, "They made their first big blunder. It was a total give away."

"What happened?"

"Guess? It is a typical 'who did it'. If you know what happened next, it would be easy for you to see how the intelligence agencies guessed quickly as to which flight would be involved. Can you guess what blunder they did?"

"Let me guess…" Rajesh said. "They shifted the pickup device to Kabir's house. And Kabir Dravid was already on the intelligence list of terrorists. And surely he already had his flight tickets booked on Eastern Airlines Flight 001 from Dubai to Chennai. It was a flight owned by Steve Mehrotra; arch-enemy of Mr A! They nailed it!"

The Captain paused and looked at Ken, who looked overawed.

"That was a very nice analysis indeed. You are an investigative reporter as well?" Ken asked.

Gabriela just gasped.

"Nope!" Rajesh said. He felt proud of himself… for a short while at least… until he heard the next sentence by the Captain.

"That was really good thinking. But no, that was not what happened!"

"Shit! You almost made me proud, Captain!" Rajesh forced a short chuckle.

"No, I am serious, that was great thinking!"

"What actually happened Captain?" Gabriela asked. She was impatient. "What blunder did those thugs do?"

"The GPS of the pickup device showed that the device had been moved to Hong Kong…"

CHAPTER 74

Both Gabriela and Rajesh were stunned into silence.

Rajesh had thought of this possibility before. *Gabriela was on the wrong side of the law. She had got the bomb inside. But why would she agree to bomb her fiancé's flight? Was she double-crossing him?*

Gabriela spoke up after almost a minute's silence. "Rajesh, believe me. I have no idea about any of this. I am not involved. I swear to God!" Her hands were trembling.

"No one said you were!" The Captain said. "But it is true that the Compressor entered the flight in your checked-in baggage. We suspect that it was introduced in the bag even before it entered the Hong Kong airport."

"But that's impossible. It was with me the whole time. I had packed it. And then... wait a minute. The hotel bellboy rang the bell and offered to take the bag down! Come to think of it, I was surprised at that time as I had not informed the front desk that I was ready to check out! I next saw my bag entering the hotel car to the airport! It was away from me all the time from the time I locked my room, got to the reception, checked out and until the moment I entered the car. After that, it had been with me up to the airport! Shit. They had put the Compressor in at that time!"

There were too many twists in the tale already! One part of the brain of Rajesh thought that it was a well-made up story by Gabriela. *She most probably just put it in herself!* She had allowed her bags to be checked-in and at the last moment got herself deplaned so that the bags still remained on the flight! *He* was just extra baggage! To make people believe that she was genuinely ill. The entire pulling out of Dubai was just a coup. She had to be brought back safely to Switzerland. She would now pull out a gun and point it at him. His part in the mission was over. He would be killed now.

He looked at her. She had totally lost her composure, however. This was not acting. She genuinely was flabbergasted to hear what had happened. The ISIS had used her as bait.

"It is easy to guess why you were chosen!" the Captain said.

Gabriela said, "Mr A and Steve are against each other in some way; in business perhaps. So Mr A decides that the ISIS should use the bomb to blast the first Eastern Airlines flight. Two stones in one. One, they would announce the arrival of the most powerful bomb on Earth. Second, they would permanently destroy the airlines' future. Steve would lose billions of dollars he had invested in it and would no longer be of any competition to Mr A! And guess what? Who better to trap than the unsuspecting fiancé of Steve Mehrotra herself? Should the plan fail and the bomb be traced, the first suspect would be me and then Steve! What a fucking plan! Tremendous!"

"Yes, it was; wasn't it? The pickup device stayed in Hong Kong. It was last switched on three hours before you boarded the flight. Although there were members of the Interpol who were posted in Hong Kong to trace its further activities if any, it was never put on again until date. However, the Interpol managed to intercept communication between the terrorists! We knew we were on the right track. The compressor was in the checked-in baggage of Gabriela Fabregas and was scheduled to compress the object to its Schwarzschild radius somewhere around 5:45 pm Dubai time. The target was clear. It was to blow the Eastern Airlines flight EA001."

"Then, if it was so clear, why was all the drama staged?" Rajesh alleged. "You could have found her checked-in baggage at Hong Kong or Dubai airport; identified the Compressor and spared all that happened!"

"That's where you come into the story!"

"What!"

"As I said before, the Interpol was sure that Mr A had been linked to sponsor the terrorists. *But you know these chaps!* These billionaires will never leave a clue, or they will make sure they wipe it all with all the money they have!"

"How am I involved in all this?"

"We found a weak spot in the billionaire, Mr A. After all, they are not terrorists. They too are normal people with normal emotions; except for the time when they talk business. They favour some people and hate some others." The Captain paused.

"How am I involved in all this?" Rajesh repeated. "It's still not clear!"

"Because unfortunately for him, Mr A had a friend of his on the same flight; something that he had not anticipated. Something we had not anticipated, either. We had to take the chance that he would bail him out of the flight. It was taking a chance, but it worked."

"I don't know any billionaires in the world, leave alone American billionaires!" It was Rajesh's turn to tremble.

"You don't know him as a billionaire. But special teams have traced every move of Mr A in the recent past. He and you spent a significant amount of time with each other. Mr A is none other than your long lost pal, Manish…"

Chapter 75

"No. You must be mistaken!" Rajesh said. "Manish is from a lower-middle-class family in Pune. We were neighbours. We lived in one-bedroom apartments damn it! He moved to the US in nineteen eighty-eight, and their family was not well to do in the US either; for quite some time at least... He did an MBA and now works as an academics events' organizer in Johns Hopkins in Baltimore. He is not your man. No."

The Captain laughed. "He is our man alright. He is not the man he painted himself to be. His parents had moved to the US from Pune, that's right. His father started a restaurant in New Jersey, which became quite famous. They earned decent money. His son was not so bright in school. He forced himself into a Management College, but he was not enjoying that either. He was into partying and had many girlfriends..."

"He said he had only one girlfriend, Cynthia!"

"Maybe that is right now, but it certainly wasn't true before. The turning point was when he was twenty-one. He entered his first Casino at the Atlantic City. He played Roulette..."

"How would you know that much detail of his life? You must be kidding! You can't be following him for that long!"

"Only through enquiry. It's not often that someone who is a first-time entrant into a casino wins nearly fifty thousand dollars. He was quite remembered by the staff and all the regulars there!"

"But they would have informed him that the Interpol is on the lookout for him!" Rajesh was still trying to desperately protect his friend.

"Come on. The detectives are not naïve. They will do their enquiries without revealing identities. They have their own methods for doing that! I don't know, so don't ask me how!"

"Okay…"

"Manish Kumar soon became the wonder gambler. He had some equations worked out in such a way that he always won more than he lost; turning this into a really profitable business. He had earned his surplus of one million dollars by the age of twenty-three. Besides gambling, he turned his attention to the stock market. There too, he hit the jackpot. His finances soon hit the roof. He became an angel investor and started funding small start-ups. Again, lottery; or dare I say, shrewd business analysis all through. Most of the businesses he funded were profitable.

"He was introduced to the world of weaponry by his new-found multimillionaire friends. He was now buying and selling arms to people in Nigeria and Somalia; often to both sides of the law. He had hit a personal valuation of more than a billion dollars by the age of thirty. Thereafter, he had entered the Elite group, the members of who guided him to be one of the world's most powerful decision-makers!"

"What the hell?"

"Now excuse me, people, I need to use the washroom. Ken, can you help make an extra round of coffee?"

This break was also given on purpose surely. But Gabriela also decided to use the washroom.

Introspection time again.

How things had changed in the last few minutes.

First, they had believed that they were rescued and brought here so that Rajesh could write a ground-breaking article on Science vs. religion.

Later, Rajesh was almost made to believe that Gabriela was the terrorist, who had checked-in the compressor onto the flight and she had escaped; all the way from the flight to the hotel and then to Switzerland via Qatar. Rajesh was the innocent distractor in the entire story.

Now it was quite the contrary. Gabriela was the innocent victim here. She had the bomb 'placed' into her check-in baggage by the terrorist organization. She was to check into the first flight of Eastern Airlines; an airline that belonged to her fiancé Steve Mehrotra, who was the arch-enemy of Manish Kumar. Manish Kumar had deplaned Rajesh, and Gabriela was the innocent distractor here…

Wait a minute!

Why would Manish want to deplane Gabriela of all the people?

Gabriela got back from the washroom. She was clearly upset by the recent revelations. Rajesh sensed that.

"Look, Gabriela. I swear by God! I personally am not involved at all! I only know Manish as a nine-year-old kid. It was supposed to be a 'cute' meeting between two friends who were estranged at the age of nine! I am not responsible for anything!"

To his relief, Gabriela said, "I figured as much. Your bloodsucking friend has decided to show his humanitarian side by saving your life. Paradoxical. He saves one life and almost kills hundreds of others!"

"Still, I don't get it, why did he save you? You apparently belong to the enemy party!"

The Captain returned. Ken was still in the kitchen.

"Well, Gabriela, can you answer his query?"

"It's simple! He had to deplane me. It was a good cover had the mission been unsuccessful. If there was a leak of information, and the compressor was found, it would have been found in my bag! And guess what? I had deplaned myself at a crucial time! Steve and I would have been screwed anyway!"

"Again, awesome analysis!"

It was Gabriela's turn to feel proud; although she knew she was in deep trouble. "So, it is clear that Mr A, aka Manish Kumar, had deplaned us both. Mark Andrews, Ken and you have done your bit to smuggle us to Switzerland, whereas Manish and Kabir tried to stop us from getting here."

"Manish is a financer for war! Yet he cared for his friendship and had me deplaned. Strange," Rajesh said.

"So there is some force that is as strong as money. A close friendship and a close love!"

A close friendship and a close love. He remembered Manish's girlfriend's name; Cynthia. *Did she even exist?* If she did, he would have done the same for her, he guessed. He didn't know how to judge Manish; good because he saved him or really bad because he had been and would be indirectly involved in the killing of so many people!

Gabriela intervened. "In my case, it was not money, not friendship and not love; just a fucking business deal. Rajesh's pal versus my fiancé!"

"What if I say that you were wrong?" the Captain blurted

"How could I be wrong? I don't see how I could be wrong!"

"You are wrong!"

Oh, come on! Gabriela and Rajesh knew that another twist in the tale was coming. What now? Ken entered with the tea, and there was an uncomfortable pause as he placed the teacups on the table.

"Shoot Captain!" Gabriela said sarcastically, "This story of yours is not for the faint-hearted for sure!"

Again, the Captain laughed. *It had become a trademark!* "Manish pulled you out because of the same emotion that he had for you as he had for Rajesh; true friendship and true love!"

What? Manish liked her in secret? He had a crush on her? She must have met him in one of the lavish Friday night parties that Steve threw. She met countless of Steve's business associates and even rivals. *She did not remember Manish!* "Ha! He surely knew that Steve and I are engaged to be married!"

"He knew!"

"But still, he wanted to save me because he liked me? I don't believe it. He knew I was a dead duck if the police caught me. If they hadn't caught me, I will anyway marry Steve!"

"No, you would marry Manish Kumar for sure!"

"Why do you say that?"

"Because the real name of Steve Mehrotra is Manish Kumar..."

Chapter 76

"What rubbish! No one knows Steve better than I do!" Gabriela exclaimed.

"Well, that's apparently not true, I guess!" the Captain said.

"I repeat, it's rubbish. You are telling me that my fiancé is an evil Elite group member who finances terror and war?"

"I'm telling you, your fiancé is an evil Elite group member who finances terror and war!"

"No…"

"Where did he tell you, he was born?"

"India."

"Where in India?"

"West India, he said."

"He was born in nineteen seventy-nine at the Poona Hospital in Pune. Did you know that?"

"No. Why should I know which hospital he was born! He didn't ask me which hospital I was born!"

"Well, okay. He was born as Manish Kumar. He was the childhood pal of Mr Rajesh Rajesh. As I have already told his story to you, I won't repeat it fully. He moved to New Jersey with his parents, was a poor student, and made his initial money in gambling, moving on to stocks, then angel investing and finally warfare."

"I know my fiancé is an angel investor!"

"At least he didn't lie to you on that part!"

"Why would he change his name? Don't be ridiculous!" Gabriela was in a continuous mood for negation. She was not ready to believe this at any cost.

"As you know by now, Steve aka Manish is a very emotional man when it comes to friends and family. Before they came to know from any other source, he himself told his parents about his latest business investments. And before they could reprimand him, he himself decided to move out of the house and give himself a totally different identity. He didn't want his family name to be in any defaming news if it came to that. He named himself Steve Mehrotra for that very sake. All his IDs were changed quickly, thanks to the free cash flow."

"Yeah! Sure! He told you all that! Family name and all…" Gabriela smiled with sarcasm.

"He didn't tell me. I am a nuclear scientist in Switzerland, don't forget. This is the information I have received from the investigating officers, who have received the same from the intelligence agencies of many countries. I believe they have their own methods."

"If the intelligence agencies know about him, why didn't they arrest him much before?"

"How could they? They only suspected him. No concrete evidence was ever forthcoming."

Gabriela was silent for a while.

Rajesh spoke now, "I remember Manish telling me that his girlfriend was leaving to Hong Kong the day after. He meant you, Gabriela!"

"Shit! That's all I can say!" Gabriela said.

"Wait a minute!" Rajesh said. "Why would Steve aka Manish allow the ISIS to bomb the airline that he invested in? As far as I know, he has invested heavily in it!"

"Can't you see why? He is a shrewd businessman. After the airline blew, the world would be scared of the ISIS, but be sympathetic to him. The initial few days' news would be concentrated on the bomb and the devastation. But surely, after a while, it would focus on a young billionaire who would lose a lot of money as his airline would be shut down after the jinx; the jinx of the very first flight being blasted by terrorists! The entire business world would really feel sorry for him! No one could point fingers at him for anything!"

"Why would he send the Compressor with Gabriela? If the plan had failed, she would be caught with the compressor!"

"That's what I said earlier. It was a blunder. A major blunder. Overconfidence. He and the ISIS team were sure to get the bomb on the flight in this way. They were then sure that they would easily manage to pull out the ladylove and the long-lost pal at the very last moment. This would ensure that no ISIS member was killed in a suicide mission.

"Remember, the ISIS wanted to use this as a dress rehearsal. The ISIS usually claims responsibility quite quickly after any terror event. But in this case, they didn't want to do so. They didn't want the world to know yet that they were in possession of the world's most potent bomb. So, this entire drama would ensure that the investigations would never be able to point fingers at the ISIS! It was a well-thought-out plan and was almost executed to perfection!"

Chapter 77

Finally, some clarity was being reached.

Rajesh said, "So let me get this straight. Steve Mehrotra, the fiancé of Gabriela and Manish Kumar, my childhood friend are, in fact, the same person."

"Correct," the Captain said.

"He is a horrible person. He funds terrorists so that he can create war. He asks them to blow up a flight of his own airline…"

"Not any flight, the maiden flight!"

"Yes, the maiden flight of his own airline. He also funds the getaway of Suleiman Schmidt and the Compressor from the highly secure CERN!"

"Correct."

"All this is an upfront capital business expense. His real money will come by the number of weapons he will now sell to the ISIS and the countries of the world who will be out to get rid of them."

"Yes!"

"But unforeseen things happened. Suddenly he realised that his friend Rajesh and his fiancé Gabriela are going to be on that flight!"

"Correct."

"So, he uses this fact to his advantage. He allowed the terrorists to send the bomb through Gabriela's check-in baggage so that no ISIS member directly needed to be present to do just that! The ISIS cannot be directly linked!"

"Yup."

"He then arranges for chemicals to be sprayed into the eyes of an unsuspecting duo, that is, Gabriela and me! He makes sure that we are deplaned! But what if we were not?"

"I guess he made sure you were! As per the report from the airport…"

"You received a report from Dubai airport?"

"I did not, I am just a…"

"Yeah, yeah. I know. You are just a nuclear physicist in Switzerland. The investigation team received the report and they have their ways of doing it!"

"Yes. Smart boy." The Captain smirked. "As per the report from the airport, the person who screened your passport at the gate had completely missed your red eyes. That means it was not at all severe. Steve had made sure of that. Later, the security head came to know that two passengers had conjunctivitis. This was possible because 'someone' noticed them on the CCTV on the aerobridge of the flight. *This is a really unlikely story!* It is so unlikely that someone was actively seeing all the CCTVs installed at the airport and happened 'just' to notice you! Apparently, it was someone who was bought out! The security team came to know about it when they were supposed to know about it; just before the pushback of the flight. The amazing thing that was understood later was that there was no one in the CCTV surveillance room at the moment the incident occurred! It was a pre-planned phone call by someone unknown; someone known to Manish!"

"All this, in turn, was to ensure that they do not deplane your checked-in baggage. As per security norms, a passenger who does not board the flight, their baggage will be deplaned. In your case, you had boarded the flight and were forcefully deplaned from a flight that was all ready to go. I guess, in larger airlines like Emirates, they would have removed the baggage anyway, but here they didn't! They didn't want their first flight to be delayed!"

"A costly mistake. Hundreds of passengers could have lost their lives!" Gabriela said.

"Kabir is made responsible to oversee that all this happens as per plan!" Rajesh guessed. "After we reached the hotel, he was supposed to escort us back to safety. I was supposed to be sent to India, and Gabriela was supposed to be sent back to the US. And we thought he was out to kill us! He only wanted us alive and Mark dead, I suppose!"

"But anyway, you would be suspect number one, right? They would block your passports anyway!" Ken spoke up. He had been silent for quite some time.

"Yes!" Rajesh said. "Maybe he was supposed to take us back to Steve aka Manish."

"But right before Kabir reached us, you reached Rajesh on the phone!" Gabriela said. "You made sure we panicked, trusted Mark, and made a run for it. We never had our phones with us, so Steve could never ever reach us! Excellent planning!"

"Kabir set out in our pursuit, but could never reach us! You wanted us here, and here we are!"

"Poor Mark! A sacrifice!" Gabriela cried.

"But it was odd that Manish sent Kabir Dravid of all the people in the world to rescue us! Kabir is a man who had such a torrid past with me!"

Gabriela said coolly. "It is clear. Steve had photos of me. He had none of you. The only way a terrorist could confirm both our identities was if he knew you already! Kabir bloody well knows you!"

CHAPTER 78

It was Rajesh's turn to take a washroom break.

As he got up, the doorbell rang. He looked at his watch. It was four in the morning. *It was strange that someone had come knocking at this time!* Ken got up to answer the door.

Rajesh headed towards the washroom.

Well, what a twisted story it was! His life had been completely transformed. His last few days had been a roller coaster ride. He had been from Chennai to Dubai to New York to Boston to New York to Dubai to Sharjah province to Abu Dhabi province to Qatar to Geneva to Champoussin village to St Leonard. He was now to report one of the most astonishing scientific discoveries to the world; in the Captain's words, it was the ultimate discovery so far!

They were government-protected people now. *They were no longer fugitives!*

Something was odd here.

Why were they government-protected people now? What had changed? Nothing!

Why were they fugitives in the first place?

As soon as he was done using the washroom, he ran to the hall.

At the same time, Ken came back to the hall, "The man is here, Captain!"

The Captain said, "Oh, good. Ask him to be in the drawing room, and also offer him a cup of coffee. I will be with him shortly, but please shut the door between the hall and the drawing room. I don't want him to know about our guests here! Ask him to watch TV if he wishes."

Who the hell was this guest who was so welcome so early in the morning? Gabriela had half a mind to get up and see who he was, but the Captain clearly didn't want them to be seen by the guy. Moreover, it was right to follow the Captain's wishes now! Besides, Rajesh was looking too desperate to tell her something!

Rajesh waited as Ken headed back to the drawing room and shut the door behind him.

As soon as he did that he said, "No, each time we get closer to solving the mystery, it seems stranger. There is a hitch, Captain. There is a hitch."

"What?"

"The Interpol, the Intelligence agencies and surely the Dubai police might have known that we are innocent people; even much before we were deplaned! And you, the Captain, were in the core of the people who were, in fact, trying to prevent the bombing. Why on earth was it needed to smuggle us out of the UAE the way you did? With fake passports! Via Qatar; the state which is in a strong diplomatic standoff with the UAE! We also took off on an international flight from an airport that had no immigration check, damn it!"

"Oh shit!" Gabriela said. "That's true! We were smuggled out like criminals!"

Now had the good guys and bad guys changed places again in the story?

The Captain had got them out like true fugitives; there was no doubt about that! Why had he done that? That means all that he said about being part of a team that was assisting the Interpol was bullshit, to say the least!

Ken got back into the room, carefully shutting the door between the hall and the drawing room again. He just gave a thumb's up to the Captain and sat.

"And I can tell you one thing for sure," Gabriela said. "A lot of money was spent on getting us out of the country. There was a Mercedes, a Hummer, a Land Rover, a Ferry, a chartered flight damn it and to top it all, fake Great Britain passports! All this means that you too Captain are heavily financed! You, Mark and Ken! Why? Oh, why were we smuggled out?"

"I can give you one clue. We were not heavily financed for what we did now."

"You were! Bombardier chartered flight from an unknown airport strip. You were financed enough to help in illegal emigration from Qatar as well!"

"No, we were not! Does this information help?"

"Oh come on Captain..." Gabriela said.

Rajesh intervened. "Wait! That means... does that mean...?" He went silent after that. Some strange possibility had crossed his mind.

This wasn't apparent to Gabriela, "What Rajesh? What does that mean?"

"Mark was not the Captain's man! He was Manish's man!"

Chapter 79

Gabriela almost decided to call it a day. She could not digest these twists and turns anymore. Each and every time she thought the mystery in the story was solved, a new turn came in. "Mark was Manish's man? He was not a part of your team?"

"Absolutely spot on!" the Captain said. "Only Manish aka Steve could finance this!"

"Do you mean that Steve wanted us to flee the country like fugitives?"

"Yes. Both of you were deplaned. The bomb was supposed to have killed all passengers on board. The Dubai police would anyway round you both up and block your passports immediately! He had to get you out instantly!"

Rajesh said, "It makes no sense. You called me in the hotel Radan and asked me to escape. You guided us to Mark. Where is Manish involved in all this?"

The Captain laughed, "Did you recognize my voice when you saw me first in my place? Is my voice the same you heard on the phone in Dubai?"

Rajesh paused. He didn't remember the voice, but he was sure of the accent. "I remember the accent very well! It is your accent!"

"What is special in the accent?"

"Your accent…it is Americanized, but you still have the *desi* twang. You said scheduled with a 'sh' sound, not an 'sk' sound!

"Well, Gabriela do you have anything to say to Rajesh about this?"

Gabriela froze. "Rajesh, Steve definitely has the same accent as Captain. He too says scheduled with a 'sh' sound."

Come to think of it, Manish sounded bang similar to the Captain! Rajesh's head was reeling now. "You mean, it was Manish who had first messaged me and then called me? Why did he decide to call himself 'Captain' of all names? How did his name match the nickname of the famous scientist who invented the Compressor? How can it be such a coincidence? I don't believe you!"

The Captain laughed aloud, "Let's put it this way. I copied his nickname. We picked it up from all the intelligence inputs that we had. Steve Mehrotra uses the code name Captain when he speaks to his connections who in turn connect to the ISIS!"

"But you are Captain Naveen Sharma, retired from a short service commission in the Indian Army! Don't tell me that is not true!"

"It is not true!"

"Why are you guys lying so much? Who are you then?"

"Okay, chaps! I retired not as Captain but as Lieutenant Colonel in the Indian Army. I was always known as Naveen to Suleiman and Ken. The name Captain stuck only in this mission!"

"What is this mission? Why were you called Captain?"

"To create confusion! The Captain was supposed to be the person who saved you and the plane from crashing! The Captain who saved you was Manish and the Captain who saved the flight was I!"

"How did we land up with you then? Why did Kabir kill Mark then, if they both are terrorists? Why did Kabir try to kill us? Why was he out to get us the whole time? He followed us all over the place! The Dubai police captured him! Ken told us that his freedom was barter to some famous person's kidnapping. He too is a highly connected terrorist!"

"You analyse it!" The Captain was playing with them.

They had to follow his rules.

"Mark Andrews directly reported to Steve. Steve contacted me and asked us to flee with Mark. Our phones were left behind at the hotel as they would give our location away," Rajesh said.

"Right."

"Mark drove us diligently away from the Dubai police. Oh yeah. Initially, he did not seem to have any idea about Kabir, for sure! He gathered knowledge from the Captain only later! Makes any sense, Gabriela?"

"No." Gabriela shook her head. She was too confused at this moment.

"Whatever. Mark's car changes were immaculate. He made sure that neither Kabir nor the Dubai police ever managed to get anywhere close to us. He managed to get us to Qatar on the ferry, where the Dubai police could not follow us; whereas, they managed to get hold of Kabir.

"Kabir walked away from the police in return for the release of some famous personality and resumed the chase. Meanwhile, we had managed to escape to Switzerland and we reached Champoussin. We were to meet the Captain, when suddenly Kabir reappeared out of nowhere, shot Mark and was about to shoot us when Ken blasted his car between Kabir and us. We made the escape while Kabir fired two rounds, still trying to kill us!

"If Mark was Manish's man, then he must be a criminal. If Ken is the nuclear scientist, which I hope is true, then he is the good guy. Then who the hell is Kabir, the cold-blooded murderer?

"Oh, God!" Gabriela said. "Please say there is another twist in the story where we now realise that Steve and Mark are indeed nice people!"

<h1 style="text-align:center">CHAPTER 80</h1>

"Let me ask you guys another teaser question," Ken spoke up. "Why do you think the Captain and the intelligence agencies decided not to remove the bomb from the flight before it took off? Did you guys guess that yet?"

Wait! Hadn't this question been answered before?

Rajesh remembered asking this question an hour before to the Captain. If the 'intel' was sure that the bomb was in Gabriela's checked-in baggage, why wasn't it screened and removed at Hong Kong Airport itself?

To that, the Captain had answered that that's where Rajesh came into the picture. For that matter, he had also meant that's where Gabriela's presence on the flight was also important. The intelligence agencies had hoped that Manish Kumar aka Steve Mehrotra would pull out Gabriela, his fiancé and Rajesh, his long-lost pal, from the flight that was about to be bombed.

"You said that they hoped that we both were deplaned before take-off."

Ken said, "Yes. The timing was crucial. What happened next was not necessarily as per our plan. We wanted to save everyone, but unfortunately, we lost two men!

"Officer Shahid Aziz was responsible for carrying out this part of the operation. He is the security in chief of the Dubai Airport. He already had sounded the monarchies of Dubai and Sharjah of his plan. He got the flight back in time and had deplaned the passengers in time. He had arranged for a quick take-off and landing in an isolated airstrip in

Sharjah. But there were inordinate delays. The original pilots chickened out, standby pilots had to be arranged. There were some further crazy delays like some officer being in the flight when he was not supposed to be there, the two standby pilots tried calling their relatives, the doors of the flight were not locked just before take-off, and most importantly, time was lost in teaching the younger pilot about the controls. All this led to the loss of life when they should not have been dead!"

"Shit!" Gabriela felt sorry for the two innocent men who had lost their lives. "Why was it so important that we were deplaned by Steve?"

The Captain took over. "As I had said earlier, it was long known that Steve Mehrotra was involved in financing wars and terror. The only hitch was that he left no proof whatsoever. The Interpol suspected that black money flowed freely in and out of his estate in New Jersey. The Interpol believed he had massive sales in the war in Crimea, in the fight between terror and the government in Nigeria, the same in Somalia, and most recently, in the civil war in Syria. This was possibly his first investment in the world versus the ISIS war.

"As I said, it was at least six months back that the Intel had suspected his hand in the same. This was confirmed when Suleiman Schmidt was grilled in his Santa Monica residence. But again, there was no solid proof. Suleiman could only say that a billionaire from New Jersey was involved. He never knew the person. He could not be used as a witness in the court of law.

"The Interpol had picked up that the ISIS was going to use the bomb in a flight from Dubai. They also knew that Steve might have been involved. But still, there was no connection."

"Hmmm…" Rajesh said.

"Then, as I said, the ISIS and he made their blunder. The flight they had chosen to bomb was the one that had you two in it. As we knew, Steve was a little cranky when it got to friends and family. So, we sure hoped that the terrorists and he would get you both out of the plane, and at the same time, they would ensure the bomb was on the flight.

"So, one thing was sure. Steve Mehrotra, after deplaning you, would make sure that you two were smuggled out quickly and efficiently, knowing jolly well that you two would be prime suspects. He had to get you both to a relatively isolated place and make you stay there for a while. Then he would have ensured, after a while, that you got back to your countries after a short break with false identities after the period of intense surveillance was over. That's what he would do to save you both so that you guys could go on to live safely!"

"And, of course, either he had to contact you over the phone or appear personally to explain what was going on..."

"Holy shit!" Gabriela said. Rajesh and she had guessed what was coming up.

"The plan was simple now. The Interpol had to wait for you to deplane so that they could follow your path; the path that was chosen by Captain Steve Mehrotra and Mark Andrews. You would simply have to lead them to the place where Steve could finally be caught red-handed, either personally, or because he used the phone or the internet to get in touch with you!"

"Oh! That means the Dubai police were already on our tail the moment we left the airport! And that's why the Dubai police never caught us!" Rajesh exclaimed.

"The Dubai police had no clue about what happened until then. The Dubai police never caught you because Steve had planned the escape to perfection!"

"What, you just said the Interpol would follow us!"

"Well yes, but had the Dubai police been informed beforehand, they would have the moral duty to block your exit from the country. Otherwise, it would be seen as treason. It was crucial that Officer Shahid Aziz knew only that part of the story where he had to bring back the flight without casualties. That's it. Nothing more. Nothing less."

"Then who was tailing us? And who on Earth was the maverick killer Kabir Dravid?"

"The Interpol had to choose an agent who would be seen as a person who would instil some fear in you as if he was out to get you both. They chose one of the best Research and Analysis Wing Members from India, especially because of the torrid past he had had with one of you, Officer Sachin Karad."

CHAPTER 81

Gabriela couldn't connect immediately, but she realised it when she saw Rajesh freeze. "Sachin Karad. That is the real name of Kabir Dravid! Kabir Dravid is a cop! I cannot believe it!"

"A very fine one at that!" Ken said.

"Why did he try to kill us at Champoussin?" Rajesh asked.

"Who better to answer this question than the man in the drawing room?" The Captain said. "Ken, can you bring him in?"

Both Gabriela and Rajesh had guessed it. In came Officer Sachin Karad aka Kabir Dravid. Gabriela sat still, but Rajesh's reflexes were to get up and be in a position to make a run for it if necessary.

"Hello, Rajesh! It's a long time since we came face-to-face!" Sachin said.

Rajesh was too shocked and a tad terrified. "H…Hello Sachin!"

Sachin went up to Gabriela and offered his hand for a handshake. "Officer Sachin Karad, Indian Police Service."

"Officer." Gabriela shook his hand. She too was in disbelief.

"Nice blow, Rajesh. Nineteen ninety-six it was!" Sachin stated.

Rajesh shivered. "Sachin… officer Sachin, I cannot express in words how sorry I am for what happened that day! It was all in a fit of anger! I couldn't forgive myself for years after I heard what happened to you! To come to think of it, you could have had me jailed for what happened!"

"Not jailed, remember? You were less than seventeen when that happened. You would have been sent to a Juvenile reform home!"

"Shit man! It was a grievous injury! I can still see you suffer! I am feeling really shit now!"

"Dude, let's not talk about it. Remember, I was holding a bicycle chain in front of Wasim Shaikh's face. I never intended to smash his face, but I did want to intimidate him. It was absolutely wrong on my part to do that! You did what your conscience told you to do. You expected your friend's face to be smashed into a permanent deformity, and you acted as an act of defence. Let's forget it, man; right here. We cannot be sure as to who was morally right and who was wrong that day. We all behaved like pricks."

"Are you sure?"

"If I give you a hug now, will that convince you?" Sachin didn't wait for an answer. He moved towards Rajesh and hugged him. He then gave him a pat on the back with his left hand and a thumb's up with the right hand.

This seemed to ease the tension a little bit. Gabriela too felt better. She was dying to hear Sachin's story. "Care to solve some of the mysteries?" she asked.

"My assignment was clear. I had to follow you everywhere. Also, I had to make my presence felt to you so that you could panic and make a run for it... right into the hands of Manish Kumar.

"I had to make myself visible to you at the boarding gate. I did that. After that, I had an impromptu setting with a cleaner from the Airlines, Ramprakash...." He went on to explain how he and Ramprakash had exchanged places; and what offer he made to Ramprakash to get that done. "After that, I came out of the boarding area and I had to again make sure you saw me at the airport. At the Radan, I purposely held the gun.

"I had to plan in such a way that I created enough commotion when the policeman and the security came into my room for you to come out of your room and see what was happening. To be very frank, I really didn't know how I was going to achieve that. But somehow, by a great stroke of luck, you yourself walked out of your room when they were there. Neither of them knew who I actually was!"

"Shit! That was when Manish called me on the phone; calling himself as Captain!"

"We figured that as much. We had Manish's every line tapped. He was calling from England at that time. We almost knew he was going to haul you guys over to Europe, we had guessed England first."

"His number began with plus four-four," Rajesh remembered aloud.

"We do not know that number, but he did use his US number to send you WhatsApp messages if you remember. That's the number we had!"

"Oh shit!"

"You would have realised by now that he has multiple numbers. The number that he gave you when you were in the US was also different. You spoke to Manish on the day you left from Boston…"

"Oh my holy word, you had my phone tapped too…"

"Not yours, we had all his phones tapped."

"Okay…"

"Now, we knew you were going to be shuttled out of Radan. We had informers all over the place. I soon realised that you almost instantaneously had made a run for it with the concierge fellow Mark Andrews in the black Mercedes. You guys didn't give me time to shower man!" Sachin laughed.

Rajesh and Gabriela just smiled.

"Luckily, I had my car, and I had my sources. I could know which roads you had taken. I was in hot pursuit, but for sure Mark and Manish had planned an excellent getaway. After all, they too are masters in what they do!"

He went on to explain how he met officer Irfan, how he realised that they were on a Hummer, how he saw the flight disappear without a trace in front of his eyes and how he traced that the Hummer had entered the dunes. He went on to explain the great difficulty he had experienced in the camp, where Mark had changed yet another car.

"Wait a minute!" Rajesh asked. "Why was it necessary for the intelligence agencies to make sure that we knew that *you, Sachin Karad,* were following us? Couldn't they do it discretely?"

"Good question. Remember, at this moment, the Dubai police didn't know what we were up to. So our resources were limited. We didn't have enough people patrolling Dubai. So we had hoped that you buckle under pressure and make some silly mistakes on the way. Also, the second part of the agreement needed me."

"What agreement?"

"I'll tell you."

"Okay."

"Actually, there were some nervous moments before that. I had followed the tracks of the vehicle that you were in from the camp in the desert to the road, but after that, there was no way of guessing where you were heading. Luckily, the Captain had guys posted at the tollbooth. They spotted you in the Land Rover entering the city of Dubai again. I was back in the chase after that. I did a car change on the way, but by then I guess I already had the Dubai police on my tail. They knew the moves I was making, and they were playing the same game as me. They were tailing me so that I could lead to you guys.

"After an hour on the road, the Captain informed me again that they had spotted you entering Al Hamra. I followed you there just to realise that you guys had parked the Land Rover. Your footsteps led to the jetty, which made me realise that you had escaped by sea.

"Just then the Dubai police arrived. They realised that they had lost you, but they had to capture me. They did. The time had come. Officer Shahid Aziz had to be informed of the plan, and so did the defence and home ministers of the UAE. As soon as they realised the plan and the need to keep it top secret, they played their role. The deputy defence minister played a role where two actors captured him, who acted their roles of being goons to perfection. They managed to release me, without Officer Irfan, the chap who arrested me suspecting a thing!"

"Ha Ha!" Gabriela laughed. "The defence minister and the home minister allowed us to escape although at that moment we were suspect number one for the dastardly terrorist act against the sovereignty of the country! A likely story!"

"The Interpol took full responsibility to declare the two of you innocent. We knew for sure the hand of the ISIS here, who for reasons of their own, didn't want to claim responsibility for the terror act. They usually did so immediately, but they didn't want the world to know that they were in possession of the world's most powerful weapon!

"Also, we assured them that we were to use your help unknowingly to lead us to the financer in chief of the terrorist attack that was a threat to the sovereignty of the UAE. We also gave them a written promise that Manish would be first prosecuted in the UAE, after his capture!"

Gabriela shuddered. It was clear that Steve, her fiancé, was now a bad man. In fact, she had broken the engagement already in her mind. He was no longer her 'fiancé'. But still, the thought of him being grilled by the Dubai police and facing a certain death penalty gave her the creeps.

"Meanwhile, we traced Manish who used his phone from Geneva. We had people posted immediately at Geneva airport. We knew that you could enter Geneva only by air; as road or rail would take you ages. Also, intelligence agencies had already picked up a flight on its way from Qatar, which was not registered for take-off from the Al Hamad airport at Doha. Yes, we still work in close coordination with Qatar police. We don't have a standoff with them!"

"Hmmm…"

"Usually, in such situations, the flight is asked to land or return back to the country of origin, but we had to allow the flight to go on. We needed it to land in Geneva. The immigration officer who cleared you in Geneva immediately recognized you three!"

"What!" Rajesh laughed. "We thought we had fooled him easily!"

"Not at all. He fooled you guys easily! We tailed you all the way to Champoussin Village. There came the second main blunder of Manish and co; where we could consider ourselves lucky. You guys took a whole day of rest; which allowed me to catch up with you!"

"Had Manish met us earlier, he would have had us and then your mission would have failed? But I thought you had people tailing us all the while!"

"The 'agreement' would have failed. As I said, I had to be there in the picture."

"Picture this. You were going to meet the 'Captain' aka Manish Kumar. Mark, the saviour, was going to usher you to his room. At the same time, the apparent villain of the story, Kabir Dravid, would gun down Mark the saviour, and then point the gun at you. Only then Ken could make his entry and save you from Kabir, and bring you here to St Leonard!"

"You shot Mark point blank!" Gabriela recalled the gory incident that they had witnessed.

"Mark Andrews, the man with whom you spent almost a day, was one of the leading commanders of the ISIS. He deserved what he got. This was the arrangement. We get to shoot Mark, Ken gets to stage a drama to rescue you guys from me, after which I fired two shots in the air to make you think I am shooting you. The second part of the staged act could begin now. We got our man, Manish Kumar aka Steve Mehrotra. Ken and Captain Naveen got you; to help them achieve what they wanted to achieve."

CHAPTER 82

Gabriela felt a chill go down her spine. Steve Mehrotra had been captured. He was the person whom she had loved. It was unbelievable. He was the sponsor of terror. He sponsored the ISIS' weapon of mass destruction. He would then sell arms to the people, who in turn would leave no stone unturned to destroy the ISIS. He would pocket billions of dollars in profit, but thousands of people would die for his profit.

Considering the fact that Steve had gone an extra mile to save Rajesh and her from certain death, she was sure that he actually loved her too.

He would have kept her happy throughout her life.

But now, of course, all this was not possible. She now hated him. And besides, he would not be seen in the free world again. He would at least get a life term, if not a death sentence in the UAE.

"Steve has been captured and would be put to death, I am sure!" she said. Her voice sounded dejected, though she didn't still understand why. That guy deserved to be killed.

"No, not immediately. We have to hold him for some more time here in Switzerland. He has to finish a job for us," the Captain said.

"I don't understand. Why will he finish a job for you?" Gabriela stated, as a matter of fact.

"We hope he will. After all, he is not a terrorist. He won't be able to face the threat of immediate death with zero emotion!" The Captain laughed. For a moment it seemed Captain Naveen was the villain and Steve was the tortured soul.

"What job, Captain?" Rajesh asked. "What is that you have brought us here for?"

"For that, you would have to hear my story out!"

"We are all ears, Captain," said Rajesh. It was clear that fatigue was catching up. It was six in the morning.

"Mine is a short crisp story; enough time for you to hear it and fall asleep after a while. I was in the National Defence Academy in the years two thousand to two thousand and two. Right there in your hometown, Pune!"

Rajesh was suddenly a bit excited. *Really? Had he mentioned it already before? But of course, he was an engineer from the Indian Army! He had to be from the NDA, Pune! That means his story intertwines with mine somewhere! Or perhaps it is related to Sachin's life. For that matter, it could be related to Manish, who was also from Pune. It could be related to the Great Guru Amar, damn it!*

"I met my fiancé at a social gathering at the Poona Club…"

Oh Wow! A romantic twist to the story!

"I used to call her *Pari*. *Pari* means 'fairy' in Hindi." The Captain explained the meaning to make sure Gabriela and Ken were in the loop. He was sure Rajesh and Sachin knew what he meant!

"Wow! I can see from your expressions that she meant a lot to you!" Rajesh said.

"She still means a lot to me…"

Rajesh bit his lip. He had assumed that the Captain was now one scientific bookworm with no romantic inclination, except to his beloved invention, the Compressor. "Sorry!"

"Never mind! Well yes, she does mean a lot to me. Things were going great guns between us. At the NDA, we used to be let out once a week. I used to meet her each time we were let out of training. We used to meet often at Main Street or at *Chandni Chowk*.

Main Street and *Chandni Chowk*! Rajesh remembered the time he had spent with Rakhee in the same places!

"It was soon evident that she meant the world to me. I was ready to accept her as my life partner. So was she. We planned to inform our parents."

"And they opposed?" Sachin asked. It was clear that he too was hearing this story for the first time.

"On the contrary, not at all. My parents and hers were absolutely in sync. The match was made in heaven."

Wow!

"But as you must have guessed by now, the match never happened."

"Why?" Gabriela asked.

"Because of what happened in the summer of two thousand and two. Pari had fallen trap to an addiction worse than weed or cocaine…"

"What! She was into drugs?" Gabriela gasped.

"Drugs would have been easier to handle. She had fallen into a far greater trap; a trap that swallowed many a youngster's ambitions!"

What was this now? Rajesh's mind had stopped thinking. It had been a long night thus far. But what the Captain said next made him alert immediately.

"*Pari* had first visited the fucking ashram of the bloody fraudster, the Great Guru Amar!"

There came the connection! Rajesh sat up. Sachin had his eyes wide open. Gabriela scratched her head.

"Until then, I had only heard stories of youth being trapped in the ashram. They gave money in thousands and served as cheap labour. We also heard rumours of young girls being exploited sexually, although this was never proven… But this was a shocker. Within a matter of two weeks, *Pari*, my Pari, decided to give up 'worldly' things and decided to become a monk. She had been thoroughly brainwashed!"

"There was no amount of coaxing that her parents or I could do; we never got her back. She was thoroughly trapped."

Rajesh shuddered. He too hated this Great Guru. He now hated him more.

"I'm sure you sought police help?" Sachin asked.

"Of course, we did. But what was the use? There was no law banning adults to join the Ashram. They were doing so on their own conscious will. None of them were forced or locked inside! They could roam in and out freely! Besides, the Guru had never done anything illegal in the public eye! There was no case that could be made!"

"Shit!"

The Captain's changing expression said it all. Even as he just spoke out his past life, it was evident from his demeanour as to how much he hated the Great Guru Amar for what had happened. Unknowingly, he was trying to bend the spoon in his hands and break it as he spoke.

He actually managed to do the same. "My life was shattered. I never had a fight with the girl of my life, yet she split ways with me. For me, it was suddenly like the end of the world. My parents and friends tried to convince me otherwise. They wanted me to get on with life, convincing me that I would find another girl.

"My first posting after my training was at the Siachen Glacier. I thought that would be good for me, as I would be far away from the city of Pune. I would surely forget *Pari*. But no! It had the opposite effect on me. At Siachen, we, the members of the Indian Army kept the post in extreme weather conditions. The temperature was minus forty degrees Celsius. The living conditions were extreme yet we managed to keep the enemy at bay always. We could do this here, but right within the heart of the country, a prick had managed to take away the love of my life and I was not able to do anything about it. My ego had been completed battered. I wanted this Great Guru Amar gone at all costs.

"After I finished my posting at Siachen and was posted in Delhi, I tried my best to write articles and publish in various other blogs against the blind faith for Amar. But you should have guessed it by now. He was too powerful a man. I failed miserably."

"Shit. Shit. Shit." Gabriela repeated.

"Further salt was rubbed into my wounds. Have you heard of 'Rudradevi', Rajesh?"

"I think she is the assistant of the Great Guru Amar, isn't she?"

"Haven't you seen her closely?"

"Nope. She was in the meeting at Coimbatore, the one that I had to cover for my TV channel, which first turned me against the Great Guru. But she was far, and I didn't give her a second look."

"Well, do give her a proper look. She is, in fact, my *Pari*, promoted right up to that level! I wanted to rip the Guru apart personally I tell you.

"I finished my short service commission in the army in two thousand and ten. I could have got into a great job anywhere with my work experience in the Military Engineering Services. However, I had already made my mind up. I would do anything it takes to bring the Great Guru down. I thought I would join the media, but later on, I decided against it. I thought then I would join the Department of Science and Technology of the Indian Government and do anything that helps disprove what the Great Guru stood for.

"The opening at CERN was fantastic for me. I, for once, had received international backing to disprove what the Guru was preaching all the time. I could now use science to disprove Creation. And I was going to do it. I was going to recreate the Big Bang and bang the aspirations of the Great Guru Amar. And for that, Gabriela and Rajesh, you guys are going to be the torchbearers..."

Chapter 83

The Great Guru Amar read it out again.

He had heard it live on TV the last night. Now it appeared to flash on all TV channels and news apps.

A young reporter from the Channel IBC news, Rajesh, had spoken. He had spoken on behest of the Professor Naveen Reddy; the Indian professor from CERN, Switzerland. Professor Naveen Reddy, as promised, had decided to throw open the challenge to the Great Guru Amar.

He still could not understand as to why he was one of the targets of this maverick professor. The professor had decided to challenge only the Pope and him. *He could have challenged any religious leader in the world, couldn't he? Why was he after his life?*

He snapped back to reality. He read the news clipping on the IPad.

Astrophysicist challenges religion; A direct attack on the Great Guru Amar

Sources from the news channel IBC have revealed what would surely shake some foundations of belief in the Almighty. Journalist R. Rajesh from Channel IBC news spoke on behest of the nuclear physicist, Professor Captain Naveen Reddy, scientist of Indian origin, working at the Centre for Nuclear Research in Europe. According to Rajesh, the Professor has decided to reveal the ultimate victory of Science over Religion. He will reveal the exact process of how the Big Bang occurred; in a public demonstration. He would thereby prove without a doubt that it was possible that all matter was created by a point of singularity, and thereby directly disprove that God had created the universe as it stands today.

It has already been claimed as one of the largest discoveries of humankind.

What is really intriguing is that he has decided to reveal the same in India, and has directly challenged the Great Guru Amar. The Great Guru Amar as we all know has been recognized by millions of Indians to be the direct messenger of God.

Rajesh revealed the cryptic message sent by the Professor to the Great Guru Amar and said that the Professor expects the Great Guru to decode the same and be present to witness the great spectacle.

The Professor has said, sic, After the Sun enters the constellation of Pisces this year, on the day Venus will align itself at 3:00 am at the '3:00 am' position of the horizon, the origin of the Universe will be revealed at the temple of 'Creator' in the state of Tamil Nadu at Sunrise for the Hindus. On the same day, at Sunrise, the Christians can witness the same in the longitude that is half the distance from the prime meridian as the temple of Tamil Nadu is from the Indian meridian.

The Professor has clearly teased the Great Guru Amar to use his religious knowledge to decrypt this complex message. He expects the Guru to accept defeat or do something to contradict his findings.

As to why the Professor picked the Great Guru Amar to be the saviour of religion, it still has to be seen.

The Great Guru Amar turned off his IPad.

He had to plan his next course of action.

He could gather religious and political support and greatly criticize this anti-religious act. He could influence public demonstrations against the same. He could get people to riot. *But wait! Isn't it what the Professor wanted?* He wanted him to fall hard in public opinion. *What if his revelation was so stunning that it would actually silence the religious world?*

He had to act more maturely.

He had to rather preach peace and possibly accept publicly that the Big Bang had, in fact, occurred. The Pope had already done it four years back. He only had to make people believe that the Almighty had orchestrated the Big Bang. He had to contradict what he had been preaching for years; that God had created man; and the Earth and the animals. He had to accept that all of it came from atoms and quarks.

But he had to solve the crypt of the Professor as well...

Oh, who on Earth is he? Why does he want to play around with my life?

As if God had heard him directly, Rudradevi entered the room and answered his query.

"*Guruji,* I know this Professor. Naveen is the person that I was engaged to, before I entered the Ashram. He is probably trying to take revenge. I promise on you that I will always stand by you. *Jai Shri Ram.*"

CHAPTER 84

"He will be taken care of. I promise." The Guru was assured.

Two days back, the Guru had consulted his astrologist friends to decrypt the message. However, this was the age of social media. The cryptic message sent by the professor was no secret. It had already been made public.

Before his astrologist friends came up with an answer, hundreds of people had already posted their opinions online.

Most came up with the same solution.

'After the sun enters the constellation of Pisces...'

That meant the time that was referred to was after March the fourth.

'The Temple of the Creator in Tamil Nadu.'

It meant the temple of Lord Brahma at the town of Tiruchirappalli or Trichy in short. Lord Brahma was believed to be the legendary God of creation. In fact, many people in India used the acronym GOD to describe the Gods of Generation, Operation and Destruction; in other words Lord Brahma, Lord Vishnu and Lord Shiva respectively.

So the next calculation was simple. They had to find out when Venus would be visualized at the three o'clock position at the horizon at three am at Trichy.

This was going to happen on March the sixteenth of this year, 2019.

The time and place where the Professor's revelations were going to happen were clear.

The Hindu world would witness the revelation at the temple of Brahma at Trichy on March the sixteenth at sunrise.

From the calculations provided, the Christian world was going to witness the revelations on the same day in the town called 'Bath' which was to the west of London.

For the Great Guru Amar, it was simple.

He had to have a plan A and a plan B.

He went through plan B in his mind first.

Plan A would be a failure. He would then admit to the world that the Big Bang had actually occurred. The Professor would be able to prove it. There was a Big Bang. All matter arose from this point of singularity. Quarks were made first, then electrons and photons, then atoms, then molecules, larger matter and then stars and planets. On the Earth, by random chance, the particles came together in such a way that DNA and RNA were formed, and then cells came into being. Hundreds of millions of years of evolution led to human beings. Humans were all part of the singularity that was the Big Bang.

But he would state clearly that this no way disputed God's presence. Humans had merely misunderstood His role thus far. Humans had believed that God directly created the first people; for example, Adam and Eve. But now they have come to understand better.

What had led to the Big Bang? What had happened before that? In fact, there is no doubt that God existed because this level of planning in the Universe could have only happened with divine intervention; the Genius of Lords Brahma, Vishnu and Shiva.

The Guru had no doubt his explanation may come under scrutiny; especially if the professor made some really startling revelations. But at least, it would ensure that the world's religious leaders unite for his views and would create a strong counter-intuitive.

Nonetheless, he hoped that plan A worked.

He had to get rid of the professor; for the greater good of religion and humanity in general. He needed someone to execute the same.

To remain powerful, he had to be connected to powerful people in the world; some good and some bad. But for sure, his actions would be under strict scrutiny now. He could not contact the really famous people, although he was a close friend with many of them. He needed support from a powerful yet inconspicuous source.

It was indeed God sent when one of his close 'professional' associates called him; he was the ideal man to do the job, and he had volunteered himself.

In the previous decade, the Guru had supplied a large amount of unaccounted cash to this gentleman. This person was powerful. He was powerful enough to sway media and political parties all over India and some parts of the world to speak good, and only good, about the Great Guru Amar.

This gentleman was inconspicuous to the eyes of the world. He was the Indian borne US Billionaire; Steve Mehrotra.

CHAPTER 85

Gabriela was in London.

Rajesh was here, where it mattered the most, in Tamil Nadu. He was on his way from Chennai to Trichy in his press van. His colleague cameraman, Senthil, was delighted to have him back after the long leave. However, Senthil was more excited about the news they were going to cover.

As far as Senthil was concerned, it was a crazy scientist who was challenging what he was taught since he was a child. He believed in God, but he was one of those who personally didn't like the Great Guru Amar, which made him someone who had a mindset similar to Rajesh.

For Rajesh, it was something else. An army man turned scientist wanted to win his love back. For that purpose, he had gone on to discover science's greatest revelations so far. He was going to prove to the world as to how science and not religion explains how the entire universe, including humans, came into existence. It was going to be a fitting climax of the entire turmoil of his life in the month of January.

He had already become famous when he was the one who revealed that Professor Naveen would challenge the Great Guru Amar. The TRP of his channel had soared, and the boss was going to hand him a handsome bonus and promotion.

He had to handle more fame today. The Professor would release his press note to him first before the others. *That was great!*

His thoughts wandered back to January and the entire story played back on his mind. *The trip to Trichy was long anyway!* He remembered the happenings in New York. *How thrilled he was to meet Manish!*

Little did he know that his childhood friend had lied to him! Manish was a billionaire, the sponsor of terror and war. He remembered the conversations with Ken, the time with Gabriela at the Dubai airport and the real unpleasant incidents aboard the Eastern Airlines flight. Then he visualized Sanjay Sharan, the valiant operations manager airport, who was no more. He gulped.

He remembered seeing Kabir aka Sachin enter the flight and leave it too. His thoughts then raced to the time at the Radan hotel; Mark, the supposed 'saviour', the car racing and the car changing in Dubai, Sharjah, Abu Dhabi and the coast of the UAE, the ferry drive, the easy escape from Qatar in a chartered flight, the immigration at Geneva, the travel to Champoussin, the shootout, the travel to St Leonard, the tour to the CERN and the time spent with Captain, Ken and Sachin at the former's house.

Gabriela had been with him throughout. She was devastated, to say the least. She had planned to marry Steve Mehrotra, who turned out to be one of the most wanted sponsors of crime in the entire world! She was in England to help Professor Naveen and Rajesh cover the news piece the same day. But after that, she had to re-gather her life and start all over again.

He liked her. That was as simple as that. But he was unsure whether the US-born person of Argentine origin, 'almost married to a billionaire' type of girl would ever reciprocate his feelings. He was a middle-class man in Chennai living in a two-bedroom apartment. *Some feelings were better to remain a dream.*

Fate had got them together for a brief while, that's it. *What had the Captain said?* He was in the story for three reasons and she was in it for one reason.

He was there for the three following reasons, he counted. One. He was the childhood friend of Manish aka Steve. Two. He was on the flight and was almost sure to be saved by Manish. Three. He was a reporter who covered the Great Guru Amar, a personal enemy of the Captain.

Gabriela was in it for one reason. She was the fiancé of Steve Mehrotra and was also on the flight; sure to be saved.

Wait a minute!

Point numbers one and two for him were of the *same* significance as the single point for Gabriela! The Captain had made a mistake. There was no other way he was involved. Maybe he also was from

Pune. *Could that be a valid point? Unlikely! The Captain had surely made a mistake!*

Or... perhaps there was surely some other connection, which he was missing. Had he covered something about space and time in his life? Probably he had. He would look up his archives after he got back home.

Now, the moment of glory needed to be enjoyed.

Chapter 86

To be very frank, Rajesh hadn't expected this. He had expected hundred or maximum two hundred people near the Brahma temple today, but he was wrong; horribly wrong. There were probably five thousand people at the gathering. Many science enthusiasts, religious persons and media players had made it to the ground zero. A striking revelation was to be made, and fewer people wanted to give it a miss. The last time Rajesh had seen five thousand people together was possibly at Times Square in New York. *It was crazy!*

He had to give credit to the mayor of Trichy. The mayor had anticipated this and thus provided space to stand, water and adequate lighting. He had arranged a dais for a press conference, where Professor Captain Naveen Kumar would give a short interview. He had neatly arranged an area for the media and also a place where the religious leaders could sit and debate. There was a microphone in the latter area too.

The time for sunrise was nearing. What perplexed Rajesh and the entire crowd alike was that neither the Professor nor the Great Guru Amar had made their appearance yet. They expected something of an extraordinary first appearance.

Rajesh waited at the designated area for him. It was surprisingly warm already. The summer was yet to begin.

A hand touched him on the shoulder from the back. *Was it the Captain?* A chill of excitement went down his spine. They hadn't met for two months. Rajesh turned around.

It wasn't him. It was a policeman. "Are you Rajesh Rajesh?" he asked in Tamil.

"Yes, sir."

"The Police Commissioner wants you to meet him in his van now!"

"But it is time for the Professor's statement!"

"The Professor has requested this. As you know, he will give the first interview to you before the public knows about this. Your cameraman too has to come."

Rajesh's angst immediately turned to joy. He rushed behind the policeman, asking Senthil to follow him.

The van was parked in the next street. There were people all over, but the area around the van had been cordoned off just a little bit.

Rajesh's heart raced as he entered the van. He never remembered a day when he was so excited. He was going to meet the Captain, and also be the first to film what the Captain had to say to the world.

His excitement deflated a bit. Only the Commissioner of Police, Palanivel, sat in the van. Rajesh had interviewed him before and hence recognized him easily. Senthil also squeezed in with his camera.

"Good morning, sir!" Rajesh said.

"Good morning, Rajesh!"

Rajesh sounded impatient. "Where is Professor Naveen?"

"Relax. He has asked me to give the first press interview, live, on your channel. Then he will speak to you in the van. After me, it will be by the mayor to the public and then him to the public."

Some stupid protocol had to be followed here too, is it? Nonsense! Rajesh wanted to hear the Captain speak, but he had no choice. He had to follow the protocol that the dignitaries had set.

"Okay, sir! Senthil can you ready the mikes?"

A visibly upset Senthil did the same as asked for. Soon, the camera was ready to roll for the live coverage. Rajesh caught a glimpse of the Sunrays. The Sunrise was due in a minute. "Ready when you are ready, sir!"

"I'm ready." The Commissioner gave a huge sigh. The normally cool and composed Palanivel was visibly nervous. Rajesh wondered why.

The camera rolled.

Rajesh spoke first. "Good morning. Channel IBC news is proud to be the first channel to report the happenings at the Brahma temple at Trichy today. We all wait eagerly to find out what the world-famous scientist Professor Naveen Kumar has to showcase. We expect a giant revelation as to how the Universe has been created, and how all human beings were created by nature and not by God. It promises to shake the faith of many religious bodies all over the world. The specific target for reasons unknown seems to be the Great Guru Amar.

"Without further ado, let us first hear a public statement requested by the Commissioner of Police of Trichy, Palanivel sir. Following which, we will hear the Professor. The mayor of the city will also handle the public interview. I repeat, this interview is special to Channel IBC and the commissioner is speaking only to us. Commissioner, the mike is yours."

"Hello. I am the Commissioner of Police of the city of Tiruchirappalli, A Palanivel. I have an important announcement to make. Citizens of India and the world, please listen carefully. There is no scientific revelation to be made today by the Professor or anyone else."

Rajesh's heart sank. *What was he saying? The Captain was not here? Was he a hoax?*

Or did the great religious leaders silence him? Or worse still, did they buy him out?

What the hell just happened?

The Commissioner continued. "This whole drama of revelation to the world was directed by the International Cooperation of Police, namely the Interpol. This drama was played mainly to make the Great Guru Amar panic and act in haste.

"It was long believed that the Great Guru Amar had connections with the underworld. In the present situation, he panicked and contacted an important person. He contacted the American billionaire, Steve Mehrotra. From the telephonic intercepts, it was clear that the Great Guru Amar has supplied thousands of crores of unaccounted Rupees to Steve Mehrotra. This creates a criminal tax fraud case against him!"

Rajesh smirked. Senthil gasped. Rajesh imagined the millions of TV viewers who were watching this *live* would have the same reaction as Senthil now.

"But worse still. The Interpol has conclusive evidence that Steve Mehrotra diverted this money to fund terrorism and war all over the world. The terrorist group, ISIS is said to be one of the major benefactors of Steve's and the Great Guru's money. It is also believed that the highly controversial disappearance of the Eastern Airlines flight in Dubai was the result of a powerful bomb. The ISIS used this bomb as a dress rehearsal for further bombings. Guess what? This bomb is sponsored by Steve's and the Great Guru's money. Now, there is conclusive evidence for criminal charges against the Great Guru Amar, pertaining to the deaths of thousands of innocent lives.

"The Great Guru Amar was arrested en route to Trichy at 3:00 am today. After questioning, he pleaded guilty to the police at 5:00 am. Preliminary investigations suggest at least three other nexuses that exist between some religious leaders, relatively 'anonymous' businessmen and terror groups among the world. This will be revealed in due time.

"Captain Professor Naveen has said that this, in fact, was the revelation he had to exhibit and pleaded people not to fall into such traps in future. It was a stern message. He himself is safe in Switzerland at this moment and has resumed his work at the Centre for European Nuclear Research."

Chapter 87

It was nothing that Rajesh expected; or for that matter, what Senthil expected. *But who cared?* It was sensational news and it was aired for the first time on their news channel. The TRP will rise further and Rajesh's career will take another upswing.

The Captain had got what he wanted.

There was not going to be any scientific revelation after all. The Compressor was still a secret to mankind, and Rajesh guessed it would be so for a while.

Rajesh and Senthil proceeded to the public announcement by the mayor. The crowd was stunned silent for a while when the mayor made the announcement. After a brief period of silence, there was uproar.

The Captain's tactics disappointed the scientific community. They had come to see something of great significance. However, their feelings were mixed. They were happy to see what had happened to the Great Guru Amar and they smiled and joked about it.

The religious community was stunned silent. Most broke into silent prayers. Their community had been tarnished, not for the first time, by a greedy and fraudulent Guru. The Great Guru Amar had the largest following at this moment in India; in fact, in the entire continent of Asia. His connections with terror-sponsoring and funding war had devastated them. The respect they had earned had all vanished and it would take years before the majority of the people again believed in any of them; even if they were a hundred per cent genuine.

The media persons and their cameramen were having a field day. Their cameras kept rolling and they were interviewing random people from the religious and scientific communities.

The common people were the ones who were most affected. Their faith had just been questioned. The Great Guru Amar was a highly respected Guru and most people believed that he represented God in this modern world. *How wrong they were!*

Rajesh and Senthil did the same as the other media people. They interviewed and interviewed. They were on air continuously. It was not until another two hours when the channel's chief editor called him and asked the duo to have breakfast. They would not be disturbed for another half an hour.

Rajesh used the break to immediately call up the Captain.

"Hello, my dear Rajesh! Good job. You have been on TV for the last three hours now. I have subscribed to your channel here in Switzerland! I have been following you since 3:00 am, local time!"

"Hello, Captain!" Rajesh's feelings were mixed. He was thrilled to hear his voice again. He was happy for his improved position in the company, thanks to the Captain, but he wanted to scream at him for not living up to his promise of the revelation. "Why didn't you reveal the Compressor today?"

"The world is not ready for it yet, Rajesh. We had a discussion about the same in the scientific board meeting a month ago. I too agree with the decision taken. The recent string of events made me believe that the Compressor can immediately be put into disastrous use unless some safety checks were first made!"

"But the ISIS already have the Compressors!"

"Wrong. You forgot the GPS, didn't you? We traced every one of them in Hong Kong, and luckily enough for us, those assholes did not move it from there since we traced them. We made the move when we had to. Once Steve Mehrotra had been captured, we regained control of them with the help of the Hong Kong police. Two policemen were injured grievously but they survived. The ISIS chaps guarding them were not so lucky. All eight were shot dead.

"All the stolen compressors are back in custody of the CERN. They are now placed under LASER surveillance and CCTVs all around. Now, even if I decide to move them from one room to the other, at least forty people in seven different countries would know!"

"Shit. That's crazy!"

"Yeah. It had to be so."

"If you know this was the plan why did you ask Gabriela to move to England?"

"Well, everyone had to believe that things were going as per plan!"

"Have you achieved what you set out to achieve? Has *Pari*, your *Pari* been contacted?"

"You bet she has been. She will have to be a part of the police investigation where she will have to be interrogated as well! Well, the Guru has already testified against the people in his organization who knew his reality. Luckily, for us, Rudradevi has already been given a clean chit."

"Hmmm..." This was all that Rajesh could muster.

"Okay Captain, one question has been troubling me for a while. You said I was involved in the story in three ways, and Gabriela was involved in this story in one way only. She and I were both related to Manish in some way and were going to be rescued by him once he knew that we were passengers on the flight. Besides that, I am a reporter who actively covered the story of the Great Guru Amar as a media person. In what other way am I involved?"

"What have you guessed?"

"I have covered the subject of the origin of the Universe before. I can't remember when!"

The Captain laughed. "You and I are connected in more ways than one, my dear! But before I tell you that, why don't you interview Rudradevi, my Pari. She too awaits for first coverage by Channel IBC, at the Commissioner's police van."

"Really? That's great news! I will get back to you soon, Captain. Stop fiddling around with my brain! Please tell me point-blank when I call you next!"

"Sure, pal!"

Rajesh hung up and immediately called out to Senthil, who had started drinking his coffee. "Come with me da, drink the coffee later." As he rushed towards the Commissioner's van, followed by a bewildered Senthil, he called his editor in chief and explained to him the need to be live when he signalled for it.

The editor was thrilled. "Go *machan*!"

This was his day. He had to remember to call Gabriela after this. He hoped that she too was following the TV channel. He guessed she would be doing the same and would have realised that she has no further role to play in this media coverage. Nevertheless, he had to call her. *He was dying to hear her sweet voice!* He was having this vague excitement. She was only the second girl who had interested him so much. He had to control his feelings.

He climbed into the van. He vaguely pictured Rudradevi. Her face was not clear in the YouTube video that Captain had spoken about. He too did not get a clear look when he had seen her from far in Coimbatore.

But this time he did.

The Captain had said that they were related in more ways than one.

Rudradevi, the '*Pari*' of the Captain stood in front of him. She wore a saffron sari and with a huge vermillion mark on her forehead. She looked beautiful. It took him a whole minute, a whole of sixty seconds, to realise that he knew her. He knew her well. In front of him stood the *first* love of his life, Rakhee Bora.

Chapter 88

"Rakhee!" That's all Rajesh could muster.

"Rajesh!" She said.

A chill ran down his spine when he heard her voice. A few seconds were enough. The good times he had had with her flashed before his eyes. He remembered her as a cool girl with a smile on her face perpetually. In the evenings, she was a party animal, enjoyed her club times. Yet, here she was, with a frown on her face. Far from her party animal image, she was dressed in a saffron sari with a huge vermillion!

"How did you get here?" She asked.

"Well, I am the reporter who is supposed to cover your bit right now! As you would have realised already, I am a reporter for Channel IBC news, based at Chennai. It has been a long journey from Pune to here!"

"Wow!"

"The sad part is – I know how *you* got to where *you* are! You were a bright and fun-loving girl, Rakhee! I know that I couldn't get along with the fact that you used to party a lot, but I always liked you, even after parting ways!"

"Well, thanks Rajesh!"

"And believe me, if I get you back to Captain Naveen, I still will be very happy for you and for him! He is a thorough gentleman and he loves you like crazy!"

"What! You know him!"

Before she could question any further, Senthil intervened, "Rajesh boss, we have to be live in exactly a minute! We have to wire up now!"

"You mind, Rakhee?" Rajesh asked. He was easing up to the situation after he mentioned about Captain Naveen. Until then, there was a vague sort of anxiety that he had.

"I can only request you, Rajesh. Please don't reveal my true identity on air! I am Rudradevi to the world. Although I no longer intend to be…"

"I will definitely take care. That's a promise!"

Rudradevi represented all the monks in the ashram, senior and junior. She clearly mentioned that none of them had the slightest inkling of what the Great Guru Amar was up to. They had been blinded by faith and just like most disciples, they truly believed that the Guru was in direct communication with God himself. They all believed that he was, in fact, the tenth and final version of Lord Vishnu, one who had set foot on Earth to put an end to this *Kalyuga*. They were shocked, shaken and devastated. They had to find their own unique identities and continue life hereafter; after the period of disillusionment.

Rajesh asked her about her belief in God now.

She had expected the question and was well prepared for it. She and her fellow monks still believed in God but had lost their faith in God-men. She hoped that people don't make the same mistake as them, but at the same time, she sincerely pleaded to the people not to lose faith in God and pray to Him directly. She urged people not to use proxies to reach out to God. Period.

The last few statements almost summed up the ultimate moral of the entire happenings of the last three months of his life, Rajesh thought.

The interview was over.

Immediately, Rakhee asked, "Rajesh! I know I am being extremely mean to you! But I want to meet Naveen! I want to beg for forgiveness! Where is he? What is he doing? Is he married already?"

"Now, let me be selfish by including myself in the answer as well." Rajesh smiled. "Neither of us is married!"

There was a huge sigh of relief. Rakhee did very less to hide it. And she didn't know how exactly to react. "Well… why you? Why have you not married?"

"I have not found anyone in my life whom I like even a bit!" Rajesh lied; on two accounts. He had met many girls whom he liked. Only thing was that he kept comparing them to Rakhee, and none reached his expectation. Except one. She was someone who he had accepted would never say yes to him. That was Gabriela.

"Ass! Mr Perfectionist!" Rakhee laughed. There was a sudden further drop in the slight discomfort that surrounded the air. Rakhee was becoming Rakhee again, slowly coming out of the Rudradevi role. She probably had not used the word 'ass' in the last ten years she guessed.

Rajesh too had a hearty laugh. "Regarding Naveen. You cannot guess what he has been through. I think it will be better if he tells you the entire story. I need to tell you only two things. He no longer is an army man. He is now a scientist at the Council for Nuclear Research in Switzerland and has made some ground-shaking discoveries. He was supposed to reveal them today, but he has decided not to, as the time has not yet come. However, be sure of one thing – He will be a Nobel Prize winner soon."

"What! I can't believe that! I thought all this 'scientific revelation' was a farce. I thought he did that so that he could trap the Guru and also insult him in front of the public at the same time!"

"Well, yes. You need to learn a lot about him yet! He is a great man. The second thing I wanted to tell you about him is... Do you wanna hear it?"

"Yes!"

"I can't believe that of all the seven and half billion other people in the world, I am the one who is telling you this. Professor Naveen Kumar loves you a lot, Rakhee. You mean the world to him. You should be lucky to have a man who can love you so much. Go get him, girl. Go get him!"

CHAPTER 89

Rajesh was finally free in the afternoon. His engagement with live TV had lasted continuously for almost eight hours.

He grabbed a quick lunch and then he had to make a decision as to whom he would call first, the Captain or Gabriela.

He decided to call the Captain first.

"Hello, dear Rajesh!" the Captain said.

"You must have seen my interview with Rudradevi *Srimati Pari Rakhee Bora!*"

"Yes, I did! How did you feel when you saw her first?" -

"Enough of questions from your side! I want to know how you felt!" Rajesh teased.

The Captain laughed. "What do you expect?"

"Again a question! I want an answer!"

"I felt amazing, Rajesh! It was the moment I have worked my last decade for! It was the moment of ultimate glory. It was like a tennis player lifting the Wimbledon trophy or like MSD lifting the cricket world cup! It was the ultimate feeling of glory!"

Rajesh felt extremely happy for the Captain. To come to think of it, Captain Naveen and he were batch mates at the under-graduation level. So, the Captain must be the same age as him. Somehow, he always tended to give him respect as a senior. He felt really good. "Guess what! I have thanked you so much today. Now is the time you thank me again. I have spoken to her. She is dying to meet you. Unfortunately, you would have to come to India to meet her, this the first time. Her passport has expired and it will take her some time to get the necessary documents for making the same as she has been in the wilderness for long!"

"I realised. I have booked my tickets for the next week already!"

"I realised that I cannot share your number without your permission! And she doesn't have a phone for the same reason as above. So, I am going to be the first one who will make both of you speak after all these years!"

"Rajesh! You are my best pal. Without realising it, you have occupied the position of bestie!"

"Hmmm... before that! I want to know. If all you said about the public revelation of Science vs. Religion was a lie, why did you send Gabriela to England? So that things looked more authentic? If you considered me a close friend, you could have confided the plan to me, and we could have saved Gabriela the trouble!"

"Who said the revelation was a lie? It is a revelation to show how Religion and Science can coexist!"

"What nonsense! There was no revelation. Only drama today!"

"Okay, there is a revelation, but you all looked elsewhere. If there are two people who would know where to look, it is you and Gabriela. I can give you only one clue. Remember the Compressor? What does it do to particles and objects? Once you answer this, read my cryptic clue again. You and Gabriela are smart enough, you can figure out what I mean. You still get to witness the Science-Religion revelation."

Rajesh had no clue as to what the Captain meant, but he would have to give it a thought when his mind was clearer. Now, he needed some rest. He had not slept the previous night and had been at work continuously since morning. He said bye and hung up.

He dialled Gabriela.

The sweet voice answered. "Hi, Rajesh! So all this was a hoax, huh? I have been sent to England for tourism purposes only!"

Rajesh laughed. He went on to tell her about the happenings of the day; the interview with the Commissioner, the first conversation with the Captain, the meeting with Rakhee, what they spoke, the interview she gave and finally what the Captain had said.

Gabriela listened patiently. "Wow! You met Rakhee Bora! She must be one heck of a girl. The world's most famous reporter at the moment, an Interpol officer, and the Nobel laureate candidate all like her!"

Rajesh laughed loudly. In all the action, he had, in fact, forgotten that Sachin and he had fought for the same girl! "The Nobel laureate candidate is the one for her, Gabriela. He is the one for her!"

"Hmmm!"

Rajesh wanted to propose to Gabriela immediately, but he was shit scared of rejection. Also, he was sure he would lose her as a friend. "What do you make of the Captain's clue?"

"I guess he has got me to England for a reason. We have to work it out. I think we will take a day to think about it. The way he said it, I am sure the day of the revelation is not today. Otherwise, he would have hurried us both up. He has booked me in England for another week. It will be in this week for sure."

"Yes, we should think. There is something here."

"Yes."

"Gabriela?"

"Yes?"

"How about you and I go for *a dinner* after all this is done?"

"For *one* dinner only?"

"Pardon?"

"I said, for *one* dinner only?"

"You want to go for a couple more?" Rajesh liked where this was heading. Or suddenly an unpleasant doubt crossed his mind. *Was she being sarcastic?*

"More than a couple…"

"Means?"

"You idiot! You don't seem to realise how madly in love I am with you! I didn't know how else to say this to you! I wish we have some dinners together to help us understand each other better, and preferably I would like to have most of the dinners in the remainder of my life with you…"

Chapter 90

Rajesh reached Chennai late in the night. He reached his house, took a shower, wore his nightclothes and lay on his bed. Today, the 16th of March 2019, was probably the best day of his entire life. The editor in chief had already spoken to him about his promotion and raise, which was in effect from the next day. He would have an entire prime time show for himself from the next month!

And of course, there was Gabriela Fabregas in his life now! *What a feeling! What a feeling!*

Today he was on top of the world... He wanted to sing the song from the Hindi film *Khamoshi... Aaj mein oopar, asmaan neechein.*

He went into a deep contented sleep.

When he woke up, he looked at his phone. It was still another half an hour before the alarm rang. He tried to sleep again but was unsuccessful. He got up and made himself a cup of coffee. He had some time in hand so he decided to sit in his balcony and sip the coffee slowly.

What had the Captain said? He had asked him to understand what the Compressor actually did. It would help him solve the cryptic message.

As far as he remembered, the Compressor compressed any material to a size below its Schwarzschild radius, below which the object collapsed in itself to form a black hole. It would then swallow the material all around it.

What had this function got to do with the message that the Captain gave?

He repeated it in his mind; the Compressor crushed material into a singularity…

He then looked at his phone and read out the Captain's cryptic message out loud. "After the Sun enters the constellation of Pisces this year, on the day Venus will align itself at 3:00 am at the '3:00 am' position of the horizon, the origin of the Universe will be revealed at the temple of 'Creator' in the state of Tamil Nadu at Sunrise for the Hindus. On the same day, at Sunrise, the Christians can witness the same in the longitude that is half the distance from the prime meridian as the temple of Tamil Nadu is from the Indian meridian."

The message was about the origin of the universe, the beginning. The Universe began with the Big Bang, from a point of singularity…

The Compressor compressed matter into a point of singularity.

The Universe began from 'singularity'…the Compressor compressed matter into 'singularity'.

His mind wandered into one of the discussions the Captain, Ken, Gabriela and he had had.

From where did the singularity that created the Big Bang arise?

It probably was the matter from an alternate universe that had been compressed into the singularity, which now emitted material as the Big Bang and created this Universe, as we know it.

Therefore, there was some compressor that had created the singularity that led to the Big Bang.

Compression preceded Singularity, which then preceded the Big Bang.

Still, he was not able to see the relation.

He looked down at the road below that stretched from the gate of his gated community to his building. On the side of it was a temple of Ganesha, where some residents had headed out to pray.

The God of Creation was Brahma, therefore, everyone flocked there to check the scientific revelation. *What was wrong with that?*

He again went back to his theory: compression preceded the Big Bang.

Suddenly it struck him.

It struck him clearly.

Destruction preceded Creation.

He looked at the Ganesha temple. Ganesha's father was Shiva, the apparent 'destroyer' in the acronym of GOD.

Shiva's role was prior to Brahma's role in the creation of the universe, as we know it.

That was it!

The revelation was to be at the Shiva's temple in Tamil Nadu.

Chidambaram it was. The temple of Natarajan at Chidambaram was the world-famous Shiva temple in Tamil Nadu.

He quickly rang up the astrologer friend of his, the person who had helped him a bit, to solve the Brahma temple theory. He had to find out when Venus would be at three o'clock position at the horizon at Chidambaram at 3:00 am.

When his friend excitedly got to work, he pulled up the atlas.

He had to calculate where Gabriela had to be.

He looked at the longitude of Chidambaram, 79.5 degrees east.

He looked at the Prime Meridian of India. 82.5 degrees east.

The difference was 3 degrees.

He then looked at the UK map to see which city was 1.5 degrees west of Greenwich.

He looked at it carefully. He couldn't find any city of significance on the map where he had calculated the place to be.

He pulled out his laptop and entered Google Maps. He blew it to large magnification. There he found it. It read Stonehenge, the popular tourist site, which was roughly around 1.5 to 1.8 degrees west of London.

His friend called, "Rajesh, the date you asked for is March twentieth."

Rajesh immediately called Gabriela. It was 2:00 am in London.

"My, my. You must be impatient enough to hear my bedroom voice!" she said sleepily.

Rajesh smiled, but he had a job at hand. He quickly told her about his decrypt.

"March twentieth! That is the day of the spring equinox! That is the day I anyway decided to go to the Stonehenge exactly at Sunrise. There is supposed to be something special about the Sunrays' alignment on that day over there! Therein lies some clue!"

After hanging up, Rajesh decided to research on the Spring Equinox and the Stonehenge. Indeed, the Sunrise on that day was supposed to be special. It would be visible exactly between two stones at the Stonehenge. There were supposed to be some rituals that many people followed on that day, right from the BC days, since more than two thousand years to be exact.

Anyway, his turn would come almost five and a half hours before Gabriela. He would have to see what happens at Chidambaram on that day.

Should he take Senthil with him? He decided not to. If the Captain had decided not to reveal anything to the world now, he must mean something.

He set out to Chidambaram by bus the previous evening and was waiting at the temple gate just before sunrise. The temple looked majestic and luckily enough had opened already. The temple has nine *gopurams* that are really large in size and are decorated with immaculate planning. It was hard to believe that a temple of this grandeur had been built in the sixth century! The temple is spread over a 40-acre area, within layers of concentric courtyards. The inner sanctum, its connecting *mandapams* and pillared halls near it are all either squares or stacked squares or both. The complex has several water storage structures of which the Shivaganga sacred pool is the largest with a rectangular plan. The temple complex is dedicated to Natarajan Shiva and theological ideas associated with Shaivism concepts in Hinduism. However, the temple also includes shrines for Devi, Vishnu, Subrahmanyar, Ganesha, Nandi and others including an Amman shrine, a Surya shrine complete with chariot wheels.

He entered the main sanctum where he saw the shrine of lord Natarajan, the dancing pose of Lord Shiva. It was nearing sunrise. The temple priests were busy preparing the Aarti.

He didn't see anything out of the ordinary here yet. What was the revelation here?

He checked his watch. It was the exact time for sunrise.

Yet, there was nothing of significance to be seen. It was just nothing. He had not interpreted what the Captain had said at all... it was a huge anti-climax...it was...

Then he saw it.

As the sun rose over the horizon, the sun rays passed through a small hole in the inner sanctum. The hole was strange. It had a small piece of crystal on it. This converged the sun's rays in such a way that the rays fell right in the space between the Lord's index finger and middle finger of the right hand, the hand which seemed to bless the devotees as they watched the dance pose. It seemed very clear, the Sun's rays almost collapsed to a point of singularity between the two fingers of the Lord.

The Silver statue was aligned in such a way that the sun rays that passed through the two fingers suddenly dispelled the light in all directions in front of the statue.

Rajesh understood clearly what was revealed here.

He folded his hands, closed his eyes, knelt down and touched his head to the floor. He was lost in deep prayer.

EPILOGUE

Two weddings were held in the temple of the 'creator'.

The grooms were now the best of friends.

The brides had met each other for the first time, but each seemed to impress the other more.

There were two best men.

Who they were, anyone can guess.